a n o n y m o u s

Book 1

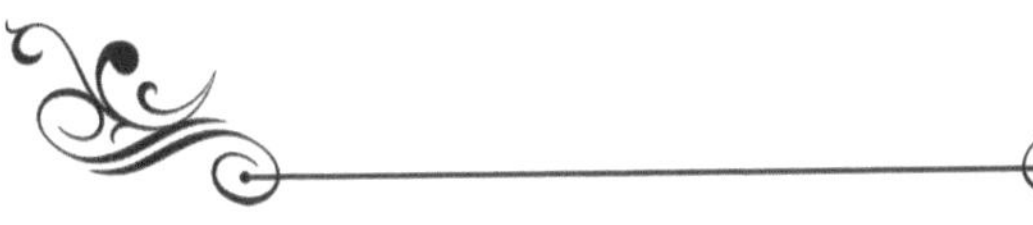

Rhoades to Bridges
series

OLIVIA BRIDGES

Rhoades to Bridges

BEHIND CLOSED DOORS OF THE MISSISSIPPI DELTA, lies a tangled web of seduction, secrets, sin, and shame. Inspired by actual events, Rhoades to Bridges is an explosive saga which defies the confines of genre. From Steel Magnolias to Ghosts of Mississippi, there have been a great many stories told about the South: her majesty as well as her malevolence. Atypical of authors who explore only one isolated facet of ties that bind or times gone by, Bridges blends history, heartbreak, and humor into a complete and captivating Southern experience. The reader, whether a Southerner or "Otherner", finds herself woven into the plot and discovers she is not a third party but a member of the Bridges family. Together they rejoice in the blessings bestowed upon them, and together they face the trials and tribulations set before them. The real story lies not merely in these experiences themselves but in the manner in which Southerners, unlike any other culture, deal with the good, the bad, and especially the unmentionable.

The series begins as Melanie Bridges wins a landmark lawsuit which rocks the nation all the way to the Supreme Court. With this victory, Melanie finds herself at the pinnacle of her legal career; yet, unmarried and childless, she is consumed with a burning desire to find deeper meaning for her life, apart from her professional persona. Taking a sabbatical, Melanie sets sail alone, bound for the Caribbean. Anticipating being far from home and loved ones, she takes with her a treasured photograph album from which her grandmother had told family stories when Melanie was a small child. She expects the photographs will give her comfort in the long hours of solitude. Surprisingly, they do much more than she could have imagined as they carry her on a journey of a lifetime, through 150 years and the complex relationships connecting seven generations. She recognizes that the Bridges have always been a unique breed, exceptionally strong, bound by faith and family, with the courageous women of each generation unifying and triumphing over the unbearable circumstances of their day. Melanie realizes the family secrets which once threatened to shatter the very core of the Bridges dynasty now serve as her salvation. From the past, she discovers she is but a solitary golden thread woven in the magnificent tapestry of a collective destiny.

Olivia Bridges was born, raised, and spent over half her life in the Mississippi Delta. It is extremely rare when a native Southerner is bold enough to seek the truth and write it with abandon. *Rhoades to Bridges* breaks the consensus of silence held by those who still cling desperately to the pride, pageantry, and plantations of a bygone era. Bridges delivers the long buried true story that now must be told.

"Hell hath no fury like the daughter of a woman scorned."

Olivia Bridges

For information about special discounts for bulk purchases, please contact Y&R Enterprises Special Sales at 1.888.649.1775 or info@yandrpr.com.

The Y&R Speakers Bureau can bring authors to your live event. For more information or to book an event, contact the Y&R Speakers Bureau at 903.253.2623 or visit our website at www.yandrpr.com.

Cover Design by Simply Defined Art
Book Design by Champagne Formats

Printed in the United States of America

Library of Congress Control Number Data

Bridges, Olivia.
Anonymous / Olivia Bridges.
1. Women's fiction—Fiction. 2. Sagas—Fiction. 3. Historical—Fiction.
Fiction. | BISAC: FICTION / Sagas. | FICTION / General. | FICTION / Historical.
PCN # 2016911674 2013

ISBN 978-1-940460-50-5
ISBN 978-1-940460-49-9

www.oliviabridges.com

anonymous

PART ONE

Melanie

o n e

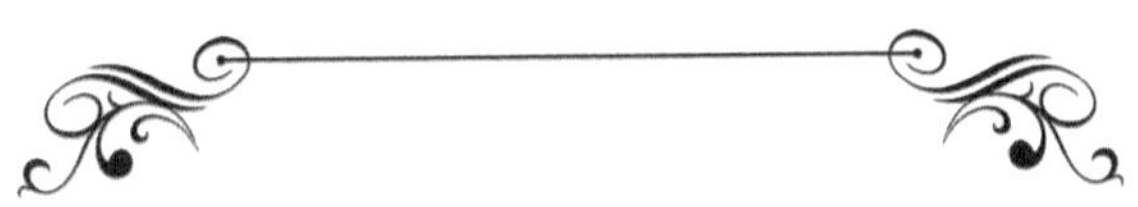

January, 2003
Dallas, Texas

"WE, THE JURY, FIND IN FAVOR OF THE plaintiff, the estate of Joshua Herbert Stanford, and order the defendant the Jack Devilland Corporation to pay compensatory damages of two hundred-fifty thousand dollars and punitive damages of thirty-two million dollars to the estate of Mr. Stanford. In addition, the Jack Devilland Corporation will pay the organization Mothers Against Drunk Driving one hundred-fifty million dollars per year for the next twenty-five years, for a total of three point seven five billion dollars, to subsidize MADD's awareness campaign against the dangers of drinking and driving."

The courtroom erupted into absolute pandemonium with reporters frantically pushing past one another, racing out to be the first television network to broadcast the history-making verdict. Some spectators cheered while others cried, and many simply sat in a state of shock. No one could have dreamed the jury would come back with such a tremendous award.

"Order in this court, order in the court!" Judge Harold Brigham's voice boomed over the room as he rapped his gavel loudly.

The courtroom fell silent.

Brigham then addressed the jury. "I thank each and every one of you for your time and commitment to the case. The bailiff will escort you through the back hallway. I have no doubt it's a circus out there. There will be a mob of cameras and reporters swarming the steps. Thank you again. Court dismissed."

Judge Brigham rose from the bench. His black robe swirled in a flurry around his large frame as he disappeared through the door to his chambers.

Melanie Bridges' heart beat double-time from the shock of the verdict. Adrenaline coursed through her veins. Enthusiastic shouts of congratulations and other bedlam surrounded her. A surreal sense of floating toward the ceiling enveloped her. The sounds all around her evaporated as her body numbed from the top of her head to the tip of her toes.

Every waking moment, day and night, week after week, month after month, she had poured her entire life, her heart, her soul, and everything she had into this case. Struggling to breathe from the jarring surprise, Melanie could not believe this epic day had finally come. Desperately, Melanie grasped to understand the impact of what had just happened. All she knew for sure was it was big.

Melanie suddenly felt his presence behind her even before he spoke. Alan Winters, the lead attorney who represented the Tennessee liquor giant Jack Devilland, breeched her personal space and towered over her.

As always, Alan was impeccably dressed in a cus-tom-tailored suit and alligator boots which probably cost more than what Melanie made in three months. To be fair, he was certainly a striking man with a physique to rival that of an Olympic athlete. Nonetheless, he'd been a pompous jerk from the first day she had met him almost five years ago. Most women found him tall, dark, and handsome, with his slicked back hair as black as West Virginia coal. Melanie was not one of those women.

"Congratulations, Melanie." Alan pierced her with his sharp blue eyes. "I must say, for a rookie, you presented a pretty good case." A smug grin stretched across his face. "Our appeal will be on your desk by eight a.m. tomorrow morning." He outstretched his hand, his absurdly expen-sive watch just showing under the cuff of his sleeve.

Melanie begrudgingly accepted his firm but clammy handshake.

Holding her hand a few seconds longer than appropri-ate, his eyes danced as if the victory today belonged to him. Yes, he was truly a first-class bastard.

Saying nothing, Melanie turned her attention from Alan and stood perfectly still amid the continued jubila-tion of her own team. Neither Alan nor his media-dubbed Dream Team mattered. Only one thing mattered. She, Melanie Bridges, small town girl from Carlton, North Carolina, had just made history. Her shoulders sagged as the months of tension eased and the hint of tears stung the corner of her eyes. History. She had made history.

How she wished her daddy was here to see his little girl take down the huge Goliath that was Jack Devilland.

Shaking her head, she knew he was indeed there in spirit, as was her mama. They were two of the three people who had given her the strength each and every day to walk into this courtroom and fight like hell.

Melanie turned around at the gentle touch upon her elbow. Elderly, wheelchair-bound widow Eliza Stanford wept openly and reached for her. Bending down, Melanie folded herself into the older woman's frail arms. The familiar sweet scent of Eliza's lavender perfume tickled her nose as she savored the moment.

Releasing Mrs. Stanford, Melanie stood and searched the crowd for the other woman. Her gaze met that of the ever stoic Sally, the only child of Eliza and Joshua. A striking woman with the classic good looks of Grace Kelly, she struggled to get through the crowd to reach Melanie.

Normally all business and rarely showing emotion, even she couldn't contain herself under these circumstances. The moment her hands clasped Melanie's, together they cried.

Sally hugged her with such force that Melanie felt she might be crushed by her overjoyed client.

"Thank you, thank you, thank you. You'll never know what this means, not only to Mom and me, but also to Dad who suffered for so long. No one would be more grateful than Josh who loved his granddaddy so deeply. Melanie you are truly an angel sent from Heaven. My family will be forever indebted to you."

"You're welcome, Sally. I'm glad we won today, for you," Melanie paused and smiled resolutely before continuing, "and for all the others too."

Wiping her own tears, Melanie bent down and once

again hugged the tiny widow Stanford for a long time. Over two years earlier, this wonderful woman and her daughter had entered Melanie's office on that fateful Wednesday afternoon.

Since that day, Melanie considered both mother and daughter to be like family. Countless hours had been spent at their home, going over facts and asking questions about events going back more than four decades. In those long hours, happy memories and many tears came back to both Eliza and Sally.

The thrill of the legal victory was suddenly replaced with something Melanie would cherish forever—the personal victory she had won for these two phenomenally courageous women.

Surrounded by her jubilant legal team hugging one another and all speaking at once, Melanie stopped and took a long deep breath. Closing her eyes, she allowed herself to simply be in the moment. God's grace rained down on her as peace enveloped her. Yes. It was a once-in-a-lifetime moment that would change Melanie's life forever.

"You did it, kiddo!" Chad Brewster, Melanie's fellow attorney and close friend, wore a broad grin, his long arm embracing her. "You did it!" He lifted her a foot off the ground.

Wrapping her arms around her dear friend, Melanie broke into laughter. "*We* did it! All of us, together. I can't believe it!"

"Believe it! Believe it!" Chad twirled her around in a circle.

"Wow! This is happening!" She hugged him tightly as he set her down.

"You had a fire in your belly from the day you met the Stanfords. A fire that turned into a blazing inferno. Those ol' boys didn't stand a chance."

Their moment was interrupted as others clamored and shared in the joyous celebration.

Josephine, Melanie's right-hand assistant, had returned to work, packing files and ready to rush Melanie out of the madness. Josephine was not only an extremely efficient administrative assistant but another close personal friend to Melanie. Over the past two years, a bond had blossomed that went far beyond their professional relationship.

From the first day Josephine had come to work for Melanie, she had been right by her side. The meticulous woman with the stylishly coiffed platinum hair took care of her every need—from scheduling her multitude of daily appointments, to filing briefs, or spending hours upon hours helping Melanie with the seemingly endless research for the Devilland case. Most evenings, she pushed Melanie out the door long after all the other lawyers and staff had gone home to their families. Melanie couldn't imagine not having Josephine by her side.

Watching Josephine busy at work, Melanie made a mental note to reward her extraordinary assistant with a handsome bonus for her dedication to this case, out of her own pocket if necessary. Unlike the vast majority in the legal profession, Melanie had almost no ego. She realized that, although this victory would be technically in her name, she couldn't have begun to try this case without the incredible support of Josephine, Melanie's fellow attorneys, the firm's paralegals, clerks, interns, and all the support staff at Hunt, Spencer & McCoy.

With the counsel table cleared, Josephine beamed brightly at her boss.

"Let's get you out of here."

"Yes, let's," Melanie said as the rush of adrenaline had begun to wear off and exhaustion filled her veins.

Moving as one, Melanie's team made their way through the small crowd of spectators who still mingled in the courtroom.

The moment the heavy doors were pushed open, bright flashing cameras dazed Melanie. An endless sea of reporters shoved microphones at her from every direction and shouted questions that crowded her ears.

A surge of excitement charged through Melanie but quickly faded as claustrophobia consumed her. Bodies closed in around her as Melanie's entourage pushed hard against the crowd, making their way to the courthouse doors looming ahead.

Over the deafening noise, Melanie could hear a few questions over all the rest. *How does your victory feel, Ms. Bridges? Are you worried about Devilland filing an appeal? Did you expect such a large award for your client?*

The voices merged into one cacophony of noise accompanied by the continuing blinding flashes of the cameras.

"Good Lord!" Melanie thought as she was squeezed tightly between Josephine and Chad. *"They must have taken more than five hundred shots of me and I'm not even out of the courthouse!"*

Finally, someone successfully pushed through the courthouse doors. A bright sun shined down on the beautiful cloud-free day.

A gasp escaped her lips as she stared at the sea of

reporters and onlookers. There had to be hundreds of people. No. Not hundreds. Thousands. All were chanting her name. Many were waving handmade signs. *VICTORY! DEVILLAND GOES DOWN! BREAK 'EM BRIDGES!*

Moments ago, the thrill of victory had been a rush but nothing compared to this. Suddenly dizzy and taking a long, deep breath, she willed herself to smile, holding back sobs of disbelief.

"Stop, stop!" Melanie said loudly to her colleagues as she motioned for everyone to give her some space.

She needed to at least give these hungry reporters something for the evening news. After all, they were only doing their jobs, just as she had done hers. Maybe if she gave them what they were starving for in this moment, they would retreat to their respective TV vans and give her enough room to make her escape to the bottom of the courthouse steps. Chad called for the impassioned reporters to settle down and give Melanie a chance to speak.

Feeling like a giant, standing all of five feet, five inches, in her two inch designer pumps, Melanie's gaze swept over the crowd of reporters and spectators who stood on the steps below her and spilled out onto the packed street. Swallowing the lump in her throat, Melanie fought to find her words, knowing they would soon be broadcast across the nation.

"On behalf of the Stanford family and my legal team, I would like to thank the jury who listened to the facts, carefully considered all the events surrounding the issue at hand, and delivered a fair and just verdict. Hopefully, this jury has laid the groundwork for others to stand up and hold these liquor companies accountable for all the lives that have been ruined and lost due to their products. At this time, I respectfully, ask on behalf of the Stanford family, that each and every reporter value the family's privacy and give them their time to reach closure on the long road they have traveled to this bittersweet victory. We must not forget what the Stanford family has lost can never be replaced by any jury award, no matter how large the sum. Thank you all for your time and hard work covering this case. I have no further comment."

Chaos erupted immediately after her statement. Melanie's entire team frantically propelled her at breakneck speed down the courthouse steps. Throngs of reporters continued to lob questions at her and the photographer's cameras whirred and clicked as they pushed past to a sleek black limousine owned by the law firm. Sammy, Charles Hunt's driver, opened the door and she slid inside where Charles and William Spencer were waiting.

Ordinarily, Melanie's preference would have been to leave in her own red Mustang convertible that was parked around the corner, but she was grateful to be whisked away from the bedlam.

Awestruck, she stared through the tinted windows at tangled mass of people, TV vans, and satellite dishes. The streets surrounding the courthouse were virtual parking lots with reporters who had set up camp there for the last week gobbling up the courtroom drama, awaiting the verdict. How could Sammy possibly get through the chaos? A few Dallas policemen were doing their best to direct traffic and move illegally parked vehicles but they were far outnumbered and not making much progress.

"A job exceptionally well done, Melanie," Charles said

with a brilliant smile. A large barrel-chested man with thick salt-and-pepper hair, Charles was admired by everyone in his firm. Dedicated to seeking justice above all else and expecting the same high standard from everyone who worked for Hunt, Spencer & McCoy, he was honest and treated his entire staff, from attorney to janitor, with respect at all times. "I don't believe I've ever seen a finer case presented in all of my thirty-nine years of practice."

"Thank you, Mr. Hunt.". The admiration in his buoyant tone gave her a shot of pride.

"I must admit," Charles continued, "I had my doubts about the jury seeing our side, much less awarding such a staggering dollar amount. You proved a great many people wrong today, including me. You mesmerized the jury from the moment you stood before them to deliver a flawless opening statement. You stayed on track, established the facts, used emotion at precisely the right moments, but not without purpose. You were simply brilliant. You've made the firm very proud today."

Melanie placed her hand on her swelling heart. "That means a great deal to me. Thank you."

Finishing his phone conversation, William Spencer turned to face Melanie.

A man of few words, William said simply, "Damn fine job, Melanie. Damn fine job."

"Thank you, Mr. Spencer. Thank you very much."

Sammy winked in the rearview mirror. "Congratulations, Mel."

Gratitude flooded through Melanie as she was happy to have the rail-thin young black man with her in her moment of joy and celebration. Melanie and he had struck up a friendship over the coffee pot one cold, rainy day when she first came to the firm. Beaming with an infectious smile and a joke to tell, Sammy lifted Melanie's spirits no matter how stressful her day had been.

"Where's Chad? Did we leave him in the chaos?" Melanie asked suddenly as she realized he wasn't in the car with them. Next to Josephine, Chad was her closest friend at the firm. He had been right beside her only moments ago and he had disappeared.

"He's in the car behind us," Josephine said.

"That's a relief. I was afraid he had been eaten by the hungry mob." Melanie eyes widened in mock horror as the others laughed.

A silence then fell among them as each savored the sweet taste of victory.

A nervous tingling spread throughout her body as she smiled at the two senior partners. Both men had been tremendously supportive of her during the preparation of the case in terms of allowing her to use all the staff and resources of the firm she needed, but neither had become involved personally in the case.

In her heart of hearts, Melanie had known the senior partners, like everyone else, considered it a case which could never be won. The liquor companies were simply too big and too powerful. The legal team Jack Devilland had at its disposal was made up of some of the best and most expensive attorneys in the entire country. Neither Hunt nor Spencer wanted to have egg on his face should the case turn out to be a flop as everyone had predicted.

Melanie had known Charles Hunt had only agreed to take the case because Eliza Stanford was the aunt of one of the firm's biggest corporate clients. Hunt had put her in first chair because he knew her research and presentation would be perfect. Melanie was certain that Charles, or anyone else, had not expected that she, the firm's petite lady with the Southern drawl, as he often referred to her, would actually take down Jack Devilland's powerhouse attorneys wholly and completely.

"Every major law firm in the country will be courting you by this afternoon, my dear," Charles said. "Rest assured, we won't be letting you get away." He winked.

Butterflies fluttered in Melanie's stomach as she realized the tables had turned swiftly for her. She had taken a lost cause and turned it into possibly one of the largest awards won for a client by the firm. Hunt and Spencer had taken the time to pick her up in Charles' own car with his personal chauffeur. She imagined few associates had ever been picked up at the courthouse steps by the man himself.

If anyone had asked her exactly how she was feeling in these precious moments, Melanie would have been at a complete loss for words. The emotions of just the last hour had vacillated from shock upon hearing the foreman read the verdict to euphoria to the current disbelief that any of this could be real.

Gazing again out the tinted window at the crowd fading in the distance, Melanie had no doubt she must be dreaming. Any minute the alarm clock would ring and she would start another routine day—due in court in two hours.

Unseen by anyone, she closed her eyes and pinched herself. Genuine surprise hit her full force when she opened her eyes and found herself still sitting next to Josephine in the luxurious back seat of the speeding limousine.

Yes! This is real. I won and won BIG. Hallelujah! Melanie allowed a tiny smile to fall upon her lips. Leaning her head back on the butter-soft leather seat and closing her eyes once again, she thanked God for all the strength He had given her on the long journey to victory. She simply couldn't believe it. Dreams of being a great attorney, like her daddy and granddaddy, had captivated her for as long as she could remember but fate had dealt her a hand of cards and led her down a very different and difficult path. It had taken her forty-one years but in this moment, she was the most famous attorney in the entire country.

Opening her eyes, Melanie breathed a sigh of relief that Sammy had successfully maneuvered out of the massive traffic jam. The car sped through Dealey Plaza on its way back to the law offices of Hunt, Spencer & McCoy. Everyone sat lost in thoughts of the glorious victory and what it meant.

Melanie's gaze fell upon a group of Japanese tourists meandering through the Plaza, gawking upward at the sixth floor of the book depository, taking pictures to share with their families and friends back home. Dealy Plaza was the most famous place in a city which had lived for the last forty years in the shadow of shame. Dallas was infamous as the place where President John F. Kennedy had been savagely gunned down.

Maybe, just maybe, Dallas would now be remembered not as the city where Kennedy had been tragically slain, but instead as the city where justice was finally won. Won for all those who had also been tragically killed, not by an assassin's bullet, but by those who made the fatal decision to drink, drive, and kill. That decision was made by someone every thirty minutes across America. Already two more lives had been lost to a drunk driver just since the jury had read the verdict. The thought remained mind-boggling to Melanie, even after studying the statistics for the last two years since first taking the case.

Suddenly, all cell phones began ringing at once. Josephine answered Melanie's phone and frowned. "Ms. Bridges is unavailable at this time." The crease in her brow deepened, anger flashed in her eyes. "I'm sorry, sir. This is a private line." Her stern voice sharpened, her words clipped. "I seriously advise against you attempting to contact Ms. Bridges again. Any future calls will be considered harassment and you will face the maximum legal consequences."

She clicked off with a huff.

"Who in the world was that?" Melanie asked.

"A reporter from the *Dallas Star* wanting a personal interview with you."

Josephine scoffed. "I'll get you a new number listed under a different name first thing in the morning.

The *Dallas Star* was one of the trashy tabloids that flew off the supermarkets' shelves. Their feature story usually had something to do with Elvis being seen at a truck stop in Arizona or an eighty-year-old woman giving birth to an alien baby.

"Thanks, Jo. You're like my own personal pit bulldog. I can't believe some reporter has already found my cell phone number."

"You don't have to thank me. Actually, I consider that fun. Those tabloid reporters are pond scum as far as I'm concerned."

Josephine often surprised people with her fighting

spirit and brazen comments. One would never expect a sweet grandmother of twelve to have such fire but this one certainly did.

"Your world has changed. You have assumed celebrity status," Charles said. "It will be more and more difficult to maintain your privacy, at least for a while."

Josephine patted her leg. "Don't worry, Mel. With ol' Josephine on duty, the scavengers will have an extremely difficult time getting anywhere near you, much less actually speaking to you." She assured her with a grin.

At that precise moment, the phone once again chirped in her hand. This time, Josephine's face brightened upon hearing the caller's voice. She handed the phone to Melanie, silently mouthing the name *Shirley Sims*. Melanie eagerly took the call.

Shirley Sims was the National President of MADD. She had lost her only son when a female drunk driver lost control of her car, crossed over the concrete median and careened into the path of Matthew Sims as he drove home from his Wednesday night Bible study. The driver had four previous DWIs and walked away from the accident without as much as a broken bone. Two days prior to the fatal crash, Matthew Sims had celebrated his seventeenth birthday.

It had been Melanie's idea to bring the lawsuit against Devilland in both the names of the Stanford estate as well as the organization MADD. This was a decision for which Shirley Sims expressed her deepest gratitude. With the award given today, the result of Melanie's choice made years earlier had proven itself priceless.

Melanie's eyes glistened with bittersweet tears for the second time in an hour.

"Thank you for calling, Shirley. Your kind words are most appreciated. Give me a call the next time you're in Dallas and we'll most certainly have dinner. I look forward to seeing you soon. Give my best to Denny and the girls."

Charles and William ended their conversations almost in unison. Both of their calls had been from fellow attorneys congratulating the firm on such a tremendous victory. Each accepted the best wishes enthusiastically but emphasized the victory belonged to Melanie. At the sound of the partners' words, she felt another billow of joyful pride.

Within minutes, Sammy turned the corner onto Turtle Creek Boulevard, one of the most prestigious addresses in the city of Dallas. Hunt, Spencer & McCoy occupied the entire top three floors of a twenty-story high rise. The sleek limo glided into the private parking garage and pulled directly in front of the firm's own elevators that would deliver everyone directly to the twentieth floor.

Melanie smiled graciously as both Charles and William stood back and motioned for the ladies to enter the elevator first. The gentlemen of the Lone Star State still treated ladies with tremendous deference. Never understanding the hard-core feminists who found it insulting when a man opened a door for her or pulled out her chair in a restaurant, Melanie accepted the gestures as Southern courtesy, pure and simple.

The elevator sped to its destination and as the doors opened, Melanie couldn't believe her eyes. Lawyers, paralegals, secretaries, clerks, and janitors were all standing in the massive marble and glass lobby of Hunt, Spencer & McCoy with champagne glasses held in the air. A huge banner which Josephine had ordered weeks earlier in optimistic anticipation of today's victory spread across the entire lob-by and read: *Congratulations, Mel.*

Accepting a glass of pricey champagne, Melanie smiled nervously as the heat of embarrassment crept onto her neck and cheeks when everyone broke out in song—*For She's a Jolly Good Lady.*

Two hours of congratulations, hugs, snapshot pictures, and office camaraderie drained Melanie completely. The ache in her neck throbbed and her feet numbed. Craving the solitude of her own office, Melanie took the first opportunity and slipped away to the nineteenth floor.

Surprised, Melanie found Josephine at her own desk and on the telephone.

"Ms. Bridges isn't available at this time but I'll be more than happy to tell her you called. Yes. I'll be sure to tell her that as well. Thank you for calling."

Josephine's phone lit up like a Christmas tree. All lines were holding. A stack of pink message slips, already at least one inch thick continued to grow.

"Thank you so much, Jo, for screening those calls. I don't think I can speak to one more person right now. I'll call them all back tomorrow." Melanie wearily filed past her assistant's desk.

Josephine flashed her brilliant smile. "At this rate, Mel, it's going to take you a full week to return all these calls. I had no idea you knew so many people!"

"Neither did I." Melanie laughed ruefully as she glanced at the growing stack of slips.

Another line rang and the ever efficient paralegal pushed the button to turn on her headset. "Melanie Bridges' office, how may I help you?"

Breathing a deep sigh of relief, Melanie walked into her office, hung her black pinstriped blazer on the coat rack and slipped out of her black pumps. Stocking-footed, she crossed the tiny space and got a can of Red Bull from the small refrigerator in the corner. Popping the top, she collapsed into one of the guest chairs.

Taking a long refreshing swallow, Melanie allowed herself to simply enjoy the peace of finally being alone. Rolling her head from side to side, she massaged the back of her neck. Her entire body ached.

Melanie's gaze fell upon her bookcase and the antique gold and jade clock her parents had given her when she graduated from SMU. That day, like today, had been filled with great joy and celebration. Melanie couldn't help but smile as she remembered how proud her daddy had been. He had been proud of all his children but her graduation from law school was a shining moment in time. She had walked through deep and dark waters before that day. In college, she had been one of the lucky survivors of a fatal car crash. Years later she had secretly endured years of violent abuse at the hands of her former husband. The day she graduated from law school had been a victorious turning point in her life. Thoughts of her daddy took her back to the day she had told him she wanted to go to law school. She had been nervous about going back to school at an age she had then considered to be late in her life. He had told her it was never too late to be what she might have been.

"You were right, Daddy. I did it. I made it. I really did." A new flood of gratitude cloaked her.

Melanie allowed herself to enjoy the release of emotion and escaped into memories when her life was completely carefree—her magical childhood. She gazed lovingly at the photo of her mama, daddy, older brother, sister, and herself standing in front of the ski lodge in Zermatt, Switzerland. The snow-covered Matterhorn towered in the background. Of all Melanie's childhood memories, those precious ten days traveling across Switzerland via the Eurail were fourteen-karat gold.

She fondly recalled the greatest part of the trip had been the fact that her daddy, usually a master planner, had thrown caution to the wind and not made a single hotel reservation for the entire vacation.

They lived the entire ten days without knowing what new experiences the next day held. It had been an amazing trip. The entire country of Switzerland reminded Melanie of a picture postcard with the trains climbing the steep snow-covered mountains and breathtaking views behind every turn.

The only other photograph in her office was of her pets, Fred and Ginger, posing with Santa Claus last year. They were Melanie's children and the center of her home life. Fred was her mixed breed, scruffy dog that she had rescued one cold, rainy night almost five years ago outside the grocery store. Soaking wet and freezing cold, the puppy huddled in the corner of a cardboard box. A soggy note had been attached to the box. It read: *Please take care of my puppy. His name is Fred.*

Her big brother Drew had always joked she had a built in "stray-dar" for any animal within fifty miles that needed food, shelter, or medical attention. Growing up, Melanie had been the one whom lost kittens or puppies would follow home from school and if no owner surfaced, the animal became part of the family.

Ginger was a beautiful long-haired calico cat that Melanie had adopted four years earlier from a paralegal in the law office with a litter of kittens.

The name Ginger had been a tribute to Melanie's maternal grandmama Yancy, a huge fan of Fred Astaire and Ginger Rogers.

She had many fond memories of her grandmama Yancy. She had spent literally hours upon hours listening to her grandmama relate tales of the actors and actresses whom she had known, the Broadway productions in which she danced, and the excitement of living in New York City in the 1920s prior to the Great Depression.

After leaving Broadway, Yancy had married and moved into a wonderful old farmhouse in North Carolina, far away from the hustle and bustle of the big city. Melanie loved to spend long weekends with her grandmama Yancy. They would have movie marathons, watching the real Fred and Ginger dance for hours upon end, and they would eat cold spaghetti with mayonnaise, a dish Melanie's grandmama had eaten all those many years ago in New York.

Yancy's favorite restaurant had been a tiny Italian café down the street from her home in Beekman Tower. She would often pick up an order of spaghetti on her way home and have leftovers the next morning without bothering to reheat it, but adding a generous dollop of mayonnaise. It sounded quite unappealing to most people but Melanie loved it to this day for one reason—because her grandmama had loved it.

On those special weekends, Melanie and her grandmama would go to the store and buy fifteen pounds of whole chickens. Together they would boil the chickens and then have a glorious chicken party for Grandmama Yancy's array of dogs, cats, the neighbor's duck, and an orphaned raccoon as well as any strays that came up to the front porch. Yancy was a wonderful, spiritual woman and her deep affection for all animals was only one of the many reasons Melanie loved her.

"A penny for your thoughts or should I say a few billion bucks for your thoughts?"

Chad Brewster leaned on the door frame of Melanie's office. He had been an associate at Hunt, Spencer & McCoy approximately six months longer than Melanie. Chad looked as if he had swallowed sunshine and had a personality to match. He could brighten any day for her. When she first joined the firm, he had taken her under his wing and shown her the ropes.

Over the years, they had grown quite fond of one another but strictly in a brother-sister kind of way. They were exceptionally close friends and would do anything for one another based on that friendship. Shortly after Melanie joined the firm, the two had discovered they shared a passion for jazz music. After a grueling day at the office they would often unwind at a little known restaurant listening to live music. Occasionally, the two would find themselves at a small concert. Their relationship had blossomed over the years and in some ways Chad had helped fill the void left by the death of Melanie's brother. The previous New Year's Eve, Melanie had helped Chad orchestrate a romantic midnight proposal to Michelle, one of Melanie's best friends whom she had introduced to Chad years earlier.

There had been such chaos after the verdict that

Melanie had barely had a chance to speak to Chad and she was glad to see him.

"Got anything cold to drink?" Chad opened the mini fridge.

"Red Bull or diet Dr. Pepper, your choice."

"No ginger ale?" He drolly complained under his boyish grin as he popped the top on a diet cola.

He flopped down in the other guest chair, held his can up to her slim energy drink and toasted.

"To my dear friend, who waltzed into court, kicked some Tennessee tail, and strolled out with the mother lode. Even ol' man Spencer couldn't have come close to putting on such an amazing performance. You were phenomenal, Mel."

"Thanks, Chad."

After a few moments of silence, Melanie allowed a smile to creep into the corner of her lips. "I did kick some Tennessee tail. Didn't I?"

"You bet your sweet little Southern backside you did, darlin'," Chad answered in an exaggerated southern drawl.

"Of course that jerk Winters said the appeal will be on my desk by morning. We're still not at the end of the road."

"I say bring it on, bubba! Mel, the case could not have been more perfect. Judge Brigham called every objection fairly. He played it straight down the middle. The whole case was textbook. No appellate court is going to find one misspoken word in the whole trial. That bastard can take it all the way to the Supreme Court and lose again, guaranteed."

Melanie sat silently as Chad continued. He had always given her wise counsel but in this instance she couldn't shake her apprehension that the worm Winters would find a way to have the verdict overturned.

"Sure, we may have a little more work to do with the appeal but it will be strictly formality. It's like having the perfect Christmas gift wrapped up and all you need to do is slap a bow on it and put it under the tree. It's a cakewalk, Mel."

"I'm certainly glad you have that level of confidence. I'm just exhausted. I'll see things more clearly after a good night's sleep. I can't remember the last time I had eight consecutive hours of sleep in the last two years. It's a wonder I haven't crashed and burned long before today."

Chad drained the last of his soda in one long gulp. "Well, I guess I need to run. Michelle and I are due at her grandmother's ninetieth birthday party. Get this. Someone had the bright idea to give the old lady a surprise birthday party. It'll be a wonder if we aren't all eating birthday cake in the cardiac unit at Baylor hospital. I mean, after ninety years, I think the old broad has earned the right not to have people jumping out from behind doors and furniture, yelling *SURPRISE* at the top of their lungs."

"Point well made, counselor." Melanie chuckled in spite of the bone-deep exhaustion that had completely engulfed her. She didn't even feel the caffeine jolt from the Red Bull.

Chad leaned down and kissed her on the top of the head. "All jokes aside, I am proud of you, Mel. You tried an unbelievable case. They gave you an old nag horse that nobody thought was worth a damn and you won the Triple Crown with her. I'm honored to be your best friend. You better not forget me when they make you partner."

"Partner, yeah right. Somehow I doubt that one is right

around the bend."

"Later, Mel."

"Goodnight, Chad. Give Michelle a big hug for me."

After Chad left, Melanie contemplated the possibility. Melanie Bridges, *partner*. That did sound quite nice.

It certainly wouldn't have been something she could have dreamed of had she been born even as recently as her own mama. The good ol' boys' network had only started changing in her lifetime.

Melanie's gaze fell upon the growing darkness outside. Glancing at her watch, she was amazed it was already past six-thirty. What an incredible day. It seemed like a week ago rather than just a few hours that she walked into the courtroom for the verdict. Rolling her tight shoulders and yawning, she decided to call it a day. She suddenly yearned to go home to Fred, Ginger, and a hot bath.

Melanie slipped on her pumps, picked up her purse and jacket, and left her office. Still at her desk, Josephine was busily organizing messages and priority files for the next day.

"Let's go, lady. There's absolutely nothing on that desk that won't be there tomorrow. I'm beyond exhausted and you must be, too."

"I guess I can finish up in the morning," Josephine said, gathering her things. "I'm meeting George for dinner at the Old San Francisco Steakhouse. We're going to celebrate this great day."

Most of the staff had already gone home. There were a few associates still grinding away in their offices or the library but the majority had taken advantage of the exuberant atmosphere from the Devilland verdict and had left.

Josephine pushed the down button on the elevator and that's when it hit her.

"Crud!" Melanie groaned in frustration. "My car isn't here. It's still at the courthouse, in the opposite direction of my condo!"

"No, my dear, your car is parked in your space in the garage. I sent Kate and Lisa to pick it up earlier. They were glad to be able to slip out of the office for a while."

"Thank you, Jo. You think of everything." Melanie sighed gratefully.

"Not everything, but I do try." Josephine grinned as the elevator doors opened to the private garage.

Melanie hugged the older woman tightly. "Thank you, Jo, for everything. Enjoy your night."

"You too, hon'. Go home; get some rest."

Once they went through the guard gate, Josephine turned toward I-35 while

Melanie took the Dallas Tollway to her condominium.

The sky darkened with the golds ushered in by the early evening. Lights of the bustling Dallas danced to life as far as the eye could see. Melanie couldn't remember the last time she had driven home from the office before dark or noticed a setting sun. It had to have been at least two years, since the beginning of the Devilland case. She made a mental promise to herself to take time to appreciate the sunset tomorrow, regardless of what she was doing. The setting sun was taken for granted by most, but the magnificent sight never failed to bring back warm, fond memories of the extraordinary sunsets Melanie and her daddy had enjoyed together.

On special Saturdays, when Melanie was a child, her

mama would pack a delectable picnic supper in the big brown wicker basket. Melanie and her daddy would wake early and drive the few short hours to the coast where they kept their boat. Once there, they set sail for what seemed like miles. They sailed to the one perfect spot where they would drop anchor, sit back, and nibble on their turkey sandwiches with homemade mayonnaise. They would have long conversations, tell silly jokes, and enjoy some of the most gorgeous sunsets ever. The colors had always amazed her—brilliant, pinks, oranges, and purples. Every one had been absolutely breathtaking.

Her daddy's hobby had been photography and often he would capture the sunsets on film. Although her daddy possessed a natural talent with his camera and the pictures were gorgeous, somehow no human was able to capture the brilliance and peace of God's daily miracle in a photograph.

The sunset sails were definitely some of her favorite times with her daddy. It was during these times they made some of Melanie's favorite memories. Her daddy had even named his sailboat after these adventures they shared. *Quality Time.*

Those stolen moments with her daddy were incredibly precious, especially in light of the fact he was the Senior Senator for North Carolina as well as the Senate's Minority Leader. Unlike many politicians, Charles Bridges never failed to make sure his family took priority over his career. God first, family second, career third had been the most valuable lesson Melanie's daddy had taught her.

Thirty-five minutes after leaving the office, Melanie turned into her condominium complex. As she rounded the corner, she hit the opener and the car slid easily into her small garage.

Without thinking, she reached across the seat for her briefcase and laughed aloud when she found the seat empty. It was odd but extremely liberating to not be loaded down with a briefcase full of files. She still couldn't fully comprehend the day's events.

As she put her key in the lock, her heart warmed at the sound of Fred running down the stairway, barking wildly. No matter what her day had been, Fred's energetic greeting warmed her heart. A man who greeted her that enthusiastically would have been even better but she would have to be satisfied with Fred for now. There weren't many men interested in a woman who worked eighty hours a week and often slept at the Stoneleigh Hotel downtown during big cases.

Melanie sighed deeply as she thought of what her life had become. She ate. She slept. She worked. Period. She quickly chastised herself for entertaining such melancholy thoughts in view of what she had achieved only hours earlier. Today she had changed more lives than even she could imagine. With the enormous settlement, Shirley Sims and MADD would be able to reach out to millions of people. No. She would not allow herself to lament the lack of a love life. She would need to get herself much more in balance before she could possibly be ready for the dating world, but right now her legal career was her top priority.

Fred jumped almost three feet in the air and ran wild circles around her as she took off her coat and set down her bag. She picked up the pup and he lavished her with wet, sloppy kisses all over her face, neck, and ears.

"Hey, buddy, we won! Mama won the Devilland case!"

Fred cocked his head in curiosity at her laughter.

From her perch atop a three story kitty condo, Ginger glanced briefly at the ecstatic Fred and jubilant Melanie and then turned back to stare into the dark night.

Melanie kicked her shoes into the corner and headed for the kitchen with Fred right on her heels.

Opening the oversized pantry, she grabbed a chocolate chip cookie for herself, a Milk-Bone for Fred, and even a cat treat for the princess.

Melanie walked into the bathroom, shedding clothes onto the bedroom floor as she went. Completely naked except for her black lace underwear, she dimmed the overhead lights and lit the small collection of fragrant candles on the shelf at the end of the Jacuzzi tub.

She turned on the water full force, and poured in a generous amount of her favorite cucumber and melon bath oil.

Returning back into the kitchen, she reached in the back of the refrigerator for the bottle of champagne. Although she seldom drank alcohol, occasionally she did enjoy something to help her relax and she almost never drank anything other than the crisp, clean bubbly.

Grabbing a crystal wine flute from her grandmama Tilly's antique china hutch, Melanie returned to the bathroom. The bubbles had reached the top of the tub. Perfect. Absolutely perfect. Melanie turned off the water, shed her panties, poured herself a glass of champagne, and slipped into the warm water. The bubbles swallowed her completely. She savored the pounding of the warm waters all over her weary body.

Relaxing in the warm water, she lost herself in the peace and tranquility. Except the bubbles being generated by the Jacuzzi, silence enveloped the entire condo.

After an hour soaking in the Jacuzzi and finishing a second glass of champagne, she turned off the jets, flipped the drain, and reached for the eggplant purple bath sheet hanging next to the tub.

Opening her large walk-in closet, she chose her favorite pair of pajamas. They were soft pink flannel adorned with yellow rubber ducks, a gift from her niece last Christmas. Despite the fact that this forty-one-year-old woman was now one of the most renowned attorneys in the country, she would forever be a little girl from North Carolina at heart.

After feeding Fred and Ginger, Melanie opened the refrigerator to see what interested her for supper. Sighing deeply she surveyed the barren refrigerator. Living at the office for the last three months during the trial had not left much time for grocery shopping. Neither the cottage cheese nor deli ham appealed to her. Looking in the freezer, she found it just as empty. Her gaze fell upon the perfect meal behind two boxes of frozen dinners—cookies and cream ice cream. There wasn't a better dinner selection after a day like today.

Melanie quickly grabbed a spoon from the silverware drawer, tossed the ice cream lid into the garbage, and turned off the kitchen light. Calories be damned after a day like today. Already savoring the first scrumptious taste of the dessert, she sat down on the sofa with Grandmama Tilly's handmade quilt and turned on the TV. Finding a rerun of *Seinfeld* she hadn't seen, Melanie settled down to enjoy the crazy antics of Kramer, Elaine, George, and Jerry.

Within minutes, the long bath and champagne caught

up with her and she fell fast asleep, Ginger curled behind Melanie's knees, and Fred curled under the covers at his mistress' feet.

Rubbing her eyes and yawning, Melanie had no idea how long she had been dozing. She sat up and stretched her arms above her head. The ache in her neck had finally subsided.

She reached for the remote control and channel surfed until she found the news. She couldn't believe what she saw, rubbing her eyes with the heels of her palms. There, on the screen, the anchorman reported the Devilland verdict. Comprehension completely failed her as she stared in disbelief at herself on the courthouse steps only hours earlier.

Of course, she had seen the cameras and reporters standing in front of her as she had given her statement but the reality of it all suddenly hit her hard and fast. An unfamiliar queasiness in her stomach rolled as she changed the channels. She found herself on station after station. It wasn't only the local channels. It was the national channels, too. Her mouth fell open as she flipped to CNN. Millions of viewers were watching her right this minute. News anchors across the world were talking about one thing and one thing only—*her*!

"Un-friggin'-believable!" Her mouth went dry and her palms began to sweat. She had been so goal driven for so long, so focused on winning that she had never fully considered this verdict truly wasn't just about Joshua Stanford. It was bigger, much bigger.

After the initial shock wore off, she scrutinized her statement as she watched it first on one channel and then the next. Typically, overly critical of herself, she was surprisingly happy with her comments. The delivery was well-done, considering she had never prepared any type of statement. Her words came from her heart and she was indeed pleased.

She then retreated into her routine criticism. "Good Lord, I look like something the cat dragged home."

That wasn't entirely true. She looked great for someone who had been working eighteen hours a day, seven days a week, skipping meals, and cheating herself out of sleep for the last two years.

The ringing of the phone broke her reverie. Automatically glancing at the caller ID and recognizing the number, she picked up instantly.

"Way to go, baby sister! You are kicking ass and taking names out there in Big D. I had no idea you could be such a ball buster!"

"Thanks, Jordie. Such polite language! Have you forgotten your Southern belle manners?"

"After a day like today, I've forgotten my own name. I'm sorry I didn't call you earlier. I've been delivering babies since four this morning. I just got my first real break of the day. I came into the lounge and saw your face all over the news. How does it feel? Is it as big a rush as you expected it would be?"

"I'm sitting here staring at the television and am in complete shock. I never even allowed myself think about how victory would feel and certainly not one like this. During the entire case I never let myself to think further than the present moment."

Jordan, Melanie's older sister, was a very successful in her own right. Living on the West Coast, she had recently been named on a prestigious medical journal's list of the top twenty-five OB-GYN's in the nation.

"Hey, Carter, that's my kid sister! Look on the tube! That's her, the hot-shot lawyer! I even have her on the phone. Want to talk to the most famous attorney in the country? She's single and even better looking than I am."

Melanie giggled as her proud sister gushed enthusiastically to someone who had obviously just walked into the doctors' lounge.

"Jordie! Who are you talking to? Please don't start matchmaking again. You know I hate when you do that. You started when I was in the ninth grade and haven't given up yet." Melanie laughed, although she was dead serious.

"Somebody has to take control of your love life. You're too damn busy busting balls to take care of anything else."

"Thanks a lot. How are Nate and the boys? When are y'all going to come visit me? I miss y'all terribly."

"Everyone's doing fine. Nathaniel's completely absorbed in basketball. Hunter's enamored with our new neighbor Kara. Jake's growing like a weed. Nate's doing great, too. He's done a few preliminary interviews with some of the universities around here, nothing serious. He's just testing the waters. This past weekend we finally decided once he gets his doctorate, we're going to make the big move. We're leaving California and going back home."

"Wow! I thought y'all loved it out there. I never imagined you would consider leaving the fun and sun."

"We do love it, or we did. When we first moved here, it was great. I think mainly because it was a big city and had the glamour appeal. Now we're both looking for somewhere a little more real and not so plastic. Even the boys are excited about the prospect of coming back to the South. As much as we've enjoyed living here, I finally realized most of the people we consider friends are racing through life, spending money they don't have to buy things they don't need to impress people they don't like. That's not us. We all want to go home."

Hearing that Jordan and her family were planning to move home was the icing on the cake of her wild and fantastical day.

"That would be fabulous. I miss y'all so much."

A beeping suddenly shrilled into the receiver.

"Not another one!" Jordan wailed. "Baby sister, I just got paged 911. I need to run so I can bring another baby into this crazy world. Take care of yourself. We're all proud of you! I love."

"Thanks, Jordie. I love."

It was one family tradition most people found odd but Melanie's family didn't say "*I love you*", they said "*I love*" to one another. Melanie had asked her mama about it long ago. Elizabeth Bridges had explained that when Drew was a toddler, he would say "I love" when his mama and daddy kissed him goodnight. Melanie's parents adopted the phrase and followed it through when the girls were born. It was little things like this that were the threads of the bonds which held Jordan and Melanie so close.

As she hung up the phone, Melanie turned to Fred and Ginger. "Okay guys, I think it's time for us to hit the sack."

This was the first night in what seemed like forever she hadn't taken the Stanford case to bed with her. Her long time habit had been to fall asleep either reading her notes from the day or jotting down additional points she needed

Josephine to research for her.

Crawling between the soft covers, Melanie plumped her pillow. Every single muscle in her body melted.

Absently, she petted Fred on the belly as she stared at the ceiling. Today had been an emotional roller coaster. There hadn't been a single emotion she hadn't felt at some point today. In a little less than twenty-four hours, her entire world had changed. What would the next twenty-four hours bring?

t w o

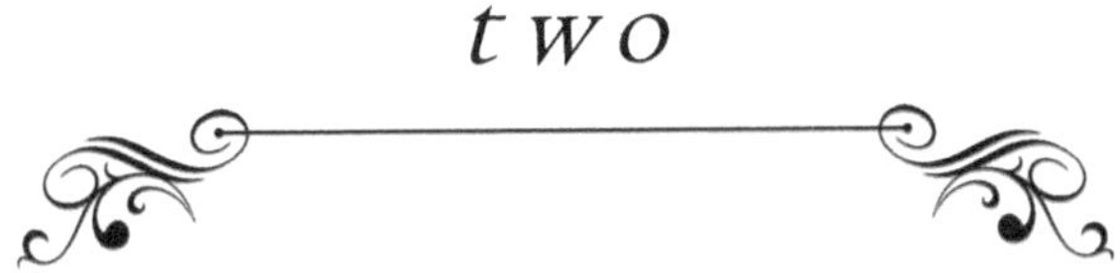

The next morning-January, 2003
Dallas, Texas

"ANSWER THE PHONE, Jo," MELANIE MUMBLED. "Why aren't you answering the damn phone?"

The incessant ringing roused Melanie from her slumber as she sat bolt upright in bed and tossed back the covers. She padded into the living room, yawning. Without even glancing at the caller ID, Melanie answered the phone.

"Good Morning, Sunshine!"

"Pauline!" Other than Melanie's cousin Sue Ellen, Pauline had been her dearest friend in college. Melanie often woke to Pauline's bright smile as she stood next to Melanie's bed with a fresh cup of coffee and those same words, *Good Morning, Sunshine!*

"Omigosh, I can't believe it's you. How was Europe?"

"Europe is wonderful. I'm still here. More importantly, how is my best and most famous friend?"

"How in the world did you know about the verdict?"

"Marco's sister in New York called earlier this evening

and left a message for us at the hotel. I hated to call so early but I was afraid I wouldn't catch you if I waited any later."

"I'm so glad you called. It's been absolutely crazy for me for the last three months. I think this is the first morning I haven't been at my desk by sunrise. I still can't believe the victory but it feels great, actually better than great. I have so much to tell you but I want to hear about you too. Are you still in Rome? Are you still madly in love?"

Pauline laughed. "That would be yes on both accounts. We're having a marvelous time but I can't wait to see you and catch up on everything. We'll be coming back to New York on the twenty-second and will be back in Dallas by the end of the month. Now that you're famous, your calendar will be full but make some time for you and me. I'll call you when we get back to the States and we'll pick a date. I hate to cut this short but Marco has the taxi waiting. We're meeting his boss for a nightcap. I have to run."

"That sounds wonderful. Take care and I'll see you soon. Thanks so much for calling. I love you!"

"I love you, too."

Still smiling, Melanie hung up the phone. She hadn't realized how much she missed her Pauline until she'd heard her voice.

They had one of those special bonds of friendship which are few and far between. They could go months without talking to one another, usually due to the demands of their careers, then one of them would call and they would pick up where they left off as if they had spoken to each other that very morning.

"Coffee." Melanie rubbed her eyes. "I need coffee."

She opened the patio door to let Fred out for his

morning rituals before heading to the coffee pot.

Reaching for the filters, she stopped and stared at the bright red numbers on the digital display—6:34.

"No coffee. Sleep. I need more sleep. I deserve more sleep." Melanie padded back across the condominium.

Crawling into the still warm bed, Melanie closed her eyes and fell asleep only a few short minutes after her head hit the pillow.

Two hours later, Melanie's eyes flew open and she sat up in the bed.

"Crap! What time is it? What day is it?" Melanie glanced at the brilliant sunbeams dancing across the room.

Relief washed over her as she finally found her watch and saw it was only ten minutes before nine. Fred never failed to wake her by 6:30 every morning.

"Fred, where are you?" She raised the covers in search of the pup.

"Outside. I let him outside."

Melanie hopped out of bed and headed for the kitchen.

As Melanie quickly started the coffee pot, the reality of yesterday hit her anew.

"Wow, I did it. I really did it." It was so unreal. All of it. The verdict. The national news coverage.

She poured a healthy dose of cream and two heaping teaspoons of sugar before filling her cup to the brim with steaming coffee.

She inhaled the rich aroma and sat at the small dining table. Watching Fred chase a squirrel from the birdfeeder, Melanie's thoughts drifted back to sitting at Grandmama Tilly's kitchen table all those many, many years ago. Her grandmama would pour one part coffee to one part milk and add two teaspoons of sugar into Melanie's tiny demi-tasse cup.

"You don't like coffee, Mellie. You like colored sweet milk." Her grandmama would chuckle as the two of them sat down at her kitchen table.

Outside the bay window, multitudes of birds flocked to feeders throughout the enormous yard. Grandmama Tilly had taught Melanie the name of every bird that flew into the beautiful yard and had entertained her with stories of the birds, their babies back in the nests, and their bird adventures. Young Melanie knew her grandmama told tall tales but she loved it anyway.

On occasion, a cardinal appeared at the bird feeder and Grandmama Tilly would stop whatever she was doing and make sure Melanie did the same. They would both spend the entire time in silence watching the glorious red bird feed until it took flight. It didn't matter what was going on in Grandmama Tilly's kitchen, when a cardinal flew into the yard, everyone, young and old alike, knew to be quiet, still, and admire the exquisite visitor.

Grandmama would say, "Child, no matter what's going on in your life at any particular moment, never forget a cardinal is God's way of reminding you to stop and be thankful for all the gifts He has bestowed upon you. The Lord is with you—always."

Still to this day, when Melanie would see the rare and exquisite red bird in the trees or flying across her path, she'd remember those precious times with her grandmama. More importantly, she still maintained the ritual of stopping whatever she was doing, watching the cardinal for as long as he stayed and saying a quiet prayer to God, thanking Him for all He had blessed her with in her life. Often, a cardinal would visit her when she found herself at her lowest point and needed reassurance that all would be well. In these dark times, she'd take it as a sure sign that God was indeed with her.

After pouring a second cup, Melanie took her coffee into the bathroom and began to get ready for work.

A little over an hour later, Melanie walked into the offices of Hunt, Spencer & McCoy feeling refreshed and energetic. Colleagues who had missed seeing her yesterday stopped her and offered their congratulations. Feeling as if she were walking on air, Melanie smiled to herself and shook her head. Yes. It was real. She had defeated the undefeatable.

Passing Josephine's desk, she noticed where there had been one yesterday afternoon, there were now three separate stacks of pink message slips, all at least two inches thick. The entire world must have called her. Melanie shook her head in both bewilderment and dread. After all, she'd have to return those calls.

Gorgeous colors and fresh, sweet fragrance overwhelmed her as she entered her office. In awe, she stood completely still. Floral arrangements covered every available surface in her entire office. Larger plants filled nearly every square inch of the floor.

In the middle of her desk sat the most magnificent arrangement of all—dozens of yellow roses in an elegant Waterford vase.

Busy making room on the wide window sill for a lovely arrangement of exotic orchids, Josephine glanced up and smiled at her boss.

"Good Lord, this place looks like a flower shop!"

"Or a funeral home," Josephine chuckled, "depending upon the way you look at it but I'm with you, I prefer flower shop."

Taking off her suit jacket and dropping her purse next to the coat rack amid two huge green plants, Melanie gazed around the small room in complete amazement.

It wasn't yet eleven o'clock and there were at least four dozen different floral arrangements and plants, all sent personally to her. She slid into her chair behind her desk and plucked out a large, cream-colored envelope tucked in the middle of the yellow roses. Her heart swelled and tears filled her eyes as she read the enclosed card.

"There are forty-five single Texas yellow roses. One dozen for each billion dollars you won for the cause. Congratulations! We're so proud of you and will be in Dallas to celebrate with you soon. With much love and admiration, Patsy and Matt Landers".

Patsy and Matt Landers were the brilliant husband-wife legal team who first conceived the legal basis behind the Tobacco Master Settlement Agreement originally between the attorneys generals of forty-six states and the four largest U.S. tobacco companies. Although the case never reached a jury verdict, the Landers and their legal team had been victorious in reaching the settlement agreement with the tobacco companies, in effect holding the tobacco giants liable for their harmful and all too often fatal products. Just as Melanie had, they had been awarded billions of dollars, over two hundred billion. They had laid the groundwork for her case and no doubt many more to come in the future.

Patsy and Melanie were introduced by a mutual friend

shortly after Melanie took the Stanford case. Patsy and her husband had become close friends of Melanie's and they were both extremely generous with their knowledge and time in discussing legal strategy while Melanie prepared her own case.

Often, Patsy would call Melanie on Saturday afternoon and spend literally hours talking to and supporting her. Matt had even sent their Gulfstream to Dallas one Friday as a surprise to pick up Melanie and bring her back to their home in Clarksdale, Mississippi for a weekend of much needed R&R. They were both not only incredible attorneys but also two of the most genuine people Melanie had ever met.

Rising from her chair, Melanie took her time walking around her office and reading the cards on each of the floral arrangements and plants. Once she had read all the cards, she buzzed Josephine and asked her to come back into her office.

"Jo, these are all lovely but I won't be able to get any work done with them in here. Please do me a favor. Make a list of the type of arrangement and the sender so we can write thank you notes. Choose an arrangement for your desk and disburse the rest among those who worked with us on the case. The only arrangement I'd like to keep in my office is the yellow roses from the Landers."

"I made an inventory of the arrangements and senders as they began arriving this morning. I'll have the thank you notes for you to sign by this afternoon."

Josephine easily chose a gorgeous silk arrangement of Texas bluebonnets, Indian paintbrushes, and other native wildflowers for herself. She then set about the task of delivering the other arrangements first to the associate attorneys and then to the support staff who had worked so diligently on the Stanford case.

Melanie answered her emails for the next two hours. Most were from friends and associates congratulating her on the unprecedented victory.

"Mel?"

Glancing from her computer, Melanie smiled at Grace Sullivan, one of the many paralegals who had worked on the Devilland case, standing in the doorway.

"Hey, come on in and sit. I had no idea you were still here. Shouldn't you be on leave?"

Grace rubbed her hand over her very pregnant belly. "Actually, I'm on the way out the door. This baby seems to have no immediate plans to be born so I'm going to the hospital first thing in the morning and the doctor is going to induce my labor. I hung on until after the verdict but now I need to have this baby. I wanted to stop by and thank you for the gorgeous flowers. That was sweet of you to think of me."

Melanie's heart warmed at the thought of the young woman delaying her delivery to hear the verdict.

"You worked as hard as any of us. Make that the two of you." Melanie grinned.

"Well, thanks again. I should get going."

The all too familiar lump immediately rose in Melanie's throat as she watched the pregnant woman waddle out the office. Biting her lip to fight back a surge of tears, Melanie reached far back in her desk drawer and pulled out the dog-eared envelope.

With a trembling hand, she removed the sonogram

dated almost fifteen years earlier. The tiny black and white image was all she had of the child she had lost—one of her life's greatest heartbreaks.

Melanie's heart ached as it did every time she thought of Stephen and how things had gone so terribly wrong for both of them. No. Maybe things had not gone terribly wrong for her. Grandmama Tilly taught all of her children and grandchildren that God never wasted one single heartbreak. Had her child lived, she would have stayed with Stephen forever, trapped in a hellacious marriage. No. God had known exactly what He was doing. If her child had been born, Melanie would have never made it here, today. She may have lost her own child but she had saved countless other children with the defeat of Devilland.

"No pity party today." Melanie resolutely forced herself to smile as Josephine brought in two more floral arrangements.

three

The same week-January, 2003
Dallas, Texas

WASTING NO TIME, MELANIE DOVE HEADFIRST back into work after the Devilland verdict. True to his word, Alan Winters filed his appeal and the process which would likely consume the next few years had begun.

Absolute bedlam consumed the next days for both Melanie and Josephine. The phones rang nonstop. Calling were the *Dallas Morning News*, the *New York Times*, the *Washington Post*, *USA Today*, *D Magazine,* and a whole host of other local and national newspapers and magazines. Everyone wanted the same precious thing—an interview with the victorious Melanie Bridges.

"They can use the statement I gave at the courthouse for one more day. Buy me some time until tomorrow morning. I need some peace and quiet to decide exactly what I want to say. It will blaze like wildfire over the AP Wire so I want to choose my words carefully. I've got to get rid of these reporters so I can get back to work, real work," Melanie groaned when Josephine asked what to tell the multitude of journalists begging for a moment of Ms. Bridges' time.

"Am I interrupting?" Victor McCoy, the firm's third senior partner, asked from her doorway.

A smile crept to Melanie's lips as she looked up from the news statement she was composing. Victor had just returned from a three month leave of absence to travel Europe with his wife.

"No, sir. You're not interrupting anything at all. Please come in and have a seat," Melanie said enthusiastically as she removed her reading glasses and gestured for the man to sit.

"You're never going to drop all that Southern formality and just call me Victor. Are you?" He chuckled as he settled his large frame across from her.

Blushing, Melanie replied as she had dozens of times before. "No, probably not, Mr. McCoy. I have to blame it on my parents and grandparents. I was taught to address my elders as Mr. or Mrs. and try as I might, I can't seem to shake it."

"That's fine and well but another couple of victories like this and all of us are going to be calling you *Ms. Bridges.* You may be running this whole place before we know it."

"I seriously doubt that but thank you for the compliment," Melanie replied graciously.

"I've heard from both Charles and William that you did an outstanding job from your opening statement all the way through your powerful closing argument. They also told me you had Alan Winters stuttering and squirming in his seat by the second day of the trial. I truly hate to have missed that spectacle. I would've especially loved to watch the smug bastard break into hives when the verdict was read."

Laughing, Melanie responded, "Somehow I don't remember it exactly that way but I appreciate the generous accolades. How have you been? We've certainly missed you around here. How was Paris?"

"Big, dirty, and expensive as always, but both my wife and I were eager to see our daughter. She wasn't able to come home for Christmas so it had been over a year since we'd seen her last. I'm pleased to say she seems to be happy and started teaching at the Sorbonne. It's always a great joy to see her and the rest of the family."

"How old is your grandson Benjamin?"

It was simply polite Southern manners to ask about one's relatives and Melanie had a special talent for remembering names of almost everyone's family, especially children and grandchildren.

"Oh my, you do have an excellent memory. The boy just turned five and I swear he must have grown two feet since we saw him last and he has a vocabulary you wouldn't believe but I've taken enough of your time." He waved his hand off and moved to the next subject. "I wanted to stop in and ask you to join us all for a celebration dinner. I assumed Charles and William had taken everyone out already but it seems the old coots waited for me to get back into town. I imagine they want me to pick up their check. That's normally the only reason they ever invite me anywhere." McCoy chortled good-naturedly. "How about either Monday or Tuesday, which is the better evening for you?"

Flattered that the firm would go to the trouble and

expense for her, she smiled graciously. "Either would be fine for me."

"Well then, Monday it is. Please feel free to invite a friend to accompany you. The more the merrier. I'll have Beth make the arrangements for seven. How does that sound?"

"Perfect. I'll be looking forward to it Mr. McCoy, and welcome home."

"Thank you, Melanie. It's always good to be back in Texas."

Melanie had no intention of asking anyone to join her, mainly because since taking the Devilland case, she'd barely had any dates at all. There was no one in whom she had any interest either. She would much rather enjoy the evening with her colleagues from the firm.

That weekend, Melanie and Michelle met for lunch and spent a leisurely afternoon shopping at the mall. Michelle had exquisite taste and Melanie was grateful to have her opinion.

Melanie had tried on at least a dozen different dresses and half a dozen pairs of shoes before finding the perfect little black dress and a gorgeous pair of high-heeled black evening shoes. The heels were a little higher than she normally wore but Michelle insisted they complemented the dress perfectly. Spinning in the mirror and giddy with excitement, Melanie knew the dinner was going to be a night to remember.

four

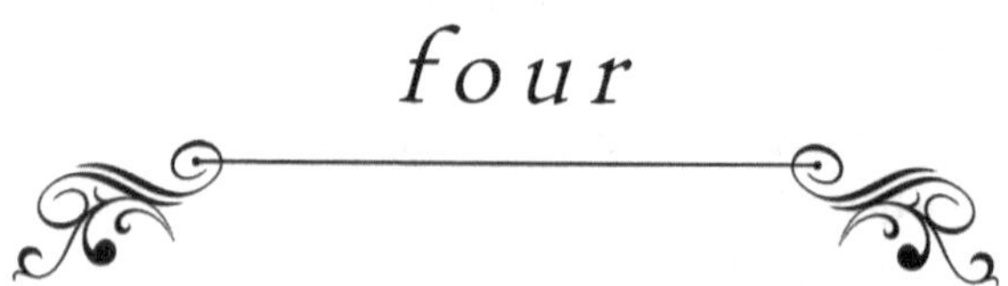

The following Monday-January, 2003
Dallas, Texas

THE FRONT DOOR BELL RANG JUST AS MELANIE PUT on Grandmama Tilly's pearl earrings. She took one last look at herself in the hall mirror, checking that the matching pearl choker was straight and that no wayward curl had escaped her hair's classic French twist. She swung the door open to Chad, dapper in his tuxedo, and Michelle, sparkling in her blue one-shouldered sequined gown, on her stoop.

Michelle held out her arms. "Wow, you look amazing!"

"Yeah," Chad said, wearing a goofy grin. "You're gonna break necks in that dress."

"Ah, thanks, y'all." Heat flushed Melanie's cheeks. She grabbed her purse off the foyer table. "I'm ready."

Thunder rolled in the distance and a light drizzle fell as Chad popped open an oversized umbrella and covered both Melanie and Michelle.

As it had been for days, shock once again enveloped Melanie as she saw the sleek black limousine at the curb.

The distinguished driver standing beside the open back door reminded the stunned Melanie of the coachman ready to whisk Cinderella to the ball.

"Chad, you didn't!" Melanie exclaimed as they slid into the car.

"As much as I'd like to take the credit, I have to admit the truth. The three fat cats sprung for it. Hunt came in my office yesterday and told me to make arrangements to pick you up in style. You are the golden child. This is your party, my love. Enjoy it." Maybe so but it was still hard for her to grasp. She wasn't used to people treating her like a star. "You've earned every luxury the big bosses want to spoil you with after the size of the rabbit you pulled out of Alan Winters' ass." Chad laughed as he popped the top on a chilled bottle of champagne and filled three glasses as the car glided easily into the evening traffic.

"Classy, Chad," Michelle said. Melanie smirked in unison with her.

"Alright then, here's to champagne wishes and caviar dreams. May they all be yours, my loves," Chad gave an amazingly accurate impersonation of Robin Leach and grinned broadly at both women.

Finishing her champagne, Melanie pulled her lipstick and compact from her purse and took one last quick look at herself as the chauffeur pulled into the drive of the elegant Mansion, the only five star hotel in all of Dallas.

Melanie had eaten at the Mansion only twice before tonight. The hotel was one of the most elegant places Melanie had ever been and she'd certainly seen her share of grand restaurants and luxury hotels around the world when her parents were alive.

Her daddy loved fine food. Her mama loved to travel and discover new places. Therefore the three Bridges children were introduced to a wonderful world of new and exciting experiences very early in their lives.

Elizabeth Bridges said the best things in life were the people we love, the places we've seen, and the memories we make along the way. Both Melanie's parents had instilled this spirit in all of their children and Melanie was grateful to be sharing this special time with so many people she'd grown to love. No doubt tonight would be a night that many memories were made.

As the silver-haired maitre d' led them to the table, appreciative glances from both men and women fell upon the stunning Melanie. She felt beautiful, if not a tiny bit uncomfortable with the attention.

When she arrived at the back of the restaurant, Melanie's hand flew to her mouth as she gasped. The firm's partners as well as the entire team of those who had assisted her on the case were already seated at large round tables, each table adorned with an exquisite winter floral arrangement as its centerpiece.

The jubilant and victorious members of Hunt, Spencer & McCoy who had crippled Jack Devilland and many spouses or significant others filled the room. Josephine reached out to squeeze Melanie's hand and give her a wink as Melanie passed her table.

The three new arrivals were guided to the larger table in the middle of the others. Already seated were the senior partners and their wives.

The waiter then appeared to take the newcomers' drink orders. Melanie ordered a glass of sweet tea. She was dizzy from the excitement of her arrival and the tall flute of champagne in the limo. The tea would soothe her nerves.

Sipping her tea and making small talk with Gretta McCoy, a waiter suddenly appeared with a bottle of Perrier-Jouet in a chilled ice bucket and set it alongside her chair. He handed his guest the tiny card embossed with the Mansion's logo.

Tilting her head in curiosity, Melanie read the card.

"Congratulations on your tremendous victory. Enjoy! An adoring fan."

Quickly glancing around the restaurant, Melanie saw no one looking in her direction. Puzzled, she reread the card. *"An adoring fan."*

Uneasiness washed over her. The sensation of someone's gaze upon her tingled down her spine. She glanced again around the restaurant, but no one was looking in her direction. Still, she couldn't shake the uneasy feeling of someone watching her.

"What's it say?" Chad asked.

She gave him the card which he read aloud.

"What an odd way to sign a card," Carolyn Hunt said. "I didn't think you lawyers had fans." Her tablemates laughed heartily. Melanie merely chuckled, troubled by the anonymous gesture.

The next hour flew as the group finished dinner. Silence suddenly fell over the room as Melanie took a sip of her tea. Curiously looking around the table over the rim of her glass, butterflies fluttered in her stomach at their expectant smiles. Confused, Melanie's gaze traveled across the room and finally fell upon a distinguished black gentleman headed toward the main table pushing a large cart carrying an enormous tres leches sheet cake topped with chocolate covered strawberries.

Everyone burst into song, singing *Melanie's a jolly good lady* as they had when she arrived back at the office after the verdict had been read.

Heat crept up her neck from the crowd's attention while her throat constricted and she fought to hold back joyful sobs of pride and gratitude.

Once the jubilant singing had ended, Chad and a few others softly chanted, "Speech, speech, speech".

The waiter reappeared at Melanie's side and made a production of popping the cork on the champagne bottle she'd been sent earlier by the mystery fan. He poured her glass first and then proceeded to fill the glasses of all those seated at the table with her. This took an additional bottle of champagne which he had within his reach. The other waiters bustled about the room pouring expensive champagne for the guests at the surrounding tables.

Nervously laughing and embarrassed by the lavish attention, Melanie shot Chad a mock evil stare. She stood and gazed around the room at her professional family. Taking a deep breath, she willed herself to not to melt into a puddle of tears as all eyes fell upon her. Melanie finally found her voice.

"I don't know where to begin or what to say. I'm truly touched by all of your kindness and support. As I said the day of the verdict, this victory doesn't belong to me alone. This victory belongs to those of you who toiled tirelessly along with me and devoted so many days, nights, and weekends to what many considered a lost cause from the beginning. I want to give a special thank you to all the spouses, significant others, and families of my devoted colleagues who ate dinners alone, spent weekends without their loved one, and assiduously supported our cause from behind the scenes. I was merely the point person. It was each of you who defeated the giant that is Jack Devilland."

Melanie raised her champagne glass and slowly turned to acknowledge each table around the room. Tearfully, she added, "Thank you all from the bottom of my heart."

After Melanie sat down, Hunt, McCoy, and finally Spencer followed with a toast, praising everyone's hard work and dedication to the history-making case.

It had been a euphoric evening for all and Melanie hated to see it end. After coffee and dessert, the guests began to depart, stopping by the main table to thank the partners for a wonderful evening and to congratulate Melanie once again.

"Are you ready to go, Cinderella? We have to get the limo back by midnight or it turns into a pumpkin." Chad winked.

"Yes. It's time for us to go. I have a deposition in the morning at nine o'clock sharp."

After exchanging parting pleasantries with the three partners and their wives, Melanie, Chad, and Michelle left the restaurant.

The drizzle from earlier had intensified and sheets of rain fell from the darkened sky as the threesome dashed for the car. Rushing to meet Melanie and Michelle, the driver held out the oversized umbrella but it was too late. Both women were already wet. Melanie's dress clung to her skin, rivulets of water dripped down her face.

"Melanie!" Charles Hunt called out to her.

Turning too quickly, her brand-new heels slick on the wet pavement, she slipped and fell, her legs wedged between the car and the curb. Immediately Chad and the driver rushed to her side, picking her up from the wet sidewalk.

More embarrassed than physically hurt, Melanie frowned at the huge rip in her hose and the bloody gash on her left knee, now throbbing in pain. Within an instant her ankle swelled as humiliation flushed her cheeks.

"I'm so sorry, Melanie. Are you alright?"

"Yes, yes. I'm fine," she insisted, completely mortified by the small crowd now gathering around her.

"You forgot your purse at the table."

She swept disheveled strands of her hair fallen from the twist out of her eyes. "Thank you, Mr. Hunt," she said quickly, eager to escape to the privacy of the waiting limousine.

She discreetly removed her shredded hose so that she could clean her knee with Chad's handkerchief and ice water.

"Good Lord! I'm so friggin' embarrassed. Could I possibly have managed to look like a bigger idiot?" Melanie wailed before bursting into laughter.

"That was quite the elegant exit, if I do say so myself, Cinderella." Chad smirked.

"Chad! Leave her alone. She feels bad enough without you harassing her," Michelle managed to say before breaking into giggles with Melanie.

"Ugh!" Melanie grimaced as she glanced down at the blood-soaked handkerchief. "I'll wash this and return it to you."

"Not necessary. Keep it as a memento of the night you busted your tiny tail right in front of God and everyone at the Mansion."

"You can kiss my tiny tail, Chad Brewster!" Melanie laughed again.

"May I walk you to the door?" the driver asked as he pulled to a stop in front of Melanie's condo.

"No, thank you. I'm fine, really."

Soaking wet with her scuffed black heels in her hand, Melanie trotted up the sidewalk, glad to hear Fred barking at the door.

As she slipped her key into the lock, something rustled the bushes. Her spine prickled with fear, her breath stilled. She cautiously looked over her shoulder while unlocking the door. No one there. Nothing. Just as she decided the noise was probably a rabbit, she caught a flash of light out of her peripheral vision beyond the hedge. Maybe there was more rain on the way. She hurried inside and chastised herself for being scared of a little creature and a bolt of lightning.

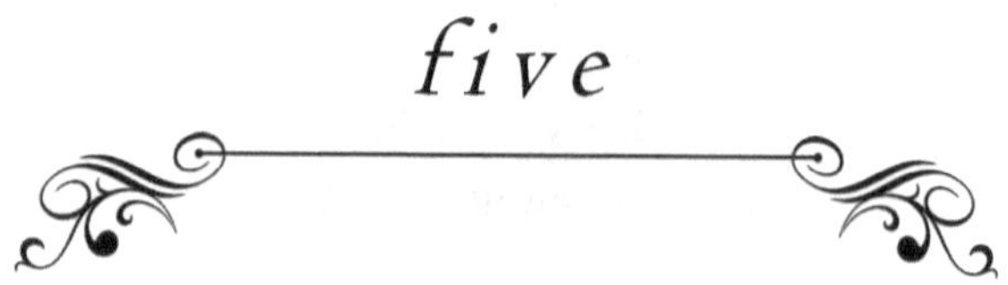

five

One week passes-January, 2003
Dallas, Texas

MONDAY MORNING DAWNED CRISP AND CLEAR and everything outside sparkled after the torrential rains of the past week. Just like rains that wash away the gray, Melanie's spirits were high without the Devilland case wearing her down. She felt better than she had in weeks, new and fresh, blooming with confidence.

Unfortunately, Melanie's tranquil mood didn't last long. Shortly after eleven, Josephine knocked on her boss' door.

"Come in."

"I hate to interrupt you. I know you're neck deep in your research but I felt it important you see this as soon as possible." An uncharacteristic sour expression creased Josephine's face.

"What is it?" An odd sense of trepidation crept over her. Melanie tentatively took the latest edition of the *Dallas Star* from Josephine's hand and her assistant quietly left the room.

Glancing at the cover of the newspaper, Melanie's

stomach roiled, air rushed from her lungs, her vision tunneled onto the headlines, sweat beaded upon her forehead with the heat of anger. Fighting the urge to vomit, Melanie grabbed her bottled water and took a long swallow.

"Bastards!"

Covering the entire front page were two photos of Melanie, both taken in the last fourteen days.

The bold red headline ran across the page and read: Melanie Bridges: Practice What You Preach.

The familiar picture of Melanie on the courthouse steps giving her statement immediately after the Jack Devilland victory covered the left side of the page. The same picture had been printed in almost every newspaper in the nation. The caption under the picture read: Jubilant Melanie Bridges gives victory speech after defeating liquor giant.

The picture on the right-hand side of the page was the one that enraged her. It showed Melanie being picked up from the sidewalk by Chad and the chauffeur after her fall outside the Mansion. The photographer had captured Melanie nervously laughing while she gazed down at her ripped stockings and bloody knee. Charles Hunt's concerned face was centered just over her shoulder. Under the picture were the words 'Drunken Melanie Bridges collapses outside Mansion Hotel after partying all night'.

See inside for more revealing photos and exclusive story was printed in an enormous bright red starburst.

Huge tears of fury blurred her vision and burned a path down her cheeks, her hands trembled.

Quickly turning to the center section of the issue, Melanie easily found the "revealing photos and exclusive story" as promised on the front cover.

Shocked by the montage of photos, Melanie carefully scrutinized the pictures. The first showed Melanie holding the bottle of the champagne sent by the mystery fan and smiling up at the young waiter. The caption read: 'Bridges begins her evening with the best champagne'.

The next picture was of her making her toast to her colleagues at the Mansion with the words *Bridges toasts her victory over liquor company.*

"The damn photographer must have captured every single sip of champagne I drank all night." Melanie cursed again.

Over a dozen different shots of her drinking, smiling, drinking, laughing, and drinking more filled the pages. From the number of different angles of the multitude of photos, one would easily assume she drank two bottles rather than two glasses throughout the evening, including the one she had in the limousine ride from her condo.

As if that weren't enough, the photographer had obviously followed her home to capture his last two shots. The first of these showed Melanie, sans her stockings and shoes, trotting up the sidewalk, still drenched from the rain. 'Miss Bridges seems to have lost half her clothing'.

The final image had captured her on the front porch of her condo, completely disheveled, and peering over her shoulder. 'Severely intoxicated, Bridges has great difficulty unlocking her front door'

"Damn that lowlife jerk! It wasn't a rabbit or a bolt of lightning. It was a scumbag photographer lying in wait for me in the bushes outside my own friggin' home!"

Melanie's mind was racing and more tears sprang to her eyes.

Quickly scanning the article on the alternate page, she read, "*Miss Bridges, hot-shot attorney at the prestigious Dallas firm of Hunt, Spencer & McCoy....blasted the evils of alcohol in her landmark case...winning a multi-billion dollar judgment against liquor giant Jack Devilland... maybe whiskey isn't her choice...but expensive champagne certainly seems to be...ironically...spotted only days after her victory at the exclusive Mansion Hotel guzzling the pricey champagne and dining on lobster tails...obviously completely inebriated...Bridges is picked up from the sidewalk outside the posh hotel....Law firm partner Charles Hunt looks on in utter disgust...Melanie...later seen leaving the limousine she shared with fellow attorney Chad Brewster...missing half her clothes...one can only assume Miss Bridges and Mr. Brewster had quite an action packed ride home from the hotel...maybe they should have retired to a room at the Mansion and not made such an obscene public spectacle...*"

Suddenly her thoughts flew from her own humiliation to a much bigger picture. What would the senior partners feel? Would the ultimate blame fall upon her for this shameful attention? Had she embarrassed the entire firm? What about the appeal? Oh, dear God, the appeal! Chad! Michelle! Rapid-fire thoughts came from all directions.

Hot tears of shame continued to course down her cheeks. How did this happen? Melanie's whole world was collapsing around her. She had been so proud of what she had accomplished, defeating the undefeatable, and now she had been reduced to nothing more than a sordid headline on a trashy tabloid.

Grandmama Tilly always said, "A lady's name should

appear in print only three times in her life—when she is born, when she marries, and when she dies." Melanie could only imagine what her grandmama, the classic Southern belle, would have to say about this disgrace.

"Oh dear God, I can't read any more of this crap! I can't believe this is happening. Friggin' scum of the earth dirt bags who print this garbage and stupid idiots who believe if it's in print then it must be true. Damn it! Damn it! Damn it to Hell and back!" Melanie cried furiously as she tossed the paper across her desk in rage, its pages scattering onto the floor.

Her head pounded a steady beat behind her temples. Reaching in her purse, her fingers quickly found two BC headache powders. She washed both of them down with a long swallow of cola. Wiping her tears with the back of her hand, she desperately tried to stop crying. Never in her life had she been so full of shame.

Gathering her strength half an hour later, she snapped up the strewn papers and tossed them into the trash. She took several deep breaths, absently wiped the last of her tears, and hit the intercom button to call Josephine.

Fortunately, she had already relayed the actual series of events to Josephine last week when she came in battered and bruised so she didn't have to go through any lengthy explanations of the truth.

The older woman entered her boss' office and softly closed the door behind her. She quietly took a seat in front of Melanie's desk.

The younger woman smiled weakly at her assistant as her cheeks still flushed with embarrassment and fury.

"Honey, I told you these guys are pond scum. These

are the same jerks who called your cell phone for a personal interview after the verdict. They'll write anything about anyone to sell their trashy papers. I thought it best if you saw it in the privacy of your own office rather than in the 7-Eleven on the way home tonight. I know this seems like a monumental disaster and I certainly don't want to minimize it. I'll tell you like I've always told my children. Ask yourself, in five years will this really matter?"

"Thanks, Jo," Melanie said in a cracked voice. "I appreciate it." Fresh tears sprang to her eyes. *Damn it! If she could only stop crying!*

"Is there anything I can do for you?"

"No, but thanks for your words of wisdom. I don't even remember why I buzzed you. I just need a little time to think. They're not going to get away with this. I will not be made a fool of by these jerks. I will crucify the SOBs, somehow, someway." Melanie said the words with more fire than she actually felt.

"That's the boss I know and love."

A familiar succession of taps knocked on the office door.

"Come in, Chad." Melanie laughed for the first time in almost an hour.

"Buzz me if you need anything, Mel. Good morning, Chad." Josephine left the office and closed the door behind her.

Melanie sat in silence as Chad went over to the mini fridge, selected a cold can of soda for himself, popped the top and flashed the familiar lopsided grin of his.

Sitting down in the chair Josephine had vacated, he dropped his rolled up copy of the *Dallas Star* on the other chair and eyed the pages in the trash can next to Melanie's desk.

"I see I'm not the first with the worst."

"No. Jo brought it in a little while ago. You know what I just this very instant realized, as you walked in here? That bottle of champagne wasn't from some mystery fan. It was from this asshole photographer to set up his first shot." Melanie fumed as she pounded her fist on the desk. Her nails dug deeply into her palm.

"I hadn't thought of it myself but my money is with you. You see, like my daddy used to say, there's no such thing as free booze."

"You're so goofy, Chad. Maybe that's why we get along so well." Melanie laughed again.

"Seriously though, I'm pissed. I mean really pissed." She frowned.

"You must be to swear like that," Chad said. "Don't sweat it. These bastards didn't only attack you. They attacked *my* good name by implying I did the nasty with you in the back of the friggin' limo. You're like my little sister, for God's sake!" Chad exclaimed in semi-mock repugnance.

"I know, seriously?" She smirked.

"I stopped by to let you know ol' man Hunt called and told me to take you out of here for a bite to eat and then he wants to see both of us in his office at one o' clock sharp."

Melanie's eyes grew wide as she stared at Chad with a mixture of shock and apprehension.

"You think it's about this?" Melanie nodded at the paper that lay next to him.

"That's my guess. I must say the gentleman sounded none too pleased. Unless you've done something else to piss him off that I don't know about, I'd say he plans to declare war on this little rag." Chad pitched his copy in Melanie's wastebasket along with the other.

"Where do you to want eat? It's on me. Actually it's on my expense account per the big man."

"I don't think I can eat anything after reading this garbage. I feel like I'm going to lose the breakfast I ate four hours ago. I certainly don't want to go anywhere around here where we'll be recognized. If some jerk looks at me wrong, I swear I think I'll kill him on the spot, in the mood I'm in right now."

"In the interest of public safety, I've got a great idea. I'll be back to pick you up in thirty minutes."

"Where are you going?"

"Don't worry about it, Mel. I've got exactly what you need in your moment of crisis." He winked as he rose from his chair.

"Thanks, Chad. I appreciate it. You're always there for me when I need you."

"It's the least I can do for a chick who so easily strips half naked for me."

"Don't push me, buster!" She glowered jokingly and playfully threw a pencil at him.

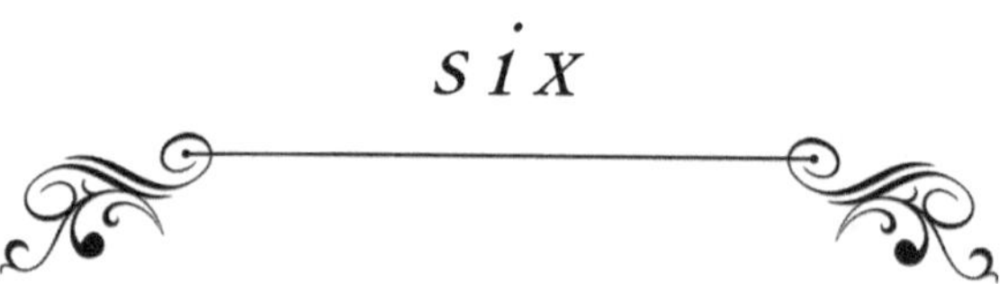

SIX

The same day-January, 2003
Hunt, Spencer & McCoy
Dallas, Texas

MELANIE DID HER BEST NOT TO FIDGET AS SHE sat next to Chad on the long sofa in Hunt's office.

The *Dallas Star* lay ominously on the glass-topped coffee table. Melanie avoided looking at it, fearful should would burst into tears of humiliation again. Instead she gazed out the windows at the breathtaking skyline. Silence hung amid the palpable tension in the air.

Hunt sat behind his desk, a second copy of the tabloid spread in front of him. He drew a long drag from his Cuban cigar. A dark cloud shadowed his features as he sat in contemplation. In addition to Chad, Hunt, and Spencer were Lou Walker and Mike Woods, two of the senior associates with the firm.

Finally, Hunt spoke. "I guess we can get down to the business at hand." He nodded toward his own copy of the tabloid on his desk. "First of all, Melanie and Chad let me say, on behalf of this entire firm, these bastards haven't only attacked the two of you, they've attacked the good name of this firm and every attorney in it. I've already spoken to McCoy and Spencer and we will absolutely not stand for this absurdity."

Melanie flinched as Hunt pounded his fist on top of the desk.

"Walker and Woods have been assigned full time to pursue a libel case against this rag. We're prepared to do whatever we have to do to take these bastards down permanently. We're going to war!" Hunt bellowed in outrage.

"Hell yes, old man," Spencer said. "Lady and gentlemen, it's times like these that practicing law becomes fun. Shutting these jokers down will be purely for sport and, of course, all the money we can squeeze out of them in the process. We can tie them up in court for so long their legal fees will break them." A smug grin broke across his face.

"Those dogs have pissed on the wrong hydrant," Hunt said as he cracked his knuckles.

"We aren't going to try this one in the media. That's their playground. We're going to play in our own sandbox where it will cost the bastards big bucks to play—the legal system." Spencer chuckled as he too puffed on one of his partner's expensive cigars.

A waterfall of emotions washed over Melanie. Less than two hours earlier she had been terrified the partners would somehow blame her for this mess, but they had her back. They had her back! Humility and gratitude filled her heart. This wasn't about her. It was about the firm. The whole firm. How had she not seen it? She had been so quick to blame herself for something that had been completely out of her control. She had done nothing wrong.

After almost an hour, the meeting concluded. Woods and Walker would be in charge of the libel suit. Melanie and Chad were to be taken out of the loop and not to be bothered with the details of the case.

Hunt had called the *Dallas Morning News* and would be issuing only one statement on behalf of the firm. Everyone agreed the less said in response to the article, the better.

Melanie and Chad headed back to their offices on the lower floor. "I think Hunt and Spencer are going to enjoy this."

"I believe they are and I'm going to enjoy watching every single minute of it. Those two are Hell on wheels. Of course, Woods and Walker will do all the grunt work but Hunt and Spencer are going to be right there all the way. I bet they close that little print shop down for good. They're bulldogs out for blood. I'd hate like hell to have them hunting me like that. Did you see the look in Hunt's eyes?"

"I did. It's funny to see them light up like that when they personally didn't want anything to do with the Stanford case," Melanie said as the two of them rode the elevator alone.

"That's because that wasn't personal. This one is personal, very personal. Those two aren't going to stand for being made to look like fools. They were both there. They know the story is a crock of shit. Feel better than you did?"

"Definitely. I don't know why but I felt so alone this morning. I didn't even consider Hunt and Spencer would take it on as a company indignity. I thought it was going to be my own battle."

"I knew better than that. You, my dear, are their

fair-haired child, the wonder kid. They aren't going to let anyone tarnish the Jack Devilland trophy you brought home."

"I haven't brought it home yet. We still have that jerk Winters to contend with and the appeals nightmare." She groaned as they both exited the elevator.

"Ye have little faith." Chad rumpled her hair and trotted off to his office before she could say anything else.

He knew she hated anyone touching her hair and therefore he delighted in doing so often. In so many ways, their relationship was in fact very much like one between a big brother and little sister.

The next morning, prominently on the front page, above the fold, thanks to Charles Hunt's connections at the *Dallas Morning News*, appeared a picture of Hunt, Spencer, and McCoy strategically posed behind Melanie and Chad in the lobby of the firm. The positioning of the partners implied unity of the firm behind the two younger associates.

The article and statement from Charles Hunt were brief. The statement was flawless, covering exactly what needed to be said without lowering the prestigious law firm to the standards of the tabloid.

"Many may have seen the preposterous photographs and blasphemous article concerning two of our associates Melanie Bridges and Chad Brewster. Ms. Bridges and Mr. Brewster are two of the finest attorneys we have ever had work for our firm. The pictures which were so flagrantly misrepresented to the public were actually taken on the evening of a Hunt, Spencer & McCoy sponsored dinner given to celebrate the tremendous victory over the Jack Devilland Company. While many attorneys in the firm devoted themselves

wholeheartedly to this case, it was Ms. Bridges who served as lead counsel and was solely responsible for presenting the case to the court. Therefore, she has become the target of this media assault. Anyone who knows anything of the Jack Devilland lawsuit knows the platform was not, by any means, one of zero tolerance for alcohol. In fact, the foundation for the Stanford case was the devastation caused by long time abuse of alcohol and subsequent addiction. Similar to the famous tobacco cases, the Stanford family sought to hold the liquor company accountable for its seductive marketing campaigns, lack of education regarding the inherent dangers of their product, and treatment for those who fall victim to the disease of alcoholism. It was not to stop the moderate consumption of alcohol by responsible parties. Apparently, the Dallas Star was either extremely uneducated about the actual basis upon which Ms. Bridges was awarded the landmark victory or more likely they did indeed know the facts of the case and subsequent triumph but chose to ignore the truth completely and wrote instead what they knew would sell their publication. Both Bridges and Brewster are above reproach and the sordid allegations that have been printed about them will not be ignored by Hunt, Spencer & McCoy. A libel suit has been filed and we will pursue this issue fully until justice is done. In closing, our firm has elected to try this case, not in the media, but rather where all legal cases belong, in the court system. Therefore, this will be our only statement issued until the appropriate court action has been taken."

With Woods and Walker in charge of the libel suit, Melanie could get back to work on her upcoming insurance fraud case. Although she'd dealt with many insurance cases in the past, she found the research for this particular one especially difficult in the wake of the *Dallas Star* debacle. She did her best to bury herself in productive work rather than stewing about the trashy tabloid. Both Woods and Walker were fine attorneys and Melanie had no doubt they would do an excellent job. Thankfully, she found herself distracted by the whirlwind that remained for the next several weeks. Every morning she'd walk into her office to another two or three gorgeous flower arrangements and stacks of cards from friends, business associates, and even total strangers.

All of the cards thanked her for bringing this case to the forefront. A few of the cards even went into great detail of how the sender's life had been severely impacted by alcohol, either by the loss of a loved one to a drunk driver or by the multitude of other ways alcohol had been the root cause for the destruction of their lives and families.

There were so many cards arriving that she couldn't read them all in the office. Every morning she tucked the new arrivals into her purse and every night she carefully read every one of them. Humbleness over the kind words filled her soul while many of the stories broke her heart. She had witnessed first-hand the devastation alcohol could cause, but reading so many different accounts gave her a much bigger picture. God had used her to accomplish something great. Really great.

On the third day after the publication of the *Dallas Star* article, one particular envelope sitting atop the huge stack on her desk caught Melanie's immediate attention. The address had been written in the familiar and careful block printing. The return address was in Georgia.

When she opened the card, she found that it was from

a box of cards she'd given him last Christmas. The front depicted a winter scene with a picture of a bright red cardinal sitting on a snow covered branch.

She gingerly opened the card and read the familiar penmanship.

"Congratulations, Mellie. I am proud of you. I hope to see you one day soon. I love."

A lump rose in her throat and her hand trembled ever so slightly as she read the name at the bottom. She tucked the card back into its red envelope and put it carefully in her top desk drawer.

Taking a deep breath, she willed herself not to think about the real reason she had been compelled so deeply to take the Stanfords' case. Aaron, her beloved Aaron. A secret she'd carried with her for so many years. She imagined she'd carry it with her for the rest of her life.

seven

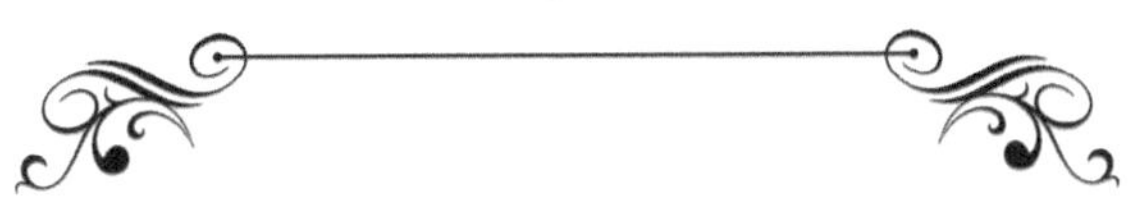

Four Years, Eight months pass
September, 2007
Dallas, Texas

CONFUSED AND NERVOUS, MELANIE TOOK A SEAT on the opposite end of the long sofa from McCoy. Hunt sat in his favorite club chair. Hunt had summoned her to his office only minutes before, saying only that the matter was important.

Both partners wore grim expressions on their faces which only puzzled Melanie more.

"Well, we got the call from George Chandler, over at Chandler, Hughes, and Watson." Hunt said flatly.

Chandler, Hughes, and Watson was the law firm which represented Jack Devilland. Melanie knew McCoy had been in touch with Chandler over the last two months in regards to reaching a settlement on the case prior to it being taken to the Supreme Court. Chandler and McCoy were the attorneys who were going to argue the case before the nine justices, should it go all the way to Washington.

As Alan Winters had promised Melanie almost five

years earlier, his firm had appealed the verdict tirelessly time and again until they were all finally looking at the end of the road. The Supreme Court opened next month and would issue the ultimate judgment, once and for all.

McCoy finally spoke. "We offered a final settlement of twenty-five cents on the dollar with each side paying its own legal fees."

Melanie's heart sank. They had settled. Her thirst for victory, complete victory had filled her dreams for the past five years. Now it was over. A settlement was good but it wasn't the same as winning. There was a tremendous difference in reaching a settlement agreement versus winning a Supreme Court appeal.

"Pack your bags. We're going to Washington!" McCoy grinned from ear to ear.

"Sir?" Melanie heard the slightest quiver in her voice. Did she hear right? Could it be true?

"We're going to Washington and we're going to win this thing once and for all." McCoy folded his arms over his chest, leaned back in his seat and gave a matter-of-fact nod.

McCoy would be the one presenting the oral argument as he was the firm's most experienced and successful attorney qualified to present a case to the highest court in the nation.

"Why in the world would Chandler take such a risk?" Melanie asked neither partner in particular.

"Well, that's exactly what Charles and I have been talking about for the last two hours. Honestly, we both thought Chandler would hold out until the eleventh hour, just for spite, and then take the settlement offer. We were wrong."

Melanie sat in silence; her emotions had completely reversed in a matter of seconds. She had been heartsick when she immediately assumed Chandler had taken the settlement and now every nerve in her body tingled with excitement. They were going to the Supreme Court, but one thought puzzled her. "Why in the world would Chandler want to push it all the way to the Supreme Court when he had lost every single appeal in the last four plus years?"

"Charles and I are in shock, too. This isn't sound legal strategy on their part. When we win in Washington, the costs for Devilland are going to be enormous, not to mention the precedent which will be set when the Court rules. Personally, I think Chandler and the boys he works with have been nipping a little too much of their client's whiskey themselves. This is nothing more than a battle of insufferable egos at this point. To decline our settlement is absurd. They can't honestly think they can win at this point," McCoy said with a confidence that Melanie didn't feel herself.

"Well, we'll let you get back to work. We wanted you to be the first one to know since this is your baby, after all," Hunt said.

"Thank you. I appreciate that. I must say I'm completely surprised. I never dreamed they'd take it all the way." Melanie sat completely still, absolutely stunned.

"Neither did we. Neither did we. Thank you for coming up, Melanie. We'll be in touch," McCoy said.

"Thank you both. Have a pleasant day." Melanie quietly excused herself.

Walking down the hall, she groaned as she realized the timing could not have been worse. She had stacks of new cases on her desks. Then there were the depositions, meetings, lunches, cocktail parties. How in the world could she get it all done, delegated, rescheduled? Anxiety coursed through her body at the thought of it all.

Absently pressing the down button on the elevator, she struggled desperately to absorb this latest turn in events. No! She would not focus on what she had on her desk or her hectic schedule. This was great. The Supreme Court would hear her case. McCoy was confident the victory would be theirs but Melanie couldn't shake the odd apprehension in her heart. What was it? McCoy was confident. Why wasn't she? They had prevailed in every single court since she had first appeared in Dallas almost five years ago, but the Supreme Court wasn't just another appellate court. Could it be that Chandler knew something that Hunt and McCoy didn't know? What could possibly make him so confident as to push this all the way to the end of the road? Maybe McCoy was right. Maybe the legal battle had shifted to nothing more than a battle of egos. Maybe.

Passing Josephine's vacant desk, Melanie walked into her own office and closed the door. She needed to think.

The Supreme Court. The Supreme Court. Those three simple words kept running through her mind over and over.

Suddenly another thought hit her. She had to make the call as she had promised.

Quickly dialing the number she knew by heart, Melanie chewed her lower lip as she listened to the phone ring, once, twice, three times.

"Hello, Melanie?" Shirley Simms asked, having seen the caller ID flash the firm's name.

"Yeah, it's me. I just got the news. We're going to Washington." Melanie forced a confident tone in her voice.

"Praise God! Finally!" The other woman cried jubilantly.

Melanie's strategic decision to add MADD as a plaintiff to the original lawsuit had proven to be an unexpected godsend.

Shirley Simms and the members of MADD had been a tremendous support. It had quickly become their personal crusade to keep the lawsuit in front of the media at every opportunity. Throngs of hundreds walked the streets in front of every courthouse when each appeal was heard. Members appearing on local and national talk shows every time the case was reconsidered fueled the public support to epic proportions. The nation literally screamed for the verdict to be upheld, according to every poll that had been taken over the last five years. MADD's dedication, influence, and connections proved invaluable through the long and laborious appeals process.

"When are we going?" Excitement laced the woman's words.

Shirley Sims had long ago assured Melanie if the case went all the way to the Supreme Court, MADD would most certainly be in DC in full force, marching, and carrying their now famous picket signs, most of which were emblazoned with a photograph of a child lost.

"I don't know exactly. I found out myself only a few minutes ago. You were my first phone call."

"I'll start making calls. Thank you, Melanie. Thank you." The other woman's voice cracked.

"Thank you, Shirley. I'll call as soon as I know more."

Melanie got up from her desk and crossed the room to the mini fridge. She had skipped lunch again and her stomach growled. Grabbing a yogurt cup and bottle of water, Melanie sat in one of the guest chairs and did her best to absorb it all.

Her earlier apprehension was now mingled with pride. Excitement tingled through Melanie as she thought about her little case that everyone disregarded over seven years ago. It was going to be ruled upon by the most powerful legal minds in the nation. During the trial she'd never allowed herself the luxury of imagining victory over the liquor giant and now she marveled that her case was going all the way to the Supreme Court. She was truly going to be a part of history.

Over the past several months, when she realized the very real possibility the JD case would go all the way to the top, Melanie had done hours of research on the justices who currently sat on the Court.

Tossing the empty yogurt cup in the trash, Melanie reflected on all she had learned. The nine justices who sat on the bench had ruled on more history-making cases than any other justices serving simultaneously on the bench. There had been a record number of 5-4 rulings made by this court. According to what she had read, there was one major factor for this phenomenon. That one major factor was the one justice hailed as the superior legal mind of the assembly. Associate Justice J.R. Williams was said to be responsible for doing such an outstanding job during the justices' private case conferences that he often swayed one or two justices to rethink their own preconceived vote on a certain case, thus changing the majority ruling.

She remembered reading about Justice Williams being a brilliant visionary who could foresee how the Court's rulings would affect the nation's future. He was dedicated to preserving the intent of the original laws and carefully ensuring new rulings were made for America's ever changing republic.

While many legal experts and even seasoned journalists could predict how a certain justice would vote on a particular case based upon the justice being either a liberal or conservative and historical voting patterns, Williams proved to be the exception. Shortly into his first session on the Court, the media dubbed him Wild Card Williams. The name had followed him for almost two decades.

Melanie had read every single decision made by Williams and still didn't have the tiniest thread of confidence that she, or any legal expert, could possibly predict how this enigma of a man would view the landmark case.

Wild Card Williams. He would be the one. He would be the swing vote. Of that Melanie was certain. The only thing she was uncertain of was which way the vote would swing.

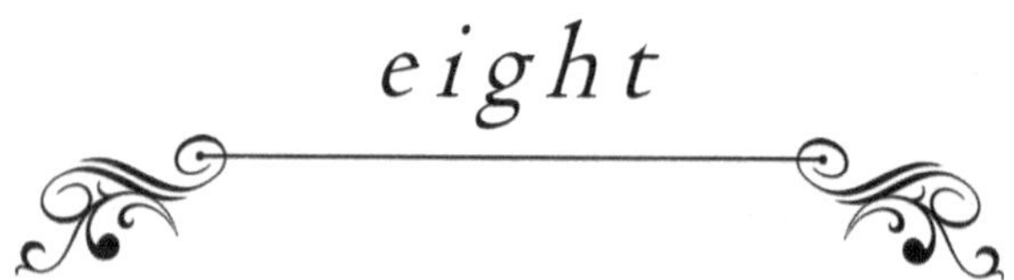

eight

That same day
September, 2007
Dallas, Texas

ONLY A FEW MILES AWAY, TWO OTHERS WERE discussing the latest turn of events. Sitting at a corner table at the Old Warsaw were Alan Winters and Seamus Chandler.

"Thank you, darlin'," Alan said absently as the waitress set his third dirty martini of the hour on the white linen tablecloth.

"You really told that fat bastard McCoy we'd see him in DC? I would've loved to have been a fly on the wall when he told the tight-ass bitch Bridges." Winters chuckled as he gazed out over the restaurant at the other well-heeled patrons.

"I'm going to trust your gut on this one. Hughes and Watson both wanted to advise Devilland to take the deal but I'm with you. I feel it in these ol' bones of mine. Despite all the pissant appellate judges, I can't imagine the Court upholding the verdict. The entire case is a damn farce. The only thing that shocks me to this day is that Stanford is still a thorn in our side almost five years later." Chandler plucked the two enormous olives from his martini.

"You and I are right on this one, Seamus. I have no doubt. It seems everyone's running scared trying to second guess how Wild Card Williams is going to vote. Let me tell you, I've known my share of men just like him. In the public eye, they are honorable, respectable, and have only the good of the nation at heart but that's all pure bullshit. Once his kind goes home, they close their fancy front doors on their expensive Georgetown homes, get drunk, and beat the crap out of their wives. Trust me. This Williams joker is no different from the rest of his kind. A leopard doesn't change his spots just because someone happens to throw a fancy black robe over his ass. There's absolutely no way he's going to swing the vote to uphold the verdict. He, of all people, will see how completely idiotic this entire fantasy case has been since its beginning. The appellate judges may not have the balls to overturn it because of the next election. This guy is on the bench for his entire fucking life. He doesn't give a shit about any damn election." Winters laughed heartily.

"Did I tell you they're running bets on this one out in Vegas? I've got a good friend who's a judge here in town. He laid down one hundred thousand the verdict will be over-turned and another one hundred grand if Williams is the swing vote with a 5-4 ruling," Chandler said.

"I'll be damned. That's some serious action,"

"Well, Alan, my boy, you and I aren't the only two who know victory is waiting in the wings. Melanie Bridges, Hunt, Spencer, and McCoy are a few precious months away from getting knocked off that high horse they've been riding for the last four years."

Alan glanced at his watch. "Shit! I've got to run. I'm due in court in less than thirty minutes."

nine

Two months pass
November, 2007
Hunt, Spencer & McCoy
Dallas, Texas

TUESDAY MORNING DAWNED WITH THUNDERSTORMS and freezing temperatures.

Melanie rubbed her neck and stared at the stack of papers in front of her. She had been at her desk since before five a.m. so she could tie up the final details before leaving for DC.

The day had come. McCoy, Hunt, Melanie, and two paralegals would be leaving on a three o' clock flight for DC. McCoy would present his oral argument to the Supreme Court on Thursday.

The excitement had been building since Hunt and McCoy had told her of Chandler's refusal to accept the settlement. Bathing McCoy's presentation in daily prayer, Melanie was confident that, at the least, they would not go down without a fight. She and the appeals team had done their best as would McCoy. The only thing she could do at this point was to continue her fervent prayers for this final victory.

That morning after Melanie had packed, dropped off Fred and Ginger at her neighbor Betsy's, and settled in behind the wheel of her Mustang, she thought of her grandmama Yancy who had danced on Broadway before falling in love with Melanie's granddaddy and settling down to raise a family. The doting grandmama had been a faithful attendee at all of Melanie's ballet recitals, Jordan's piano recitals, and even Drew's basketball games when they were all growing up in Carlton.

Without fail, Grandmama Yancy would be standing off to the side of the stage moments before Melanie's dance troupe stepped out to perform. Leaning down, looking directly into her granddaughter's bright eyes, she would kiss her three times on the tip of her tiny nose and whisper, "It's show time, my love. Give it everything you have. This moment will never come again."

"It's most definitely show time, Grandmama Yancy." She had mused.

At five after eight, she had finished drafting her sixth letter of the morning for Josephine to send out to four other attorneys and two clients.

Appearing quietly, Josephine set a steaming cup of coffee and piping hot cinnamon roll on the corner of Melanie's desk.

"You need to take a break."

"Thank you, Jo. This is exactly what I needed." Melanie inhaled the rich aroma of the coffee and sweet roll. Taking a long sip, she closed her eyes and savored the hot beverage.

"Looking at that stack of papers, I have no doubt you

were here, once again, before sunrise."

Melanie smiled grimly. "Yes, I was. Lately it seems the harder I work, the more work there is. I feel like I'm a gerbil on one of those little wheels running faster and faster and getting nowhere. I can handle the legal work fine but the social aspect is killing me. I can't count the number of lunches, dinners, and cocktail parties I have attended with the partners. That sounds trivial and possibly ungrateful, especially today when I am going to the Supreme Court—the chance of a lifetime. I would never say it to anyone other than you. I want my life back. I just want my life back."

"Hon', it doesn't sound trivial or ungrateful. You do deserve to have a life. You need balance. The fact is you are this firm's shining star, the rainmaker. I see how hard you're pushing yourself. Do you want my opinion?"

"Always."

"When you get back home, you need to sit down with Hunt and tell him how you feel. Be honest. You can't keep this pace. Nobody could. I know you're tired of the social aspect of your position but the truth is the wining and dining is the lifeblood of this firm. Bringing in new clients is vital. You have achieved a new level of success. Let Hunt know you need some help with all these cases. Nobody except me knows how much you're carrying. He'll understand. Let's get through this appeal and then let's get your life back."

"Thanks, Jo. You're right."

"Will you talk to Hunt?"

"Maybe. I apologize for my verbal vomit. I'm just tired, really, really tired."

"I know you are, hon'. Tell me what I can do to help."

"After I finish this letter, I believe everything will be buttoned down for the week. I'm in better shape than I appear." Melanie offered a wry smile.

"You have an amazing inner strength, hon'. I have no doubt you are fine for now but you will talk to Hunt when you get home." Josephine gave Melanie the stern but loving look of a mother. "Sammy will be here at noon. Hunt and McCoy want to grab a quick lunch before the flight."

"That's right. I've got four hours. I'm good. "

"Oh wait, I need to go over the Clarke file with you!" Mild panic crept into Melanie's voice.

"Mel, we went over everything last night. I promise I can take care of it. If I have any questions on the Clarke file, I'll ask Chad. I'll probably ask him anyway. I think it does his ego good. You were his protégé and now you're setting the world on fire. You know a man's pride." Josephine chuckled.

"Thank you but I don't think I personally have anything to do with Chad's recent little bout of insecurity, which I, too, have noticed. The new baby coming in spring is the reason for his peculiar behavior. Maybe it's male hormones or something." Melanie tore apart her roll and popped a piece into her mouth.

"I heard it's going to be mums the word on whether Michelle's having a boy or girl."

"Yes. Chad said they want to do it the old-fashioned way and find out the sex when the baby is born. It does make it much more exciting, not knowing if I'm going to have a godson or goddaughter." Melanie grinned brightly.

"A new baby is always exciting." Josephine returned the smile.

"Thank you again, Jo, for the coffee and sweet roll. It's truly divine and I certainly need it. I didn't get much sleep last night. All I could think about was this appeal."

"I have faith we're going to win in this one just like we've won in every other court. You watch and see, ol' Jo can feel it in her bones," she assured Melanie.

"I want to believe that too but I can't get a solid feeling about Williams other than he will be the swing vote. I think he could go either way. He's brilliant and seems to have an insight that very few judges have."

"We are going to win. Don't you worry. I need to get back to work," Josephine said firmly as she rose from the chair and left the office.

Taking off her reading glasses, Melanie rubbed the bridge of her nose. The coffee helped but the ever present exhaustion pushed her limits today, of all days."

Melanie jumped as Josephine appeared once again in her doorway.

"There's a call on line three from the nursing home. She says it's urgent."

Frowning, Melanie quickly picked up the receiver.

Josephine left quietly and again closed the door behind her. Melanie had never told her who lived in the Georgia nursing home but she always took the calls when they came—even when Melanie was meeting with Charles Hunt himself. The truth was that other than Jordan and Jordan's family, Melanie had never told anyone, not even her cousins, about Aaron. Her fear had been no one would understand the complicated situation. Judgment would undoubtedly fall and Melanie was determined that would never happen.

After the call, Melanie, cradled her head in her hands and sobbed. *Dear Lord, how much more can he take? It's always one more emergency, one more surgery. Aaron, my sweet, sweet Aaron.*

"Stop it! He needs you!" Melanie grabbed a tissue and forcefully wiped her tears in frustration. She jabbed the intercom.

"Jo, can you please come in here?"

As she entered her boss' office, Josephine slowed as she took in the sight of Melanie's red and blotchy cheeks, she assumed from crying.

"Are you alright, Mel? What can I do?"

"I'm fine." Melanie snatched up the crumbled mascara-streaked tissue on top of the desk.

"The nursing home will be faxing some papers over in the next few minutes. I need to sign more damn papers. Please watch the fax machine."

"Absolutely. Can I do anything else?"

"No, that's all," Melanie said dismissively.

Within minutes, the fax machine outside her office hummed and soon the pages were in front of her.

Scanning the documents, Melanie hastily signed her name and the date on the last page.

"Please return these to Margaret. One more thing, call the florist and send flowers and a teddy bear, preferably a panda. Those are his favorite."

"Consider it done. Will there be anything else?"

"No, but please close the door."

Melanie quickly picked up the phone and dialed the first five digits of Jordan's cell phone number before placing the phone back in the cradle.

Damn it! Her mind was so foggy. Jordie was at the medical convention. There was nothing she could do but worry. Melanie had that covered for them both. She'd call her after the surgery when everything was fine. It was going to be fine. He was one helluva fighter. He had certainly proven that.

Staring out the windows, Melanie began to pray aloud. "Dear Lord, give him peace. That's all I ask. Peace. Just peace, please."

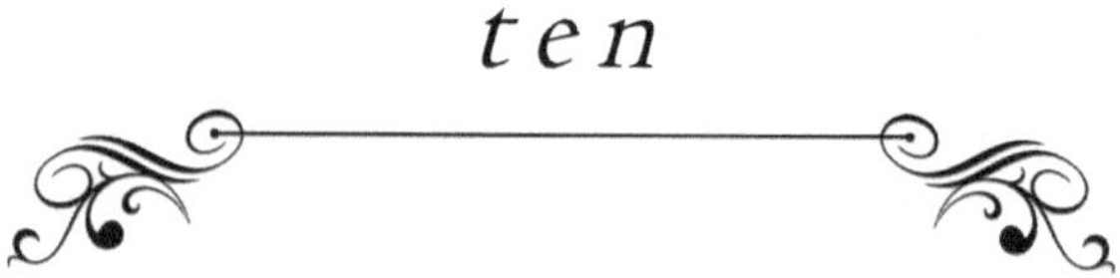

t e n

Seven months pass
May, 2008
Dallas, Texas

THE ALL TOO FAMILIAR TINGLING HAD BEEN THERE all morning and was increasing its intensity. Soon it would settle behind her left eye and eventually all the way down into her neck. Melanie had been experiencing excruciating migraines since the age of sixteen years old and this one was coming on with a vengeance.

Her daddy Charles and both his brothers Jimmy and Eddie had suffered from the debilitating migraines as had their mama Tilly. Melanie and her sister Jordan had both inherited the ailment.

Melanie could still remember the shadow box frame with the gold plaque that read: *In Case of Emergency: Break Glass.* Behind the small glass pane was one Viceroy cigarette and one folded packet of BC headache powder. The frame had hung in her daddy's study until his death and now hung in Jordan's home office. The girls' mama had given the framed cigarette and pain reliever to her husband as a sort of joke shortly after he quit smoking. Growing up, Melanie thought the shadow box was silly but as an adult she fully appreciated her mama's humor.

Of course, there was medicine that could be taken, but anyone who suffered from migraines knew in reality the medication only served to sedate you enough so you could ride the horrific wave of pain. The only real remedy was to lock oneself into a completely quiet and pitch-black dark room with no communication with the outside world until the worst had passed. Only those in the exclusive club of Headache Hell, as Jordan had long ago christened the agonizing condition, could understand the full extent of the pain and the need to, like a wounded animal, climb into a cave and pray for sleep until the migraine passed.

Melanie's mama had noticed, once the girls were grown and Grandmama Tilly had passed away, that either Melanie or Jordan seemed to be either getting over a terrible migraine or had one coming on but the two sisters never had one at the same time. Elizabeth Bridges used to joke and say their grandmama must have had a migraine the night she passed away and accidentally left it on earth and together her daughters were doomed to carry it around with them.

"Thanks, Jordie." Melanie massaged her temples, mumbling. "At least I know you're feeling fine because I have the damned thing, probably for the next friggin' week."

Melanie cradled her head in her palms and willed the pain to subside long enough for her to finish her conference call scheduled in less than twenty minutes.

"Uh-oh, I know that look."

Melanie jumped at the sound of Josephine's voice.

"I'm sorry I startled you. Have you taken anything, hon'?"

"No, I have to hang on until after the conference call with Austin and then I think I'll have to throw in the towel and go home." Melanie moaned as she laid her head on the desk and closed her eyes.

Melanie didn't realize Josephine had left the office.

Returning a few minutes later Josephine set a glass of ice water, two packets of BC headache powder, and a blueberry muffin on Melanie's desk.

"Do you think you can get this down, hon'?"

Looking up, Melanie managed a weak smile.

"Jo, you're the best. What would I do without you?"

Opening her mouth wide enough to get both powders as far back as possible in her throat, Melanie swallowed the aspirin and caffeine, drank the entire glass of water in one long gulp, and then took a few small bites of the muffin to kill the horrific aftertaste of the powder.

"No matter how many times I watch you do that, it never ceases to amaze me how you can swallow that stuff."

"After almost thirty years of practice, I'm pretty good at getting it past the majority of my taste buds." Melanie winked with all the energy she could muster considering her ever increasing pain.

"I'll get you some more water. Your phone will be ringing in a moment with the conference call."

No sooner had Josephine left Melanie's office, the phone buzzed and she picked up the receiver.

Mercifully, the call lasted less than thirty minutes and by then the aspirin had taken the edge off the pain. The relief would be short lived so Melanie quickly packed her briefcase and prepared to go home for the day.

"You know where I'll be. I'll call you in the morning, if I'm still alive." Melanie attempted the joke as Josephine came into her office to make sure she was headed home.

"Are you sure you can drive? I'll be glad to run you home."

"No thanks. I'll be fine if I leave now. I'm afraid this one may prove to be a Category 5."

Over the years, Melanie had learned to describe her headaches in the same terms weather forecasters described hurricanes. That made it easy for the fortunate souls who never had a true migraine to understand the varying degrees of severity. With a tropical storm migraine, Melanie could continue working if absolutely necessary but when a Cat 3 or greater hit, it put her out of commission for two to three days. Thankfully, the majority of her migraines were what she classified as Cat 2 or less.

"You go home and get some sleep. Don't worry about a thing. I'll call Betsy and let her know to check on you."

"Thanks, Jo." Melanie wearily headed for the elevator.

Once home, Melanie managed to eat a bowl of chicken and rice soup with saltines and drink a full glass of water before she took her painkillers.

After turning off the lights, both phones, and closing the blinds to block out the sunlight, Melanie padded into her bathroom to take a long, relaxing hot bubble bath and let the medicine take effect.

Within thirty minutes, the warm welcome fuzzy feeling of sedation enveloped her. Slowly she got out of the tub and dried herself off with a towel. Slipping into her favorite gown, she groaned as she crawled between the cool sheets on her bed. After she put her sleeping mask over her eyes, only minutes passed before she drifted into a deep, dreamless slumber.

As Melanie had predicted, the migraine proved to be one of the worst she had had in months. She phoned Josephine the next morning to touch base and said she would be out of the office for at least the next two, if not three, days. Josephine assured her everything was under control and to call if she needed anything.

For the next three days, Melanie existed in her own twilight zone, waking long enough to eat a light meal and take another round of painkillers. With the phones and TV turned off, the blinds drawn, and not even the bathroom nightlight on, the entire condo took on a primitive cave-like atmosphere.

Finally, on the fourth morning after the migraine first gripped her, Melanie had stirred back to the land of the living. As she stood in front of the bathroom mirror brushing her teeth and running a hot shower, her doorbell rang.

It wasn't yet seven o'clock. Who in the world would be on her doorstep at this hour? Whoever it was, they weren't going to go away. The bell continued to ring incessantly.

Melanie laughed in spite of the still slight throbbing of her head. Chad, dear Chad. No one else she knew could ring a doorbell to the tune of the *William Tell Overture*.

What in the world could have possibly brought him over at this hour? Michelle must've had the baby and she had all the phones turned off for the last three days!

She hastily rinsed the toothpaste from her mouth and rushed to the door, not caring she was still in her flannel granny-style nightgown.

As she threw open the door, Chad, dressed for work in a three-piece navy pinstripe suit, immediately picked her up, twirled her around, and gave a loud whoop of joy.

He sat her down and, almost in unison, they both shouted, "Congratulations!"

Startled, she eyed him in confusion.

"Well, do I have a godson or goddaughter?"

Grinning from ear to ear and without saying a word, Chad unfolded the morning edition of the *Dallas Morning News* in his hand.

Melanie burst into tears, wild happiness flooding through her.

WIDOW WINS 5-4
WILD CARD WILLIAMS TIPS SCALES OF JUSTICE

PART TWO

The Justice

eleven

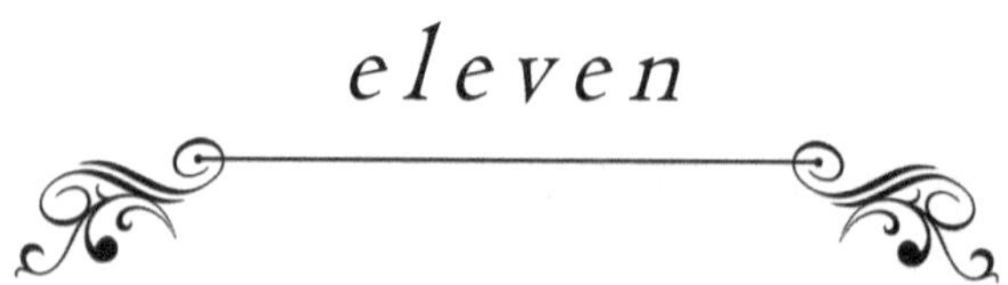

July, 2008
Charleston, South Carolina

J.R. WILLIAMS CLOSED THE MAGAZINE UPON THE plane's descent. Removing his bifocals, he rubbed his weary eyes. It had been a pleasant enough flight from DC but he was eager to get to his hotel, have a hot shower, and a good steak.

Exhausted from an exceptionally long and grueling week in the Court, he welcomed the summer recess more so this year than normal. Lately, he simply couldn't keep the pace he once had. His wife Gloria had reminded him that he would be fifty-eight years old next year and his body was not equipped, as it once had been, to work eighty hour weeks, play eighteen holes of golf at the Congressional Country Club twice a week, and run on his standard six hours of sleep per night.

He had little doubt his loving wife was right but frustration still nagged at him. Eighteen years after taking his seat on the Supreme Court, he should be coming into his prime. Rehnquist had sat on the bench until the age of eighty, after all. J.R. decided he would call Dr. Lee to schedule a checkup when he got back to DC. Maybe his cholesterol was high or something. Gloria had been complaining recently about his diet.

Resting his head on the soft dove gray leather headrest, he waited for the plane to land. After touchdown, J.R. gathered his briefcase, suit jacket, and hanging bag before exiting the plane with the other first-class passengers.

This would be a quick trip. He would be staying in Charleston only overnight to visit his grandmama at the nursing home and would be returning to DC tomorrow evening. Gloria and he had a wedding to attend on Sunday and he hoped to slip in at least nine holes of golf at the country club later in the day.

The sleek black Lincoln Town Car waited at the curb as he exited the airport into the mild summer night.

"Good evening, Justice." The young chauffeur took the older man's briefcase and luggage. "I hope you had a pleasant flight."

"Yes, I did. It's good to see you again, Bradley. I hoped they would send you. I missed seeing you last time I was in town."

As the driver pulled into the evening traffic, J.R. asked, "How is everything going for you?"

"All is well. I received my scores on the LSAT, sir." The blonde-haired, blue-eyed young man beamed.

J.R. had known the young man for a little over three years, since Bradley had begun working at the car service J.R. used when in Charleston. He knew the boy well enough to recognize he was bursting with pride and eager for J.R. to ask him about the results of his LSAT.

Smiling to himself, J.R. recalled the day he had received his own scores from the law school admission test. He still remembered his grandmama's joy when he called to tell her the results. He had made a perfect score, an extremely rare achievement. With his LSAT scores and impeccable recommendations, he had easily walked onto the Harvard campus. He purposefully sat in silence for the next several minutes, staring out the window.

Out of the corner of his eye, he noticed Bradley's anxious glances in the rearview mirror as the young man expertly guided the sleek car through Charleston's evening traffic. He had toyed with the young man long enough.

"Well son, that's good news. What did…"

"I scored in the ninety-ninth percentile, Justice." The boy's fair skin immediately turned crimson as he realized his faux pas.

"I apologize, sir. I didn't mean to interrupt you. It's just that I've been waiting all day for you to arrive so I could share the news with you."

J.R. chuckled heartily. "Don't you worry about it, son. I shouldn't have joked with you like that. I'm the one who owes the apology. My grandmama always told me I had my daddy's sense of humor. Ninety-ninth percentile." J.R. gave an appreciative whistle. "I do believe you have written your own ticket to my alma mater."

A bright smile broke across Bradley's face as he turned into the drive of Charleston Place.

"With a score like that, I guess you won't be needing this letter of recommendation from me. My secretary did spend quite some time typing it so maybe you could go ahead and keep it. Actually, it's only a copy. I have the original on my desk, ready to be mailed, with your permission, of course."

He handed the speechless young man a thick envelope embossed with the Supreme Court seal in the upper left-hand corner.

Taking the envelope, Bradley cleared his throat as if choking back a rising lump. "I don't know what to say, sir. I mean thank you, thank you, thank you very much, Your Honor.

The young boy's blue eyes clouded over with tears. He quickly jumped from the car and ran around to open the back door.

Upon opening the door, the young man had managed to regain his composure.

"Sir, I can't find the words…"

J.R. held up his hand to stop him. "You don't have to say anything, son. You have no idea how thankful I am to be able to do this for you. I didn't get where I am today without God's blessing and the generosity of a great many people. You're going to be a wonderful attorney one day. Who knows, you may even be sitting next to me on the bench within the next, shall we say, fifteen, twenty years?"

Awkwardly, Bradley put out his right hand to shake hands. As he did so, the tall elder Southern man took the boy into his arms and gave him a warm hug.

"I'm proud of you, Bradley."

"Thank you, sir."

He released the boy from his embrace and smiled brightly. "Can you pick me up at ten in the morning? I need to be driven to Eden Manor to see my grandmama."

"Most definitely, sir. Ten o' clock it is. Thank you again."

"Have a good evening, son." J.R. waved to Bradley as the

liveried doorman rushed to open the door of Charleston Place.

The next morning, rested and refreshed, J.R. entered the door of Eden Manor with a bouquet of red roses in one hand and a box of imported chocolates in the other.

"Good morning, sir," the petite blonde said brightly from behind the desk. "I believe your grandmother is in the solarium. She's eagerly awaiting your arrival."

"Thank you, Mary Sue." J.R. picked up the dark purple feather quill pen to sign his name at the registration. He had to smile to himself at the great lengths the staff went to maintain the ostentatious aura of this fine facility.

"A feather quill pen, good Lord," he mused to himself.

Of course, Charleston was still the Old South, proud of her noble glory.

Nostalgically, as he signed his name, he recalled his grandmama had been the one to teach him how to first write his name. His own mama had died tragically before she was able to teach him, her only child, even this, the most basic of life's skills.

Heading down the opulent hallway, lined with antiques and oriental rugs, toward the solarium, he couldn't believe his grandmama had turned ninety-six this June and remained as alert as ever.

Gloria had already begun mental preparations for her beloved grandmother-in-law's one hundredth birthday celebration. It seemed like only a few years ago his grandmama and he had moved to South Carolina from Mississippi.

Immediately, he spotted his grandmama as she sat next to another attractive elderly lady and laughed. It didn't matter that he was one of the most influential men in the entire country. His heart always skipped a beat when he saw the face of his grandmama. In his heart, he would forever be her little boy.

"There's my boy! Baby, you remember Rosalyn, don't you?" his grandmama asked as J.R. approached the two ladies.

He had to smile to himself. His grandmama had never been one to put on airs or to be impressed with status. Of course, he remembered Rosalyn. She was the former First Lady of South Carolina, but to his grandmama she was simply a good friend at the retirement home.

Reaching for Mrs. Conner's outstretched hand, he kissed it lightly. He had always been the epitome of a true Southern gentleman. Leaning down and giving his grandmama a warm hug, he kissed her on the forehead.

"Good Lord, child, what have I told you about spending your hard-earned money on me? You should be saving your money for yourself!" The woman shook her head as J.R. handed her the box of chocolates and roses.

The elder Williams considered any discussion of one's financial worth vulgar. Therefore, he chose not to remind her that in addition to his own successful career, Gloria, his wife, was one of the best, and consequentially, one of the top paid legal advisors in the nation.

Unlike most, Gloria had never been lost in the shadows as the wife of a Supreme Court Justice. As the senior partner at Williams, Clinton, and Feldman, she was a dynamic force of her own.

In addition, J.R. and his wife had made many wise financial investments over the years and were financially secure, but money was something discussed only by the lower classes, according to his grandmama. He had learned early to be thankful for monetary blessings but to never be braggadocios about such.

"Oh, how beautiful those roses are!" Rosalyn said. Grandmama Williams held the flowers out to her friend and they both inhaled the wonderful fragrance.

"They are gorgeous and probably cost a small fortune. Boy, you can't squander your money on an old woman like this."

"Spending money on you makes me feel good, Grandmama. How many times do I have to tell you that? You deserve every luxury in the world as far as I'm concerned. Humor me. Enjoy the candy and the flowers, please."

"He's right, my dear," Rosalyn said. "Enjoy the pampering. You deserve it." She excused herself to let her dear friend and her grandson spend some private time together.

"Glory sends her love. She's sorry she couldn't make it this time but she's working hard on the opening of the new wing at Children's hospital which is scheduled for the end of this month. She's busier than ever. She wanted me to tell you she'll be down here at the first of September and you two will have some real girl time."

"You tell Gloria that I understand but I miss her and will hold her to coming soon. I couldn't have hand-picked a better woman for you. The Lord definitely smiled on you that day."

J.R. chuckled as he reached for his grandmama's arthritic hand. "The good Lord smiles on me every day. I'm one lucky man to have two such wonderful women in my life."

"Don't you ever forget it." The elder Williams shook her index finger at her grandson in jest. "Please take me back to my room so I can freshen up for lunch."

After placing the box of chocolates and roses in his grandmama's lap, J.R. wheeled her out of the solarium and down the short hallway to her private room. In reality, it was not simply a room. It was a luxurious suite with a private bedroom, bathroom, and a large sitting area, complete with a kitchenette, and large plate glass windows overlooking the azalea gardens.

In the spring, the view was absolutely breathtaking. The gardens overflowed with the pink, red, and white blooms that his grandmama loved so dearly. She said seeing the lovely flowers reminded her of growing up in the Mississippi Delta. She could close her eyes and be transformed back in time ninety years. Memories of swinging on the old rope swing hanging from the massive oak tree in front of her home were some of her most cherished. The yard back home had been covered with hundreds of magnificent, blooming azaleas.

It cost J.R. a pretty penny for his grandmama to have the best living quarters available in the home but he insisted she was worth every cent. If it hadn't been for her, he had no doubt he wouldn't have reached the pinnacle of success he had. He thanked the Lord every night that he was able to provide for his beloved grandmama in her later years as she had sacrificed so much for him early in his life. His grandmama had supported him not only financially but also, and more importantly, emotionally for as long as he could remember. She had been right by his side, encouraging him to study hard and be the best he could be. She had been a firm disciplinarian but he knew it was because she loved him so deeply. He couldn't remember it ever being anyone but the two of them against the world as he grew up, first in Mississippi then in South Carolina. They had left the Delta shortly after his twelfth birthday. The two of them had loaded up everything they owned and moved from the only place either of them had ever called home.

After graduating from high school, J.R. went to college at Boston University and then went on to earn his law degree. Upon graduating from law school, J.R. wanted a career in government. He wanted to be instrumental in making changes for the advancement of the country. He had fulfilled his dream by being one of the most celebrated Supreme Court justices in history. Known for not only his brilliance but also for his strong code of ethics, he had never been one to be swayed by public opinion or his own political ambition.

Upon entering her suite, the elderly Mrs. Williams rang for a nurse to come assist her in changing clothes for lunch. J.R. took the time to wander down the hall and take a look at the new dining hall under construction. They had made considerable progress since the last time he visited. When was that? Had it been only eight weeks ago for Mother's Day?

Lately he had lost all track of time. This term had been especially intense as there were several cases in front of the Court which were quite controversial. None more than the Devilland case, the final decision had been issued in May but Devilland had weighed heavily upon J.R. since he first became acquainted with the case. The country had gone absolutely crazy and had been trying this case in the public spotlight for the last five plus years. While no real precedent existed for the case, the plaintiff did bring to light many thought-provoking issues. After hearing the oral arguments, J.R. had spent many long hours studying everything from the original case to the progress through the appellate system as well as doing extensive additional research of his own. He couldn't remember the last case he had been as fascinated with as he had been with this one. Early on, he had concluded his decision would more than likely be the swing vote, as he was confident how the other justices would decide on the case. He had felt the votes would be split evenly as many of the suits had been for this particular group of justices. This only added to his determination to carefully consider all aspects of the case. He not only studied the facts diligently but also prayed for the wisdom to make a fair and just decision. He had no doubt in his heart he had done exactly that.

J.R. realized he must have been staring at the one particular bulldozer clearing land for quite some time. Something about the man driving the monstrous machine brought a flash of déjà vu. J.R. often found himself curious about the men who made their living constructing buildings, roads, and bridges. What a different lifestyle it was from the legal profession. Still thinking about the power of the mighty piece of equipment, he turned and headed back to his grandmama's suite, intent to not keep her waiting.

Looking absolutely stunning in a bright pink silk blouse and long skirt that was slightly darker in color than the blouse, Grandmama beamed brightly at him. Around her neck she wore the gold filigree cross with a single diamond in it that he had given her on her seventy-fifth birthday.

Her luxurious salt-and-pepper hair had been swept back into a chignon.

"You look simply gorgeous. I feel underdressed. I thought we were going to have a casual luncheon together."

"We're having a guest join us. I'm eager for you two to meet. I wanted to look my best. I absolutely love this outfit. It's one Gloria picked out for me last spring. She has such exquisite taste. After all, she picked you for her husband," the gorgeous elderly woman said with a wink.

"May I ask who this mystery guest might be?"

"Oh, he's not a mystery guest. You already know of him. I think it's time you meet him. He's the gentleman who has been handling my business affairs for the last few years. He was going to be in the neighborhood today and I asked him to join us."

As J.R. pushed his grandmama up to her favorite corner table, a handsome man approached.

"You must be Justice Williams. It's a true honor to meet you." The newcomer outstretched his arm to shake hands. "My name is Walter Frasier. I've heard so many wonderful things about you, both from your grandmother and from others. I can't tell you how much I've been looking forward to meeting you in person."

"You are too kind, Mr. Frasier." J.R. humbly nodded.
"Call me Walt."

"Alright Walt, my friends call me J.R. It's a pleasure to meet you as well."

Frasier then bent down and shook the hand of Mrs. Williams. "You look lovely as always. If I weren't a happily married man, I would be courting you every day."

Laughing merrily, Grandmama made a motion as if to

push her old friend away from her.

While the other man wasn't at all what J.R. had imagined, Frasier seemed to be extremely fond of his client and vice versa. Beyond that, he knew little of the man. It made J.R. smile to think how serious his grandmama had always been about keeping her financial affairs confidential and how she had been so frugal his entire life. It was a characteristic which came from living through the Great Depression and seeing some very hard times, as did everyone in the country during those years.

Once, after graduating from law school, J.R. had offered to assist his grandmama with her financial planning but she had been quick to tell him she preferred to keep her money matters private and to handle those issues on her own. The tone of her voice told him the matter need not be discussed again. She had been extremely adamant about her own ability to handle such private issues. He had been amused. By her strong reaction, she gave the impression she had been entrusted with guarding the Rockefeller estate. Her grandson assumed she had built up a small nest egg as she had been penny-wise when he was young and going to school.

They had lived a modest life but he honestly couldn't remember ever wanting for anything. His grandmama made sure to keep a nice home for him to have his friends visit. She said she would much rather he bring a bunch of rowdy teenagers over to watch TV than be out on the street where there was nothing but trouble waiting to happen. Although he didn't have an extensive wardrobe, he definitely had nice clothes for school and church. She had even bought him a second-hand car to take to college when he graduated as valedictorian of his high school class.

He had no doubt his grandmama went without many comforts in order to provide him with the best education possible. It was but one of the many reasons why he had been so pleased he had been able to put her in the lap of luxury when she turned seventy-five and finally agreed to move from her own home. He had chosen this particular retirement home as it wasn't a nursing home in the conventional sense. The majority of the guests, as they were called, remained active and needed only minimal nursing care. They had an extensive social program and the waiting list to get into the facility was several years long. It was definitely the best in all of South Carolina and his grandmama flourished here. She had a multitude of good friends and the staff adored her.

Once everyone was seated, the waitress appeared with a pitcher of ice water and filled their three crystal water goblets. Again, J.R. had to smile at the formality of the establishment. The starched pink tablecloths, the matching monogrammed napkins, fresh orchids on every table, black tie waiters standing at the ready to service their guests all coincided to give a very sophisticated aura to even the most casual of mid-day meals.

Time flew by as the threesome enjoyed a lively conversation. As the waiter cleared the three bare luncheon plates, a pretty blonde waitress rolled the dessert cart up to the table. Grandmama Williams advised her guests that the blackberry cobbler was her favorite. Both men agreed that sounded fine to them. After the three finished the last of their cobbler and vanilla ice cream, the elder Williams suggested they all go back to her suite for coffee.

Before they left the table, they ordered the coffee to be delivered to the room.

J.R. positioned his grandmama in her favorite spot with a full view of the gardens.

Someone had arranged the gorgeous red roses in a Baccarat crystal vase and set them on a side table. The vase had been a gift from J.R. and his wife when his grandmama had first moved into the residence. He brought flowers with him on his every visit and had a standing order with the local florist so his grandmama had fresh flowers in her room every week. It was a small indulgence but one that his grandmama truly adored.

Within moments of everyone getting settled, a tall, elderly black gentleman brought in a silver coffee service.

"Son, I wanted you to meet Walt as I'm not getting any younger and the day will come that I'll pass on to be with your wonderful granddaddy, your beautiful mama, and your loving daddy. Of course, you will inherit everything I have but there are a few things I want to explain to you in person and I want to give some things that your daddy left for me to give you when I thought the appropriate time came."

Taken aback at the mention of his daddy, J.R. leaned forward in his chair and struggled to swallow the rising lump in his throat.

"You may wonder why I didn't share these things with you long before today. I can only tell you that your daddy told me to give you these things only if and when I felt in my heart it was the right time."

His heart beat rapidly as his palms began to sweat at hearing his grandmama speak of his daddy. She had told him so many incredible stories about his mama but she had been evasive anytime he broached the subject of his daddy. She had promised to tell him in time and that time was now.

Grandmama Williams paused briefly and sipped her coffee before continuing.

"I'm very proud of the man you've grown to be and never wanted to give you any reason to do anything but your very best. You've become an amazing gentleman and have achieved so much more than even I ever imagined. I held on to these things only because I didn't want to deter you from the path you were following. I wanted you to have confidence in yourself and know you could make it in this life by your own wit and wisdom and that you most certainly did."

He listened anxiously as he stirred two sugar cubes into his coffee. This was amazing. After all these years, his grandmama was ready to talk about his daddy. She had never said anything more than his daddy had loved him very much.

"I pray you won't fault me for waiting so long to give you these gifts and hope you'll understand my decision to let you become your own man first, without being confused by these issues of so many years ago. I never wanted you to feel like you were defined by your parents and the impossible obstacles they faced. You need to know the two people who gave you life were very special and they both loved you deeply. You've been the light of my life and I believe the time has come to share these with you."

As if on cue, Walt opened his briefcase, and took out a thick manila envelope and passed it to J.R. who slowly opened it and found a small worn leather-bound journal, several photographs tied together with a small piece of twine, and a yellowed handkerchief with the single letter *B* monogrammed in navy blue. The cloth had been folded in a manner to hold something inside it.

Confused, his gaze met his grandmama's. She merely nodded for him to open the tiny bundle. Inside the aged cloth lay an exquisite heart-shaped locket on a delicate gold chain. A tiny diamond sparkled on the front and the back had been engraved with two sets of initials. He knew the first set were his mama's but did not readily recognize the second set. Before he could ask to whom the initials belonged, his grandmama continued.

"The locket belonged to your mama. Your daddy gave it to her on the day he found out she was expecting you."

J.R.'s eyes grew wide as excitement tingled through his body. His grandmama had told him so many stories about his mama but he had never seen or held anything that personally belonged to her. As he held the small golden piece in his massive hand, warmth washed over him. Staring at the small heart, he shook his head in awe.

"The journal is from your daddy. He wrote me a letter and tucked it inside the journal and it said he wanted me to give it to you. I've never read the journal itself. That is private between the two of you. The pictures are mainly of your daddy and you but there are two of your mama before she was taken from us."

"You see, son," Grandmama said, "our family had secrets. There was a wonderful woman named Sarah. She was a relative of your daddy's. She showed up on our doorstep one cold winter day. She had a small white box with these things in it. Our visit that day was brief but Sarah explained that, while helping the family sort your daddy's personal possessions after his death, she had run across the box and its contents. She was certain your daddy meant for you to have them. I could see it in her eyes. Sarah understood and would never betray our confidence. That's the kind of woman she was."

The weathered journal contained entries dating from 1950 until over a decade later. As he tentatively read the first entry, he looked up once again at his grandmama.

"Go ahead, baby. Read it… slowly."

His eyes misted as he read the first few pages of the journal. The handwriting, the easy flow of the wording, a whisper of something familiar. The moment he read the name of his daddy, the room spun and a lump rose in his throat. He stopped reading and took a long, deep breath. How could he have *not* known? After quickly pouring himself a glass of cold water, he drained it in one long swallow. He had spent his lifetime not knowing who his daddy was, but, in truth, he had not only known him but also loved him deeply for so many years—a lifetime ago.

J.R. placed the journal on the coffee table, cradled his head, and began to weep. He couldn't ever remember being as completely stunned as he was in this moment

Finally, J.R. found his words. "*He's* my daddy…oh dear God in Heaven…how…I always thought…" He choked back more tears and quickly poured himself another glass of ice water.

"Yes, he was your daddy and loved you more than I have ever seen any man love a child."

Biting his lip, fighting back a second flood of tears,

he took a long breath and gathered his thoughts. As he glanced up at his grandmama, his heart broke when he saw the pained expression on her face.

"I should have told you earlier, son. It was such an impossible situation. I could never find the right time. I am so sorry, baby." Tears glistened in her brown eyes.

Stunned, he slid from his chair, knelt in front of her wheelchair, took her in his arms, and held her close.

"No, no, Grandmama. Don't you ever regret holding this from me. You did the right thing. I did need to become my own man first. No. You always told me faith in God includes faith in His timing. My emotions are with myself. How could I not have known? The long hours we spent together. The love he showed me. How did I not feel that natural bond?"

"You were just a young boy, son. There was no way you could have known. It had to be that way. The relationship between your mama and daddy was complicated by so many other people and circumstances beyond anyone's control. It was so hard on your daddy but we both did the best we could for you. Please know that."

"I do, Grandmama. I really do."

Frasier cleared his throat. J.R. had completely forgotten the other man was there. He wiped the last of his tears unashamedly.

Obviously embarrassed to have intruded on such an emotional family moment, Frasier flashed a nervous smile. "I'll leave your grandmother and you alone. I know she has a great deal to tell you. However, I felt it was important that I provide you with this affidavit signed by both your grandmother and me. It states you couldn't possibly have had any prior knowledge of this information until today. I also have a copy in your grandmother's safe deposit box as well as another copy in my office. I sincerely doubt you will ever have a need to produce this but felt that, in light of your position, it was best to protect you completely.

Perplexed, he perused the page Walt handed him. "I'm sorry but I don't think I understand the necessity of this document."

"Well, I felt the need to prepare it several years ago. Specifically, when the original Devilland verdict was announced. Melanie Bridges was the lead attorney on the case."

The full ramification of Frasier's words hit him like a sledge hammer. *Melanie Bridges!* He would have never made the connection and still couldn't tie it all together.

"Melanie Bridges. Yes, of course I recognize the name but how would… Who… who is she in all this?"

Frasier continued by explaining exactly who Melanie Bridges was and how she related to all J.R. had discovered only moments earlier.

"This affidavit, the precaution you took. You changed the entire course of history. I would never have heard the case!"

Fear gripped him. What would happen if this got out to the public? He had the affidavit but would it be enough? The ramifications could be monumental. No! He had done nothing wrong. He had no way of knowing who Melanie Bridges was. She was still only a name to him. This was beyond comprehension. What were the odds? One in a million? One in a hundred million?

"This is definitely the icing on the cake as far as finding

out about my daddy. Shock doesn't even begin to cover it all but I appreciate your forethought on the matter. You're a very wise man, indeed, Walt. I can see why my grandmama has trusted you for so many years. Thank you. Thank you very much."

Grandmama then spoke. "There's the matter of my will and the tedious financial details but all that's straight forward and quite dull as far as I'm concerned. You two gentleman can discuss that on another day." She waved her hand dispassionately.

Walt handed him one of his cards. "It was a pleasure to meet you, J.R. Please call me if there is ever anything you need."

"Thank you, Mrs. Williams for a lovely luncheon." He shook the elderly woman's hand before collecting his things and leaving.

The two Williams sat alone quietly for a long time. J.R. held his grandmama's frail hand in his massive one and struggled to process all he had learned. He didn't fault his grandmama or his daddy. He understood the impossible circumstances of his daddy's world. His daddy had had no other choice than the one he made.

Standing and stretching his massive frame, he looked lovingly at his grandmama who grinned brightly at him.

"Wow! If I were a drinking man, I would say a shot of whiskey would be in order, but since I'm not a drinking man, I think I will have another cup of coffee. May I get you a second cup, Grandmama?"

"That would be nice. Only make it half a cup or I'll be up all night."

The two talked for several hours. He had so many

questions and his grandmama had all the answers. His emotions had run the full gamut from disbelief at the identity of his daddy to sorrow for all the years he had missed with his daddy to deep gratitude for all his grandmama had done for him.

"Grandmama, I love you and never want you to regret keeping this from me. God knew exactly what He was doing. If I had known about my daddy, I would have never been able to rule on the Devilland case. As many years as I have set on the bench, there has never been another case that made me feel the way I feel about Devilland. It's going to change lives, millions of lives. For once, I believe I have helped make a difference in this dark world."

"You've always made a difference in this world. You never give yourself enough credit."

The grandfather clock chimed five times as the two finished talking. Of course, they still had so much more to say. After all, they had almost sixty years to catch up on with questions, answers, and memories but Grandmama had tired and he was just as exhausted. They decided to take a break from the emotional subject.

After freshening up, J.R. wheeled his grandmama through the massive gardens, taking time to soak up the beauty and tranquility of nature. A slight breeze blew and the air was heavy with the fragrance of the countless flowers that bloomed throughout the grounds.

"Look, son! Stop!"

His gaze followed his grandmama's and he smiled brightly as his eyes fell upon the gorgeous cardinal perched in the magnolia tree.

The two were silent for the next several minutes as they

watched the magnificent bird cock his head as if conveying a silent message to them before taking flight.

"Can you stay for supper, son?"

"Absolutely."

They shared a poignant dinner together and were sad to see the day end.

He was catching the last flight back to DC and imagined Bradley was already waiting for him so he took his grandmama back to her suite.

"Grandmama, I'll never be able to thank you enough for all you've done for me. My parents may have given me life but you made me who I am today. For that, I am eternally grateful. I love you." His lip quivered like a small boy.

"I love you, more than you will ever know. Please give my love to Gloria. Have a safe trip and God bless you, my baby boy."

Leaning down, J.R. hugged his grandmama for a long time and kissed her gently before finally leaving her room.

As he reached the hallway, he turned around once more and said, "I love you, Grandmama."

"I love you, baby." She smiled softly.

twelve

That same night-July, 2008
Justice and Mrs. Williams' home-Washington, DC

J.R. REMOVED HIS KEY FROM THE LOCK AS GLORIA hurried into the foyer to greet him.

"Hello, darling. How are you? How's Gram?"

"I am exhausted, dear. Grandmama is quite well and sends her love. We need to talk." He grinned mysteriously as his wife.

"Talk?" Curiosity creased Gloria's brow.

"Yeah, talk. I need to talk but first I need to take a hot shower."

"Would you like a nice cup of tea? Are you hungry at all?"

"Tea sounds wonderful but I'm not hungry. I'll meet you upstairs for tea, if that's alright." He gently kissed his beautiful wife of thirty-one years on the lips.

"Take your time and I'll be up soon. Here, sweetheart, let me take your briefcase."

"No. I'm going to take it upstairs."

"Upstairs?" Her forehead crinkled in disbelief. "Don't

tell me you are going to work tonight."

"I have no intention of working tonight." Williams grinned. He couldn't wait to share with her all he learned.

He and Gloria had a wonderful life, envied by many. They were blessed with an incredible marriage all couples dream of having on their wedding day but few ever truly have. They weren't only husband and wife but best friends and partners in every sense of the word. The only misfortune of their long and happy union had been that they had never been able to have a child together. Therefore, they lavished all their love and attention on one another as well as their very spoiled and fat cat, Prince William.

Far too soon their idyllic world would be shattered.

J.R. came out of the bathroom in his navy blue terry cloth bathrobe and slippers. The Siamese-Burmese mix cat waited for him on the other side of the door.

"Hello Prince, my man." J.R. knelt down to pick up the purring cat.

In answer, the enormous feline nuzzled his neck and purred even louder. He sat Prince William down on the mint green chaise lounge, the cat's favorite spot in the bedroom. Williams then turned to take the wicker bed tray from his wife who had just entered with their Earl Grey tea.

Placing it on the tiny table which sat under the front window and overlooked the quiet street below, he pulled out the chair for his beautiful wife, already in her favorite pink lace nightgown and robe which he had given her this past Christmas.

"You look lovely, my darling," he said as she poured their tea.

"Thank you, sweetheart. You look refreshed but still

extremely tired. I want to hear all about your trip but are you sure you don't want to get some rest and tell me about everything tomorrow?"

"Definitely not, sweetheart. I've been counting the minutes until I could get home and tell you about today." A smile crept across his face.

"Okay," she said hesitantly. "So tell me about your trip. How did Gram look? Did you explain to her why I didn't come with you? Did she get the package I sent to her last week?" Her questions came rapid-fire.

"Amazing, gorgeous, yes, and I'm not quite sure, ma'am." He laughed lovingly at his wife.

She was so effervescent and always interested in his day, no matter if he had spent it issuing an opinion regarding a controversial case or had merely played a round of golf at the club. She made him feel so complete. She was truly a remarkable wife and partner. He couldn't imagine his life without her and she felt the same about him.

"I will say this trip was like no other. I finally met Walt Frasier, Grandmama's financial advisor, and the three of us had an enjoyable luncheon. Afterwards, we retired to her suite and Grandmama gave me some special gifts she's been holding onto for over five decades. I have so much to tell you but don't know where to start. You aren't going to believe the magnificent, yet heartbreaking, tales Grandmama shared with me."

"I don't understand." Her dark eyes danced in confusion.

"I met my daddy today." He grinned while sipping the hot tea.

"Oh dear Lord, this is wonderful! After all these years,

I got the impression it was too painful for her to talk about but never understood why."

"You are exactly right. It is wonderful and it was painful for her to talk about him."

Reaching down beside the chair, J.R. opened his briefcase and retrieved the gifts his grandmama had given him. First he took out the yellowed handkerchief and carefully unfolded it.

The gold locket caught the light as it spun from the chain. "It's the prettiest I've ever seen," Gloria said.

"Grandmama gave me this today. My daddy gave it to my mama on the day she told him she was pregnant with me."

Standing, he walked around the table and carefully placed the necklace around his wife's graceful neck and fastened the tiny clasp.

When she turned back to him, her eyes were filled with tears, as were his. He then shared with his wife all he had learned on his visit with his grandmama, showing her the journal and the photographs as well.

His wife's loving comfort flooded through J.R. as they talked, laughed, and cried for the next several hours. It was an incredible story held secret for over half a century.

"There's one more thing. Possibly the most unbelievable of all."

"What could be more unbelievable than all you've told me?" Gloria frowned with a shake of her head.

"Devilland." The name was flat on his tongue.

"What? What in the world would Devilland have to do with…" Realization crept over her and her eyes grew wide.

"Bridges! Not…Not the same Bridges as…as in…

Melanie….*Melanie Bridges!*" Gloria's hands flew to her mouth as she stared in disbelief at her husband. A sudden uneasiness washed over her.

"Yes. The same Bridges."

"Oh no, darling!"

"I know what you're thinking but I'm covered. At least I'm fairly sure I am. I need your opinion, not as my wife but as the best attorney I know."

J.R. produced the affidavit and explained about Frasier.

Gloria's eyes fell upon the page as she read it carefully, twice.

"What do you think?"

"What do I think? I think this Frasier is a brilliant man. You're fine, J.R. You didn't know. There was no way you could have known."

"What if this gets out to the public?"

"J.R., as usual, you are selling yourself short. You are known as the most ethical and honest man to ever sit on that bench. Nobody would think otherwise. I promise. That's your attorney, not your wife, speaking," she said firmly.

"Thank you, darling." J.R. blew a long breath of relief upon hearing his wife's expert words. His uncertainty of the past hours vanished as optimism that all would be fine filled the void. I think we should probably give it some more thought. And I think I should take it to the Chief Justice or maybe to the President."

"Okay. I agree but let's save that for tomorrow. I'm exhausted and I can only imagine how you must feel after all you've been through today."

"Yeah. Let's call it a night."

Falling into bed, J.R. pulled his wife close and breathed in her sweet vanilla scent.

"Goodnight, my love," she whispered sleepily.

"Goodnight, my Glory."

As he held his wife in his arms and faded off to sleep, J.R. dreamed of being a young boy growing up in the Mississippi Delta. Fond memories long forgotten surfaced and he vividly recalled the people, the sights, and the smells of a time long, long ago.

thirteen

The next morning- July, 2008
Washington, DC-Charleston, South Carolina

THE RINGING OF THE PHONE JARRED J.R. FROM HIS deep slumber. Turning over and peering at the clock, he saw it was just after six-thirty.

"Who in the world is calling at this hour on a Sunday morning?" Gloria moaned as she rolled over to see J.R. sitting on the edge of the bed reaching for the phone.

His voice thick with sleep, he answered, stifling a yawn.

"J.R. Williams," he said into the receiver.

"I'm so sorry for calling at this hour, Justice but I wanted to catch you before you left for church."

"Mary Sue?" An odd sense of confusion mixed with uneasiness washed over J.R. as he did his best to shake the heavy fog of sleep.

The soft voice then delivered the worst blow J.R. Williams had experienced in his entire life.

His body numbed. His mind spun out of control as a cold sweat broke across his brow. As his heart thundered in his chest, nausea consumed him.

No! Please dear God, no, no! His thoughts roared as he struggled to speak.

Finally, the only words he could find the strength to utter were simply, "Thank you for calling. I'll be in touch."

Tears rolled down his cheeks as he bit his lip to fight back his volcano of emotions. As the full impact hit him, he, the stalwart Supreme Court Justice J.R. Williams, broke into racking sobs.

He flinched under Gloria's tender embrace as she pulled him close and gently rocked.

"J.R.? What is it?" She lifted his head and he met her gaze filled with anguish.

He couldn't. Just couldn't say the words. He shook his head and leaned into her.

Gathering the will and swallowing the lump in his throat, he managed a cracked whisper. "She's gone. Grandmama's gone. She's gone, Glory." He cried with all the heart-wrenching emotion of a young boy.

She whimpered, breaking his heart further. "How? When?"

Scrubbing his face, breathing deeply, he fought to find the words.

"The night nurse was making her last rounds…before going off shift at seven… Grandmama… she slipped…she slipped away… peacefully…in her sleep… sometime during the night…" His words came in short staccato phrases.

Rising from the bed, J.R. paced the bedroom with his hands on his hips. He caught a glimpse in the mirror of someone he didn't' recognize. The bloodshot eyes, the vacant stare, he was a man who had withstood more emotions in the last twenty-four hours than most could bear.

After almost thirty minutes of sitting in anguished silence, Gloria finally spoke.

"Can I get you some tea, a little breakfast?"

"I can't eat anything but I'll take some tea. I need to get my thoughts gathered so I can begin making arrangements."

The grandfather clock in the hallway struck eight o'clock, but the chimes meant nothing to him.

Lost in his own thoughts, sipping on his third cup of tea, he gazed blankly out the window at the pedestrians below. His tormented thoughts consumed him. There would be no more visits, no more special occasions. How he would miss her melodic laugh, the singing of the old hymns on Easter morning. So very much had vanished in the blink of an eye.

The ringing of the phone ten minutes later caused J.R. to flinch as it broke his trance.

"Thank you. He's right here."

"It's Walt Frasier." Gloria handed J.R. the phone.

Clearing his throat, J.R. took the phone from his wife's hand.

"J.R., I can't tell you how sorry I am. She was an amazing woman."

"Thank you. That she was. I appreciate your calling, really I do."

Neither Gloria nor he had made any calls. How in the world would Frasier have already gotten the news?

"How did you know?"

"Your grandmother left explicit instructions with the staff at Eden Manor to call me when this time came."

"I don't understand. Why would they call you?"

"Well, your grandmother has taken care of the details for her arrangements. She told me that when the Lord called her Home, she didn't want you to be bothered with the mechanics of planning her funeral. The only thing we need to decide is the day and time for the service. When you feel like talking, please give me a call and I'll take care of everything from here."

Only the slightest of surprise pricked J.R.'s heart. Of course, she would have taken care of her own arrangements, to spare him. She had always thought of him first.

"Thank you, Walt. This is far above and beyond your duties as a financial advisor."

"Your grandmother was more than a client to me. She was a dear friend. I'm taking care of this last wish as a friend, not as her advisor. I'll wait for your call."

"I'll talk to Gloria and will call you back this afternoon. Thank you again, Walt."

"Call me anytime, J.R. My thoughts and prayers are with you and your family."

As he hung up the phone, Frasier's last words hit him in the gut like a Louisville slugger. Your family. J.R. suddenly realized his family now consisted of only his beautiful wife. His grandmama had been the only family he had ever known and she was gone.

His heart was breaking into a million irreparable tiny pieces.

Of course, he had known this day would come, but not today…not today. He had seen her only a few hours ago. She had been so vibrant and healthy. He simply couldn't get his brain to wrap around the fact that he had lost her.

Gloria came into the bedroom with the wicker tray once again. This time she carried fresh tea and blueberry bagels.

"I know you don't think you can eat anything but please try to eat a bite or two. You've got to keep your energy up and not eating isn't going to do you any good."

Absently he said, "Thank you, dear." She poured him a steaming cup of tea and added two cubes of sugar, exactly the way he liked it.

"You've been running on empty for these past few weeks, working indefatigably to end the court term. You haven't been well since right after Christmas. Would you like me to call Dr. Lee for something?" she asked.

"What do you mean? Tranquilizers?" He frowned, not liking what she suggested. He wasn't weak.

"Yes, darling. It will help you through these first few days." The compassion in her eyes did nothing to temper his sudden anger.

"No," he barked, leaning away from her. "I don't want to take any drugs. You know I don't take anything stronger than an aspirin."

He rarely, if ever, had used that tone of voice with her. Tears brimmed in her eyes and the shame ate at him. He wasn't the only one who was grief-stricken.

"I'm sorry, darling. I didn't mean to speak to you that way. I know you're hurting, too. I need to have my thoughts clear. I need to walk through this."

She swiped the tears with the back of her hand. "It's okay, dear." She nodded. "Really it is. This is hard for both of us.

Gloria had adored her grandmother-in-law. All of her own grandparents had passed away by the time Gloria graduated from college so she had treated Gram, as she called her, as if she were her own.

The next several days passed as if J.R. were moving underwater and he was immensely grateful for the support of his loving wife and friends.

An intimate and poignant affair, the funeral was attended by Walt Frasier, a handful of close friends from Washington, and two dozen staff and residents from Eden Manor.

Grandmama was laid to rest next to her sister in a plot surrounded by magnolia trees that overlooked a small duck pond. She had chosen the site herself almost a decade earlier, unbeknownst to J.R. or Gloria.

After the services, everyone came back to Eden Manor for something to eat and to visit with one another. The day proved extremely emotional for everyone, especially for J.R.

Gloria had wandered from the crowd and stood in the suite Gram had called home. Staring vacantly at the gorgeous azalea gardens, Gloria jumped as she felt her husband's hand on her shoulder.

"I'm sorry, dear. I didn't mean to startle you." He kissed her lightly on the cheek.

"She loved this view so much," Gloria said quietly.

"That she did. Look!"

"What?" Gloria followed her husband's gaze.

"I bet it's the same little fella Grandmama and I saw the other day." J.R. grinned as he pointed at the red cardinal perched on one of the bird feeders in the azalea garden.

An intense rush of pure tranquility fell over J.R. and Gloria. Without looking away from the bird, he slipped her hand into his.

"It's the most peaceful sight I think I've ever seen. It's

almost like Gram put that red bird there to let us know she's still with us."

"I have no doubt she did. Grandmama loved watching birds. The cardinals were her favorite. I guess because they are rare compared to the others you see every day. She was so enthralled with them that I gave her a book on birds when she was first learning to read, a year or so after we moved from Mississippi. She had always been so self-conscious that she was unable to read but never admitted she was illiterate until I asked her the meaning of a word while I was doing my homework one night. I couldn't imagine not being able to read. I'd been reading every book I could get my hands on since the age of five. I remember saving my allowance for two whole months to pay for that book. Each night after supper, we would sit together for an hour or more and I taught her to read it. I remember how proud she was when she read it cover to cover all by herself for the first time." J.R. smiled, recalling his grandmama's joy.

It had been so long ago but now felt like only yesterday. He could still taste the cocoa and smell the sugar cookies baking as he, a thirteen-year-old boy, taught his fifty-two-year-old grandmama to read.

"After that, she read constantly and studied tirelessly. She became fanatical about words, their meanings, and most especially about the correct pronunciations. Grandmama became a connoisseur of the English language and it all started with that one book about birds."

"How beautiful. You never told me that story."

"I hadn't thought about it in a long time until right now. I do imagine that was Grandmama bidding us her own fond farewell." He drifted away, content with the peace.

"Excuse me, Justice." A petite brunette stood inside the doorway.

"Yes?"

"Some of the guests were looking for your wife and you. They're preparing to leave."

"Thank you. We'll be right there."

For the next half hour, J.R. and Gloria exchanged parting pleasantries with those who had come to pay their respects.

There were only a handful of people left when Walt Frasier approached him.

"How are you doing?" Frasier asked with genuine concern in his eyes.

"I'm doing okay. I don't believe it's sunk in yet."

"I understand. There's a final matter you and I need to discuss but you can call me after you've had some time to grieve."

J.R. was certain it would be a long time before he came to terms with his loss. "If possible, I would prefer to meet with you tomorrow and take care of whatever matters there are. I don't want to make a second trip."

"Whatever you need, J.R. How about eight in the morning at my office?"

"That will work fine. Gloria plans on taking care of things here. I'll see you in the morning."

The truth was J.R. didn't know if or when he would ever be able to return to South Carolina. Nothing remained here for him except the memories of his dear grandmama. Of course, there was her grave site but she wasn't there. He had never understood people who had a need to return to a loved one's grave for birthdays, anniversaries, and holidays.

His grandmama wasn't in the cold dark ground. She had gone on to a better life and he would carry her in his heart until he saw her again. He had arranged for flowers to be put on the site year round but he doubted if he would ever return himself.

The next morning, J.R. and Gloria woke refreshed and eager to finalize their business in Charleston and return to Washington. Gloria would be going to Eden Manor to oversee the packing and shipping of Gram's personal belongings back to DC.

Many of the possessions would be either given to friends at the home or donated to the Salvation Army. There were only a few items Gloria said she wanted to keep—like Gram's pink hat. It reminded her of last Easter when Gram had worn the hat with her pink linen dress. Gram had sung "The Old Rugged Cross" in perfect harmony with the choir.

Finally, with everything sorted and packed away, Gloria picked up the Baccarat vase and walked out of the suite for the last time and headed for the main office.

She asked for Laverne Shipley, the administrator for the residence. Laverne had been running the home for the last thirty years and had become a close friend to all three Williams. Gloria explained she would like to leave the Baccarat crystal vase at the home in honor of Grandmama Williams. Gloria wanted to do something unique for the people who had been so very special in Gram's later life by keeping the standing order with the local florist for fresh flowers to be delivered weekly to refresh the arrangement. J.R. agreed. His grandmama had made a great many friends at the place she called home these last twenty years. The fresh flowers would help keep their dear friend alive in their hearts.

While Gloria attended to affairs at Eden Manor, J.R. met with Walt Frasier across town.

"You grandmother shared with you the personal matters about your father the other day," Walt said. "I'm going to assume she didn't explain anything more simply because she told me long ago she didn't want her will discussed until this time came."

"No, we didn't discuss anything about her finances. We never did," J.R. said dismissively.

"Her will is pretty straight forward. She left everything to you. Years ago, your grandmother was named as a beneficiary in the Bridges' estate. She inherited a tremendous amount of money along with landholdings in the Mississippi Delta. The landholdings are farmland which has been leased out to area cotton farmers since your grandmother inherited it. The leases on the land have provided a healthy income stream over the years. Your grandmother lived very modestly and invested very wisely. The original inheritance has grown substantially over the years."

"Grandmama owned land in Mississippi?" J.R. asked in bewilderment. Chuckling, he shook his head and threw up his hands.

"Yes. Quite a lot of it, actually."

"How much are we talking about here?"

"This is a copy of your grandmother's last financial statements."

Williams scanned the documents quickly. Shocked, he slunk back into his seat. He stared at the words and numbers on the page in front of him. The room beyond the paper he held blurred.

J.R. and Gloria had both worked hard through their life together and were financially blessed beyond most people's imaginations but nothing compared to this.

Taking the glass of water proffered by Walt, J.R. drained it in two long gulps.

"I'm going to tell you what your grandmother told me," Walt said. "It was when she explained to me who your daddy was. The enormous wealth was what motivated her to keep that secret for as long as she did. She said money had a way of changing people, not necessarily for the good, and she wanted to make sure you could handle such tremendous wealth."

"Grandmama was exactly right. How in the world does one handle that kind of money?" J.R. whistled and shook his head.

"There is one more final matter."

"Oh no…no…no… You can keep it to yourself. I have had quite enough." J.R. tossed the financials on the coffee table and buried his head in his hands. He didn't think he could handle one more emotion.

"I promise this is one is not nearly as monumental as all the others. It's something your grandmother wanted to do for you and Gloria."

"As if this isn't enough?" J.R. laughed heartily and again threw his hands into the air.

"This is personal. It goes beyond any dollar value. I can't take no for an answer. I promised your grandmother I wouldn't." Walt had a sparkle in his eyes.

"Okay." J.R. blew out a long breath of air. "Hit me with it."

"Your grandmother's greatest wish for this time was

neither Gloria nor you spend time grieving for her. She wanted you to celebrate her life."

"I don't understand."

"Gloria and you are to leave for Italy as soon as possible. The funds for the trip are being held in a separate account and will pay for everything. I only need to know the dates you would like to go. Your grandmother said she never got a chance to see Italy herself and she wanted to go with you now in spirit. I'll call you next week after you have a chance to talk to Gloria. Your grandmother insisted you take fourteen days and I cannot accept excuses about you being too busy to get away for a while. Gloria and you are to indulge yourselves and celebrate Mrs. Williams' blessed life. Those were her exact words to me." Walt was firm but wore a broad smile.

"Italy? Of course, it would be Italy. Grandmama had stacks upon stacks of books about Rome, the Sistine Chapel, the Colosseum, all of it. She and Gloria would spend hours poring over those books and somehow we never made the time to go." His heart filled with sadness that he had never made the time to take his grandmama to Italy. There were so many things she hadn't done for herself. He should have done more for her. She had guarded his inheritance closely, invested wisely, and sacrificed so much for him. In awe of her fierce inner strength and pure heart, J.R. shook his head and stared into the distance. Had she really known how much he loved her, how much he admired her?

"You're going to make the time now. You won't deny your grandmother's last wish. I promised her I wouldn't let you."

"No, I won't. I won't deny Grandmama or Gloria. We

need this. Grandmama was right. We need to celebrate her life. Please, please tell me that you don't have another rabbit in a hat somewhere." J.R. chuckled. The tension of the past days slipped through him and a warm peace unexpectedly fell upon him.

"No more rabbits."

"I can't thank you enough for all you did, Walt. You are truly a kind and amazing man. My grandmama was lucky to have you in her life."

"I was the lucky one."

"We all were."

Rising to his feet, J.R. grimaced as pain pinched his back.

"J.R.? Are you okay? Sit down and let me get you another glass of water."

"I'm fine. Really. I've had a helluva week. Cut an old man some slack." J.R. mustered up a weak smile.

The two men said good-bye and Frasier promised to expedite the Trust process and he assured J.R. he would be in touch soon.

As J.R. headed to the car, he rubbed his lower back. He couldn't remember how long it had been aching.

"Damn it! I'm too young to feel this way," he muttered as the ever present exhaustion took hold.

After pulling into traffic, his thoughts swiftly traveled to how excited Gloria would be about Italy. Fourteen magical days in Italy. Just the two of them. They deserved it.

"Thank you, Grandmama," he said wistfully. "It's going to be perfect."

fourteen

That evening-July, 2008
Washington, DC

YAWNING, J.R. STIRRED AND RUBBED HIS EYES AS the flight attendant who was walking down the aisle smiled at him. Glancing over at his wife who was deep in thought, he curiously looked at the book which held her entire focus. He recognized it immediately. It was a first edition of *Gone with the Wind* that she had collected from Grandmama's personal belongings. J.R. recalled fondly the day he had bought it for his grandmama over thirty years ago. It had been a wonderful day. Gloria and he had taken his grandmama shopping shortly after they were married. His grandmama's eyes had lit up instantly when she spotted the dusty book on a small table under a tiny pair of antique spectacles. J.R. had insisted on purchasing it for her and she had been overjoyed. She said she had heard so much about the story but had never seen a copy of the book. Being a first edition, the book carried a hefty price tag. J.R. had been taken aback by the price when the dealer told him what it would be. Gloria and his grandmama were already sitting on a bench outside the tiny store. At any price, the book was a bargain as it was so precious to her. His grandmama had made sure he grew up in a home where books were never in short supply. He had devoured every book he could get his hands on in his teenage years. It had tugged at his heart that this wonderful woman should ever want for anything after all she had done and sacrificed to raise him. His heart warmed as Gloria carefully turned the page. Completely absorbed in the tale of the Civil War, she was oblivious to his loving gaze.

The flight attendant announced they would be landing at Reagan National shortly as Gloria glanced up at her husband.

"J.R.! How long have you been staring at me?" She chuckled.

"Not long enough," he replied, grinning.

She cupped his face. "That's the same smile I fell in love with over thirty-four years ago."

J.R. had not yet had a chance to tell Gloria about his meeting with Walt Frasier. She had been so busy at Eden Manor and they had barely made their flight back to DC It certainly wasn't the kind of conversation he could squeeze in at the baggage claim. He was still trying to absorb it all himself. Excitement tingled up his spine as he thought of telling her about Italy. She would be thrilled. He chastised himself now that they hadn't taken more opportunities to travel and see the world. They had both been so driven in their careers that travel was something they were going to do when they retired. Not this time. He would fulfill his grandmama's last wish, no matter what.

Within the hour, the driver pulled up to the Williams'

elegant home and quickly opened the back door of the car before getting the luggage from the trunk.

As J.R. stepped out of the car, a wave of nausea hit him and he raced up the steps, unlocked the front door, and ran to the bathroom.

Bile burned up his throat just as he dropped to his knees. He heaved, vomiting over and over. His gut wrenched from the uncomfortable effort, sweat beaded on his brow. At last, the anguishing pain subsided and he flushed the toilet.

Neither Gloria nor the driver had noticed J.R.'s hasty exit. Gloria had been preoccupied with finding her wallet to tip the driver as he took the bags into the foyer.

Once the driver left, Gloria realized J.R. had vanished. She then heard the anguished noises followed by the flushing of the toilet down the hallway.

"J.R.? J.R.?" She called as she raced to the bathroom.

"I'm okay, Glory. I'm okay." He sat on the floor with his head hung over the toilet.

"No! You're not okay, J.R! I'm not going to take one more excuse from you!" She cried as she fell to the floor next to him. "It's not work. It's not Gram. Something is going on with you and you have to see Park."

J.R. wiped his mouth and finally admitted to himself what he had been denying for so long. He was ill and had to see the doctor.

"I'll go see him. I promise. I'll have June call first thing in the morning. I promise, Glory."

Rising quickly, Gloria grabbed a washcloth and ran it under the cold water. She handed it to J.R. who gratefully took it only moments before a second wave of nausea hit and he vomited violently into the porcelain bowl.

After a half hour, Gloria managed to get him cleaned up and into bed.

The next morning, J.R. retreated to the back patio and found Gloria with her head bowed, praying aloud as she rocked back and forth in the wrought-iron chair.

The tiny courtyard was pure tranquility. Thick ivy climbed the brick walls. A babbling cherub fountain sat in one corner. Feeders were scattered throughout the garden for the ruby throated hummingbirds that traveled over two thousand miles from Central America every spring. A plethora of greenery and flowers attracted the tiny birds as well as dozens upon dozens of butterflies. His wife had put in a great deal of research, time, and meticulous effort when choosing the gorgeous flora for the area. She had long ago pictured it exactly as she had created it—a virtual fairy tale garden. She seemed to notice none of it this morning.

"Good morning, Glory."

"J.R.! How do you feel?"

"I feel better, much better," he said honestly.

"Evelyn has the tea kettle ready. Do you think you could eat a little something?"

"I am a little bit hungry. I could eat an egg, maybe a piece of dry toast. Let's have breakfast out here. We need to talk." He forced himself to smile. "Grandmama had a few more tricks up her sleeve."

"What?"

"Yeah, there's a lot more to the story. I'll tell you about it over breakfast."

As they ate, J.R. told his wife all about the fabulous fortune his grandmama had left them as well as the trip to Italy.

When he finished, Gloria sat motionless. A slow grin crept across her lips. She chuckled before breaking into a full burst of laughter.

"Gram was something else. I had no idea. Imagine keeping a secret like that for almost sixty years. Amazing, simply amazing! And a trip to Italy on top of everything else! What are you thinking?"

He was delighted by her reaction, quietly sipping his second cup of tea. "Honestly, I feel like my life has been one huge jigsaw puzzle and now I'm trying to put all the pieces into place. Daddy. Melanie Bridges. The inheritance. Italy. All of it. I can't ever remember being this overwhelmed. We have so many decisions to make. I'd like to have June go ahead and get me in to see the President. I know I'm covered but I'm going to feel a lot better once I bring it to his attention. Given our long years of friendship, I feel more comfortable going to him first before I go to the Chief Justice. As far as the inheritance, we both need some time to think about it. I have no idea what to do with that kind of money."

"I agree on both accounts. You should see the President as soon as possible. Frasier is the only other one who knows about the Bridges connection but if word were somehow to leak out, we could easily have a nightmare on our hands. The President needs to know as soon as possible. Let's take all of this one step at a time."

Glancing through the window at the clock in the library, J.R. was shocked to see how quickly time had flown.

"First things first, I need to get to the office and before you even say a word, yes. I will have June set an appointment with the doctor. I know you don't want to hear it,

Glory, but it could be as simple as I've run this old body of mine too hard for too long. Let's not build any bridges we may not have to cross. Maybe Park will tell me I need some good old-fashioned R&R and we're off to Rome."

"You're right, dear. You have been working harder than ever since the Court opened. Promise you'll make the appointment and I promise I won't build any bridges."

fifteen

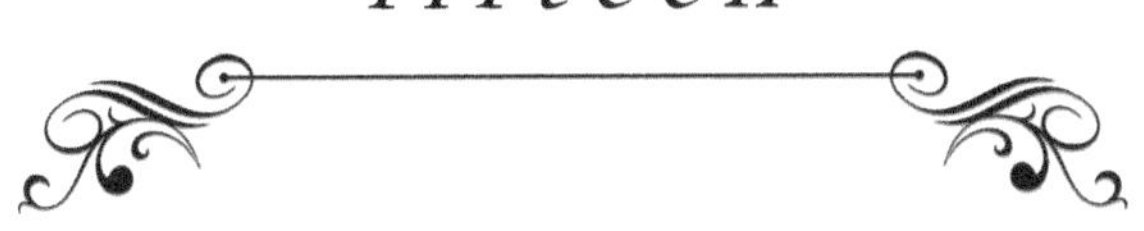

The same morning-July, 2008
Washington, DC

J UNE, J.R.'S EXECUTIVE ASSISTANT, KNOCKED ON HIS door with a fresh cup of steaming tea in her hand.

"Come in, come in." J.R. placed the brief he had been reading in the file and smiled at the young woman.

"Good morning, sir. I was so sorry to hear about your grandmother. I lost mine a little over two years ago and I know how hard it is. There's no one else in your life like your grandmother. I know you two were especially close."

"Thank you. Did I ever tell you that my grandmama's name was also June?"

"Yes, sir. You did mention that." June smiled warmly.

"Before it gets too crazy around here, I have a couple of appointments I would like for you to schedule for me. The first is with the President, at his earliest convenience. I believe he's out of the country but I need to see him as soon as he gets back to Washington. Call Ruth. She's the one who runs the ship over there and will be able to get me an appointment quickly. Tell her it's a private matter of some urgency and will take less than an hour of the President's time. If he would prefer, I can meet him in the evening. It's important I speak to him as soon as possible."

"Yes, sir."

"Please call Dr. Lee and get me an appointment as soon as possible. I promised Gloria I'd see him."

J.R. caught the immediate flash of concern in June's eyes.

"There's nothing wrong with me. It's a wife's job to worry." He flashed an easy smile, hoping his young assistant didn't detect his own worry.

June left and reappeared in the doorway of the Justice's chambers within minutes.

"Excuse me, sir."

"Yes?"

"Dr. Lee is leaving this afternoon for a medical seminar. He's going to be gone for ten days but his nurse said she could get you in this morning at ten."

Glancing at his watch, J.R. realized he needed to leave immediately in order to make it across town.

"Tell her I'm on my way."

Traffic was light and he made good time to Park Lee's office.

"Good morning, J.R. Come in, come in."

The doctor stood from behind his desk and came around to give his friend a warm hug.

"I've not seen you in ages. I was so saddened to hear of your loss. How are you holding up, J.R.?" The doctor's brow creased with compassion.

"I guess I'm doing as well as can be expected. Of course, I always knew this day would come but we all fool ourselves into thinking we'll have our loved ones with us forever. It's been a tough ten days. That's for sure."

After a few minutes of catching up with one another, the doctor got down to business.

"What brings you in to see me today?"

"I'm sure it's nothing. I first thought maybe I needed some vitamins but now I think I may have a kidney infection because I've got a nagging pain in my lower back. I feel like I've run the Boston Marathon by noon every day. It seems no matter how much rest I get, I don't have the energy I used to have. Don't remind me that I'm no longer a spring chicken. Gloria has already put that bug in my ear." He chortled and shook his head.

"So you need vitamins or treatment for a kidney infection. When have you had the time to go to medical school?" Lee jovially peered over his black rimmed glasses with a smile.

"I assume it has to be something like that. I don't have any symptoms other than incredible fatigue, a slight decrease in appetite lately, some vomiting, and this troublesome pain."

As he heard his own words, the long list of symptoms that he had been denying, J.R. swallowed hard. He should have come to see Park sooner, much sooner.

"Okay, let's get you on the table and let me take a look at that machine of yours."

The two men walked across the doctor's office and entered a side door to one of the exam rooms.

"Strip down to your skivvies and put on that cute little gown. I'll be back in a moment," the doctor said. "I'm going to pull your chart."

Lee had noticed his friend had lost weight when he first came in but seeing him in the thin gown made him realize how much weight his friend had actually lost.

"Good Lord, J.R., doesn't that wife of yours feed you anymore?" Lee asked in an attempt to mask his deep concern.

"I'm doing my best to go for the lean and mean look lately." It was a weak attempt at humor. He had known Park Lee for too long to be fooled by his quip. And the troubled look on the doctor's face elevated his concern. J.R.'s his mouth went dry and he struggled to swallow the lump rising in his throat.

"I've been telling Gloria maybe I've run myself into the ground. I admit I've been pushing myself pretty hard. Maybe I need some good old-fashioned R&R. What do you think, doc?"

"I think you need to be quiet so I can listen to that ticker of yours."

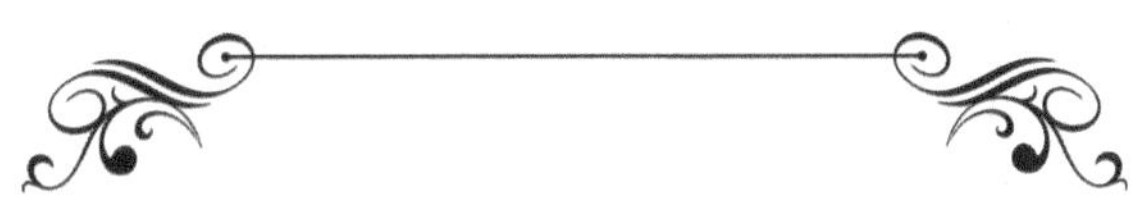

sixteen

Two weeks pass-August, 2008
Justice and Mrs. Williams' home-Washington, DC

THE CHERUB FOUNTAIN BABBLED AS J.R. STARED blankly into the twilight. He and Gloria had decided earlier in the day that he would step down from the bench. Both wanted to soak up every single precious moment they had left together in privacy, far away from the eyes of the public.

He jumped as her hands rested upon his broad shoulders.

"J.R., I've been looking all over for you. You are supposed to be resting. Oh, honey." Gloria wiped the tears coursing down his cheeks with her delicate hand before sitting next to him on the long swing.

"I tried to rest but I needed to come out here. To sit. To think."

"What are you thinking about, darling?"

"Since the diagnosis, my emotions have run the full gamut. At first I was confused as the why this is happening to me. I hate to admit it but I held some anger, real anger against God for taking me too early. I should be in the prime of my life. When I prayed, I had the sensation of literally being held. Held tightly. I believe I understand. I don't know why I couldn't understand it sooner. Grandmama always told me God has a perfect plan for each of us. When I look back over my life, all the way from the Mississippi Delta to a seat on the Supreme Court, I think I finally understand His plan for me."

Gloria bit her lip, fighting back tears as she waited for her husband to continue.

Silence hung in the warm air for several minutes before J.R. found his voice once again.

"Devilland. Grandmama said there is no such thing as coincidence. God always knows exactly what He is doing—even when we don't. God put Melanie Bridges exactly where He needed her to be. He put me exactly where He needed me to be. He gave her the guidance and wisdom to win the suit. He gave me the guidance and wisdom I needed. The first vote was 5-4 to overturn the verdict. When I wrote the dissenting opinion, I prayed more than I ever have over a case. Of all those in the majority, Patterson was the very last one I thought would change his vote. In all my years on the bench, I cannot recall one single time that he changed his original vote. I have no doubt God was indeed there. When I think of what Melanie Bridges accomplished, it's truly nothing short of phenomenal. When I think what she and I accomplished together, it's extraordinarily phenomenal. Until Devilland, I had been blessed with an amazing life. With Devilland, I was blessed with an amazing purpose. His purpose. I've fulfilled His purpose. I've run my race, Glory. I feel like I'm truly going home. I have a childish perception of Heaven which I'm nourishing. I know that none of us knows what Heaven is like. Heaven may be all of being a sparkling drop of dew on a blade of grass in the morning sun. It may be a place where we are all so well pampered and taken care of that I can't even imagine, but it doesn't matter to me. That's the way the end of life is. It's a big mystery and none of us will know what it is like until we experience it. I'm looking forward to it. For me, it really is going home. It's Grandmama. It's Mama. It's Daddy. I finally have peace, but then I feel so very selfish. So very selfish with so many regrets." He bit his quavering lip and gazed deeply into his wife's dark eyes.

"What do you possibly have to feel selfish about and what could you possibly regret?"

"I feel selfish about leaving you behind. I'm leaving you alone. I can only imagine how I would feel if the roles were reversed. I regret not having children. We should have adopted half a dozen kids and you wouldn't be alone. That's the one thing in which there is no peace. Leaving you." His voice cracked and the all too familiar pang tore at his heart.

"Honey! Shhh. Don't you worry for one single minute about me. We're all waiting at the same airport for our flight Home and you have gotten a first-class ticket. You're going Home early. I will miss you every single day for the rest of my life but I will find peace in the arms of the angels because I have no doubt you will be waiting at those gates when God calls me Home. As far as any regrets about not adopting children, that's a choice we made together a long time ago. Our careers were so hectic we agreed we didn't want children to only have them raised by one round of nannies after another but since you brought up children, I do have something I want to run by you," she said anxiously as a tiny curl crept to her lips.

"What?"

"Well, with the diagnosis and everything, we never talked much about the inheritance and something came to me earlier this morning."

"The inheritance? That's all yours now, Glory."

"Well, that's the thing, J.R. I don't need it, any of it. Not a penny."

"Not need it? You're young, Glory. I want you to live out your life comfortably. The inheritance will take care of you." He struggled to comprehend what she was saying.

"J.R., listen to yourself. I have enough money to live to be four hundred and twelve without the inheritance. I want you to light a torch for me so I can carry you with me every single day."

"Light a torch? What do you want to do? Start your own Olympic games? Actually, you probably could with that amount of money." He chuckled at his jest.

She squeezed his knee. "That's the first time I've heard you laugh since the diagnosis. It's the sweetest of melodies."

It was true he hadn't found much humor lately but it was therapeutic to laugh a little. "The sweetest of melodies, huh? Maybe you should have your hearing checked." He winked and she just shook her head, grinning slightly.

"Hear me out on this one. What is the most important thing your daddy gave you?"

"Love? I didn't know he was my daddy back then but I did know he loved me."

"That's true. What I'm asking is what is the most important thing the inheritance gave you?"

"Glory, I don't understand."

"Education. The money allowed Gram to send you to the best schools to get the best education possible. Without education, you couldn't have achieved all you have."

"I still don't understand."

"Let's take the Trust Fund and provide college educations for kids who wouldn't have a chance at one any other way. We could even take it a step farther and make a thousand more lawyers, just like us!" It was Gloria who now chuckled.

Amazed, J.R. simply stared at his wife. She never once thought of herself before others and she was right. They were financially secure. She would have plenty of money to live out the rest of her life without the inheritance.

Several moments passed before Gloria spoke. "J.R.?" Her brows knitted in anticipation of what he thought.

"I think it's a wonderful idea. How would you feel about throwing a few doctors in the mix?" He gave her a sly smile.

"Of course we could. Light the torch, J.R. For the rest of my life, I will have a part of you to share with the world."

"If you're sure that's what you want to do."

"It is, darling. It truly is. Think of how many children we could bless just as you were blessed." She smiled as she folded herself against his body.

"I love it. Grandmama would've loved it. Daddy would've loved it."

"Then it's settled."

"There's one thing. Daddy left the Trust in my name. I think we should change it to honor him."

"I think we should change it to honor both of you."

"Both of us?"

"Yes. I even have the name."

"What do you want to name it?"

"Rhoades to Bridges. It wouldn't be only your name and your daddy's name. It would be symbolic. As we give children educations, they will be able to travel roads and cross bridges into a much better life than they would have had without an education."

"You are so very clever, my love. It's perfect." His heart warmed as he thought of how proud his daddy would have been.

"Great." She snuggled even closer to him, desperate to breathe in his scent so she could carry it with her once he was gone.

"Rhoades to Bridges," J.R. whispered. "Rhoades to Bridges."

seventeen

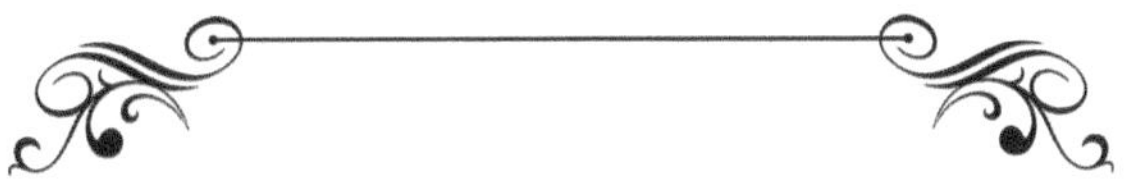

The following morning-August, 2008
Supreme Court, Washington, DC

"GOOD MORNING, SIR," JUNE SAID CHEERFULLY as set her boss' hot tea on his desk.

"Good morning."

"Ruth called earlier and said she would have to reschedule your appointment with the President for next Monday at four, if that meets with your schedule. He's been out of the country and got back to DC last night but then he left this morning to visit the families of the soldiers who died in the bombing. He'll be in Crawford for the rest of the week."

Looking up from the sheaf of papers he had been studying intently, he gave June a blank look.

"The President?" he asked, confused.

Gloria and he had made the decision yesterday. How in the world had June known to schedule an appointment with the President?

"Yes, sir." June frowned, uncertain at the Justice's reaction. "You asked me to make an appointment with him but Ruth hasn't been able to get you in to see him as he has been traveling extensively. You said it was a private matter of some urgency."

He had indeed forgotten. So much had happened in the past weeks.

"Of course, thank you. Next Monday it will have to be. Please get me an appointment with the Chief Justice, too, any time after I see the President."

As they went over the day's schedule and matters in progress, the Justice struggled to keep his focus. He had to ask her to repeat herself more than once. As she talked, he did his best to listen. His thoughts kept traveling to another world as he stared past June at something far in the distance—what the all too near future would bring.

"Will there be anything else, sir?" June gathered her notes and the files.

"Please make an appointment with Stuart Weldon, my investment banker. I'd like to see him sometime in the next day or so if possible. Tell him I'd like to have at least two hours of his time. Offer to treat him to a meal. That gets his attention every time. The man does love to eat." J.R. smiled for the first time all morning.

"Yes, sir."

"One more thing, before I forget. Things are going to get somewhat hectic around here pretty soon but Gloria and I would like to invite Gregory and you to join us at the inauguration in January. I believe our man will indeed win the election and it will be a historical event which none of us, especially Gregory and you, should miss. I imagine I'll have some pretty good seats for the show." The Justice grinned broadly. "Gregory and you have poured not only your hearts but also countless hours into working on the presidential campaign. You deserve to be there to share the taste of victory."

June's mouth fell open at his words. Speechless for almost a full minute, she finally found her voice. "Thank you, Mr. Justice. I have no doubt there are many other people you could invite. This is an incredible honor. I speak for Gregory and myself when I say joining Mrs. Williams and you for the inauguration will be an experience of a lifetime, truly."

"Gloria and I will be honored as well and neither of us can imagine anyone else we would rather have with us."

One more thought flashed in his mind as June stood to leave, he asked her to make another appointment for him.

"Please call *Time* magazine and get in touch with Katie Sawyer. Ask her to join me for dinner any evening but it will have to be after my meetings with the President and the Chief Justice."

"Yes, sir."

The flash of curiosity in June's eyes wasn't lost by the Justice. He regretted he wouldn't be able to explain everything to her as he had no doubt his resignation would hit her hard. His heart ached at how fond he had grown of the young woman and how much he would miss her.

eighteen

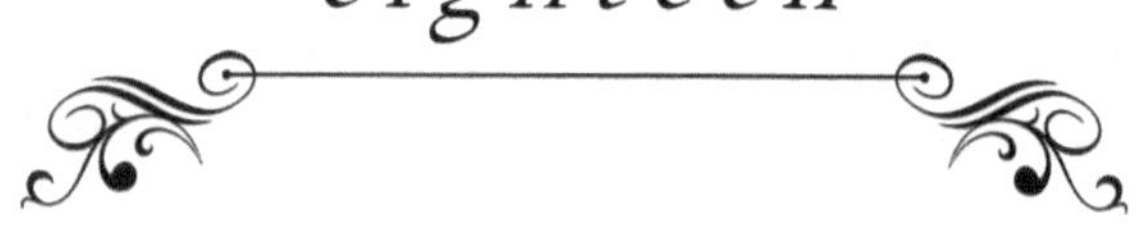

Two days pass-August, 2008
Old Ebbitt Grill-Washington, DC

UPON ENTERING THE RESTAURANT, J.R. immediately spotted his longtime friend and advisor Stuart Weldon at a corner table.

"Well, well, it's good to see you, my man." The investment banker shook J.R.'s hand.

"You too, Stuart. How's your lovely Barb?"

"She's doing quite well, busy as ever with the Special Olympics. They celebrated their fortieth anniversary last month and it was a tremendous success. How is your beautiful bride?"

"She, too, is doing well. We've both had a rather strenuous few weeks with my grandmama's sudden passing. Gloria and she were especially close."

"Yes, yes, I was sorry to hear the news. I only met her once at a Christmas party at your home but I found her to be an elegant and entertaining woman."

"That she was. Thank you. She lived a full and rewarding life. I spent a glorious day with her and later she passed

"

away peacefully in her sleep. Our last day together was a true blessing. She looked and acted like a woman twenty years younger. I guess that was what made her sudden death such a shock. As I told someone else, intellectually I knew we wouldn't have her with us much longer but emotionally I don't think anyone is truly prepared to lose a parent. I never knew my mama or daddy so my grandmama was both mother and father to me for my entire life." J.R. forced himself to swallow the lump rising in his throat as he realized his last sentence wasn't entirely true. He had indeed known his daddy. While the man he knew had certainly been active in his young life, it had been in a completely different way.

"Well, I believe God truly blesses those he takes during a peaceful slumber. That's how I want to go when my number is called. My mother suffered most of her entire life with her illnesses and eventually lost her battle with both emphysema and cirrhosis of the liver, after God only knows how many cigarettes and even more vodka. It was very painful to watch her suffer in those final years. Consider yourself blessed, my friend."

"I do."

Over the fine meal, the two men enjoyed catching up with one another, news of mutual friends, the hottest topics on the Hill, and their personal favorite, tales of their own latest and greatest golf games.

"J.R., it's wonderful to see you and it definitely has been too long. What do you say I have Meira arrange a tee time for Saturday? We need to play eighteen holes like we used to do before we got so damn busy doing whatever it is the two of us do." Stuart shook his head and smirked.

"Sounds great to me. I'm afraid Saturday won't be possible as I have a few things to button down in the next couple of weeks but we'll definitely get together soon. It has been far too long since we hit the greens. We should give Ned and Bernie a call. It's always a pleasure to kick their tails around the course." Williams smiled, but it was vacant. Hollow by the empty plans made.

"Sounds wonderful but you do remember it was us who went home with our tails tucked the last time we played those two."

"I certainly do. That's why it's high time we redeem ourselves. It's a date. I'll have June give everyone a call and make the arrangements as soon as I take care of a few things." J.R. prayed silently he would be able to share one last golf game with his friends. A joy he had always taken for granted. Until now.

Stuart nodded, but the frown he wore indicated he wasn't convinced, though it vanished as quickly as it had come.

Once the waiter cleared the luncheon dishes and served the coffee, J.R. pulled a legal size manila folder from his attaché case. The tab's label read simply *Rhoades Trust*.

After almost an hour, J.R. finally finished explaining his wishes to Stuart. He had explained the inheritance had come from his grandmama but had given Stuart no details beyond that. Although he trusted his advisor implicitly, there was no need to divulge the full story to him.

Struggling to keep his focus, J.R. took a long swallow of ice water. Details. All the details. He had told Gloria had found peace with the end of his life but keeping up the charade of acting as if nothing was wrong was taxing. He had caught June looking at him with concern on more than one occasion and had the same feeling earlier from Stuart. He needed to focus on the business at hand and not think of what had been weighing heavy on his heart. The conversation he would have with the President. No. He could not think of that. He would take it one step at a time. The Trust was what was important in this moment.

"Good Lord, J.R., what an incredible tale. Your grandmother's banker is right on the money. That's one hell of a fortune for a little Southern lady to amass over the last forty plus years. She was definitely an extremely intelligent woman. I know men with MBAs who couldn't have built such a portfolio." Stuart leaned back in his chair, shaking his head in astonishment. "I greatly admire your generosity in establishing this Trust but as your advisor and friend, I must say even a percentage of this amount of money would be a tremendous charitable contribution. Are you both sure you want to turn over the entire Trust?"

"I appreciate your thoughts, Stuart. I truly do but this decision hasn't been made lightly. There have been many lengthy discussions and a great deal of prayer involved. You know what our personal net worth was even before this unexpected inheritance. Gloria and I have been enormously blessed. We have more than enough money to live the rest of our lives very comfortably. Since we never had children of our own, we both are driven to provide these funds for the children who would otherwise have no other means to achieve their potential. The two of us feel strongly the money left for me allowed me to receive the best education possible and become the man I am today. We want to use every penny of the Rhoades Trust to continue the legacy."

"That's all you need to say. Gloria and you are extremely generous."

"I appreciate your kind words but Gloria and I are only giving back a small amount compared to all the rich blessings, both tangible and intangible, that have been bestowed upon us. We trust you'll make the appropriate arrangements. Once you begin to establish the new Trust, I'm certain there will be many details we haven't addressed. Gloria will be the one who will be taking the reins from here. I wanted to meet with you initially since the Rhoades Trust was left in my name."

"Well, I have a great deal of work to get done. Tell Gloria I'll be in touch with her soon. I look forward to working with her and hope to spend more time with you on the golf course. Don't forget to have June set that tee time and give Meira a call."

"I won't forget. Thank you again for meeting with me today and taking care of this matter." They stood and shook hands.

As J.R. walked to the car, he thought of Stuart, Barb, and all the dear friends he would be leaving behind. He had no doubt each of them would be there for Gloria once he was gone. In that, he found a measure of peace.

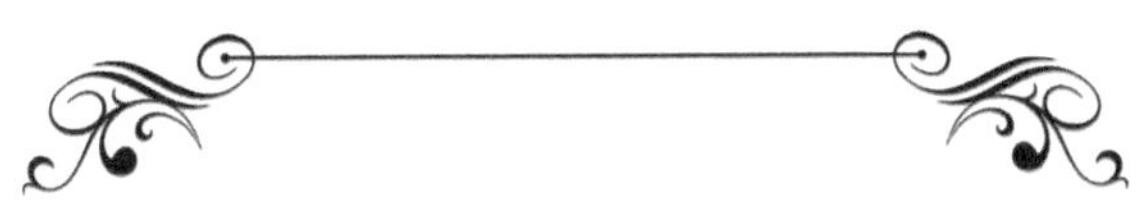

nineteen

Five days pass-August, 2008
White House, Washington, DC

PRESIDENT BARTON'S FACE BROKE INTO A WIDE GRIN. "J.R.! Good to see you! Come right in. I've been looking forward to your visit. Please accept my condolences for your loss."

"Thank you, Mr. President."

"Would you like some coffee or tea? If I remember correctly, you prefer tea."

"You have an excellent memory, sir. A cup of hot tea does sound good."

"Ruth, will you please bring the Justice a cup of tea and I'll have one as well."

"Certainly, Mr. President." Ruth dutifully closed the door to the Oval Office behind her.

"Please have a seat, J.R. Make yourself comfortable."

The two men exchanged stories of their latest rounds on the golf course and the President was ready, as always, with a couple of his latest jokes. After a few moments, a brisk knock rapped at the office door.

The President's secretary entered with a large tray laden with a full tea service, a variety of tea bags, sugar, honey, cream, and lemon. There was also an assortment of gourmet cookies on a small sterling platter.

"Thank you. Justice, do you need anything else?"

"No, no, this is perfect. Thank you."

"You're welcome." Ruth left the two men to discuss their business.

"Let's talk about what brings you to see me, J.R. Ruth said June mentioned it was a matter of urgency."

"Yes, Mr. President, I'm afraid it is an urgent matter. When June first called, I only had one issue at hand. I now have two and the second is the more urgent of the two, but I will get to that."

The Justice stopped for a moment and gazed around the Oval office. It seemed as if it were only yesterday when he had first entered the hallowed chamber when he was first nominated for the Supreme Court. It had been such an honor to have been chosen and soon he would walk away from it.

"The first matter deals with the Devilland case. It's rather complex and came to my attention only last month, before my grandmama passed. I've taken that time to process it for myself and haven't discussed the situation with anyone other than Gloria."

Reaching into his briefcase, the Justice pulled out a file containing copies of the affidavit he had been given by Walt Frasier that afternoon in Charleston.

He then explained to the President the intricacies of the matter and how Melanie Bridges played into all of it. It took him more than an hour to finish relaying the startling turn of events.

"Wow, I think I've heard it all in my sixty-two years, only to have someone show me how little I do know. This Frasier is one shrewd business man. Maybe I should give him a call and bring him to Capitol Hill. The man has uncanny foresight." The President shook his head in utter disbelief.

"This brings me to the second and more pressing matter, sir." A cold sweat broke across his brow and the room spun slowly. He had rehearsed this speech a thousand times before but the time was here. Other than Gloria and his doctors, he had not discussed the diagnosis with anyone.

"I have reached the end of my journey on this earth, Mr. President. The Lord will be calling me Home soon."

The President sat in anguished silence as J.R. explained the diagnosis he had been given.

"Gloria and I would like to spend the time we do have together out of the public eye. I'm giving you my resignation from the bench, sir." J.R. laid the cream-colored envelope on the coffee table.

"Oh, J.R., I don't know what to say."

"There's nothing to say, sir. I have found peace. Truly, I have," the Justice said quietly.

Silence hung in the air as the President gazed compassionately into J.R.'s eyes.

Finally the President spoke. "Well, as far as Devilland and the affidavit, I see no reason for disclosure at this time."

"Thank you, Mr. President. I wanted to make you aware of it as soon as possible, should it come up in the near future. I haven't told the Chief Justice of either matter simply because I felt more comfortable discussing everything with you first, given our years of friendship. I'm scheduled to meet with him later this afternoon regarding my resignation but would like to tell him that it is for personal reasons. Gloria and I strongly feel that the fewer people who are made aware of my illness, the easier it will be for us to live out the rest of my life in private."

"I'm honored you feel that way. I'll keep this file and disclose the affidavit to the Chief Justice only if and when the need to do so arises. As your friend first and your president second, I'm here to support you and will do as you wish. Of course, it saddens me greatly but I certainly will support you one hundred percent. When would you like to make the announcement?"

"Gloria and I both feel the sooner the better, all things considered. Of course, I'll do what's best for the Court and the country."

"We can schedule the press conference any time you feel ready. I'll be in town for the next two weeks so you tell me when and I'll have Ruth make the arrangements. Normally, she likes to have a twenty-four hour notice to make the necessary contacts for such an announcement but I'll have her take care of this immediately."

"Thank you, Mr. President, for your consideration. I'd like to make the announcement to the nation as soon as possible. Tomorrow would be fine."

"I'll have Ruth make the arrangements and she'll give you a call this afternoon with a time. On a personal note J.R., please don't hesitate to let me know of anything you or Gloria need. Laine and I are here for both of you."

"Thank you. I appreciate that. I've taken enough of your time. I shall be on my way."

The two men rose and the President gave his longtime friend a firm hug. When the President pulled away, the Justice caught the faint mist of tears in the eyes of the most powerful man in the free world.

As his stomach roiled, J.R. shook the President's hand and excused himself quickly—afraid he himself might break down in the middle of the Oval Office.

As he reached the door, the Justice turned once again, cleared his throat and said simply, "Thank you, Mr. President. Thank you for everything."

t w e n t y

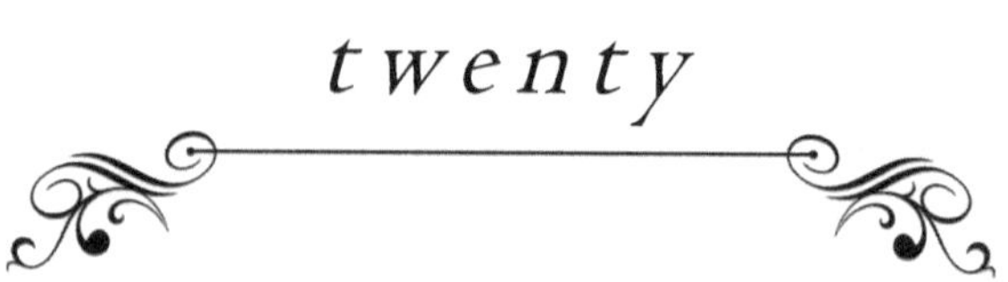

The following day-August, 2008
White House, Washington, DC

OVERCAST AND UNUSUALLY CHILLY FOR AN August morning, a threat of thunderstorms was building on the horizon. The Press Corps anxiously congregated in the Rose Garden waiting for the arrival of the President. They had all been notified late yesterday afternoon that the President would be holding a brief conference of utmost importance.

Rumors and speculations had been swarming around Capitol Hill since Ruth had told the Press Secretary to gather everyone. With the state of affairs not only in the Middle East, but also here at home, it was anybody's guess as to what could possibly be so important for the President to call a press conference with less than a twenty-four hour notice. No one in the media or the nation could have guessed the complexities discussed only yesterday in the Oval Office. The complete story would not to be told today, but it would be told.

"There he is!" The first reporter exclaimed and

immediately cameras whirred.

The President and First Lady, hand in hand, crossed the garden. A few steps behind were J.R. and Gloria. All were wearing cheerless expressions as they came to a stop behind the podium. A somber aura fell over the foursome.

Blinded by the flash of cameras, overwhelmed by the sea of faces and the whispered murmurs among the crowd, J.R. struggled to retain his composure. In a few short minutes, it would be over. Never again would he stand on the grounds of the White House. Never again. This was the moment. The final moment.

"J.R.," Gloria whispered as she nodded toward the crowd.

He hadn't heard a word the President had said as he now saw the Commander in Chief step away from the podium. His moment had come. Knowing he would be overwrought with emotion, J.R. had written his brief statement on a single index card. Reaching in his pocket, he pulled out the card and stepped forward. He read the words he had written and then it was over. It was done.

To J.R., the buzz of cameras sounded like an invasion of thousands of cicadas and continued feverishly as he grasped for Gloria's hand, turned, bowed his head and together they silently followed the President and First Lady back up the path to the White House.

PART THREE

Melanie

twenty-one

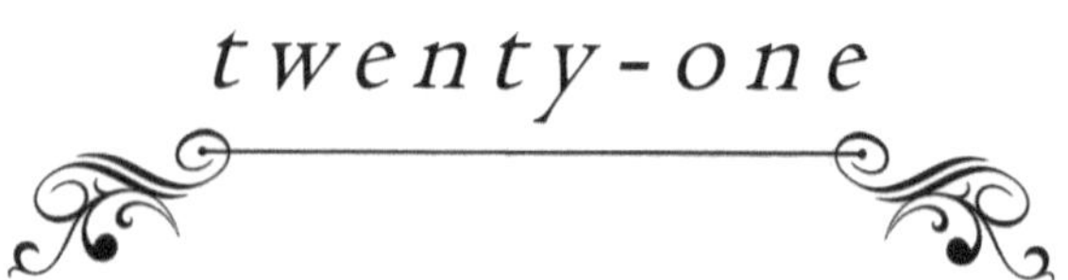

July, 2008
Hunt, Spencer & McCoy, Dallas, Texas

"CRAP! I CAN'T DO THIS ANYMORE!" MELANIE tossed her reading glasses onto the yellow pad in front of her and massaged her temples. She crossed the room and grabbed a soda from the mini fridge. Maybe caffeine would dull her headache.

Her head pounded from the bottle of wine she had drunk last night. Melanie had never been a big drinker but lately, alcohol was the only thing that could soothe her. Often, it was only one or two glasses but lately she had been drinking more and more. She knew she was walking a slippery slope. Her thoughts were coming and going in all directions. Exhaustion consumed her. No matter how much sleep she got, she was always tired, dog-tired, as Grandmama Tilly used to say. It had been years since she felt this way but she made the decision she couldn't go another day like this. Her calendar was constantly overbooked with calls, meetings, and social events for the firm. She could never get ahead or even slow down to take a break. The workload during the Devilland case paled in comparison. At least with Devilland, she had no other responsibilities and there was a finish line ahead. She had never gone to Hunt as she had discussed with Josephine. She feared she would appear weak in his eyes and kept believing she could push just a little harder for a little longer. Until now. She couldn't push one more inch. Her life had become one huge pinball machine and she was the pinball, knocking into one emotion after another. Her life had spun completely out of control.

Melanie had not confided in anyone, not even her cousin or sister, about how unhappy she had become. She would sound like an ungrateful brat. She had considered broaching the subject a few times but could never find the words. No one could possibly understand. From the outside looking in, she had everything anyone could want. Fame, fortune, no shortage of men courting her.

There was one person who would possibly understand. He had understood so much about her. She put her glasses back on and her focus shifted to her computer as her fingers flew over the keyboard. *Was he even still in practice? It had been almost twenty years since she had seen him. Would he even remember her?*

His name and picture popped up on the computer screen. "Praise God!"

Reaching for the phone, her relief was overshadowed by a myriad of emotions. Did she really want to open this door? She knew from experience the path would be complicated and difficult but there simply wasn't another option unless she wanted to continue to live her life in this prison of emotional turmoil full of guilt and endless anxiety, hopelessness. She was a failure. She couldn't handle the pressure of her career anymore and was living a lie. Drowning her pain in alcohol in the dark shadows of solitude. She had lost herself and become a hypocrite of the worst kind.

Swallowing the lump in her throat and taking a long sip of cola, Melanie dialed the eleven digit number but hung up before the call connected.

She sat in silence for the next half hour, staring out at the growing cloud bank on the horizon.

"Storm clouds. Literally and figuratively. I have to make the call. I have no other option."

"Doctors' office," the woman on the other end said pleasantly.

Melanie's mouth went dry and her palms began to sweat.

"*This is ridiculous!*" her inner voice screamed.

"Yes, I'm a former patient of Dr. Horton. Is he available?"

"Yes, ma'am. He is. May I ask who is calling?"

"Melanie. Melanie Baldwin." She said the last name without thinking.

Nervously tapping her left foot, Melanie waited for what seemed like an eternity while classical music filtered through the earpiece.

"Good afternoon, Melanie! How are you doing?"

A long forgotten sense of comfort and compassion immediately soothed Melanie at the sound of his voice. He had walked with her through one of the most difficult periods of her life—the horrific destruction of her marriage.

"Fine. Actually, no, Dr. Horton, the truth is I am far from fine. I am in a bad place, a very bad place. I'm hoping you might possibly be able to provide a referral to someone in Dallas."

"I'm sorry to hear that, Melanie. I should have known this wasn't a social call after all these years," he said grimly. "As a matter of fact, I went to school with a wonderful woman who is practicing in Dallas."

"Is she any good?" Trepidation tingled up her spine. Once again, her emotions had changed within seconds.

"She's extraordinary, one of the best as a matter of fact. She only takes patients through referral but I feel confident I can get you into see her. Let me give her a call. With your permission, I'll send her my file on you."

Instantly overcome with shame and fear, Melanie's entire body trembled with the memories of her awful past life with Stephen. Struggling, she fought to speak.

"Is that necessary, Dr. Horton?" Her voice cracked and she nervously bit her lip.

He must have heard the tremor in her voice. "Melanie, as I told you many times during our sessions together, the horrific abuse, both emotional and physical, you suffered during your marriage will never define who you are," he reassured her. "However, it did have an impact on you. The more Dr. Johnson knows about your past, the better she will be able to help you deal with whatever you're facing now."

"Okay. I'll take the first appointment she has. Thank you, Dr. Horton,"

"Melanie, whatever it is that you are facing, you can walk through it. I have no doubt. Remember, I have witnessed your inner strength. You came to me as a weak kitten and left as a lioness. The road may be rough but you're doing the right thing. I'll call Dr. Johnson immediately. I'll have her office call you and set the appointment. What's the best number for you?"

After giving him her cell number, Melanie melted with relief. She was going to get help. If this doctor was anywhere near as good as Dr. Horton, she had no doubt she had done the right thing.

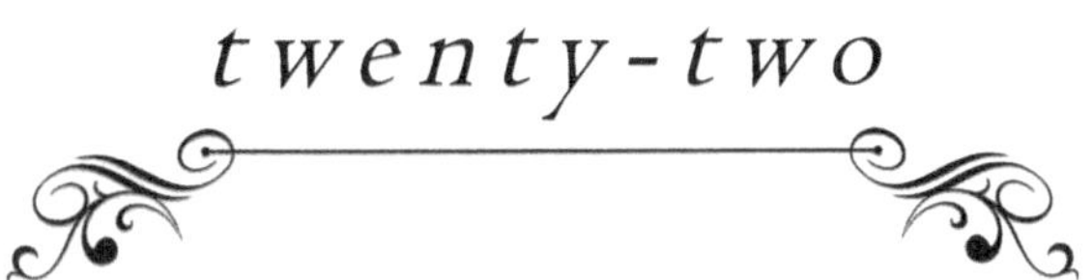

twenty-two

One week passes-July, 2008
Dallas, Texas

HER HANDS SHOOK AND HER STOMACH ROILED AS she filled out the forms. Her heart raced, doubt clouded her thoughts as the pen flew across the pages.

Melanie returned the clipboard to the receptionist. She picked up a magazine and thumbed through the pages.

"Hello," a man said as he took the seat next to her.

Paranoia suddenly hit her like a sledge hammer. Did he recognize her?

"Hello," she replied flatly. She didn't dare make eye contact.

Over recent years, her picture had been splashed over countless newspapers and networks. She couldn't count the number of interviews she had given. After the Devilland verdict, her life no longer belonged to her. She had become a magnet for every reporter, especially when another appeal approached. With the Supreme Court ruling, an entirely new crop of stories and photographs haunted her. She thought of bolting from the office. No one knew she was here and she wanted to keep it that way.

"Ms. Baldwin," the receptionist said. "The doctor will see you now."

Melanie had used her former name on the paperwork, desperate to cling to anonymity.

Without saying anything, Melanie reached for her purse and crossed into the inner offices.

A petite woman of Middle Eastern descent approached her. The woman smiled brightly and introduced herself as Dr. Johnson.

Melanie was taken aback and she immediately prayed the other woman didn't detect her surprise. The last name Johnson belied the doctor's obvious ethnicity. It wasn't prejudice. It had been simply unexpected. Melanie had formed a completely different picture of the doctor in her mind.

"Make yourself comfortable anywhere you like." The doctor opened her office door.

Melanie took in the cozy atmosphere of the doctor's office. There was a long sofa with colorful throw pillows and two overstuffed chairs. The sweet fragrance of the fresh pink roses on the small coffee table suffused the air. Brilliant sunlight peeked through the tall windows which overlooked a small private atrium filled with exotic blossoming plants. A small desk with various diplomas hung on the wall behind it occupied the far corner but the ambience of the whole room gave the aura of a comfortable sitting room rather than a doctor's office.

Choosing the chair closest to the window, Melanie grinned sheepishly as the other woman poured two glasses of water from a small crystal pitcher.

"Thank you." Melanie took a long swallow of the cold water. She hadn't realized how dry her throat was. It was as if she had swallowed a dozen cotton balls. Nerves. No. It wasn't nerves. It was the wine, again. She had polished off the rest of the bottle sometime after midnight.

Taking a second drink of water, Melanie fidgeted as her gaze fell upon the lush foliage on the other side of the window.

Dr. Johnson slowly sipped on her glass of water, patiently watching Melanie. Waiting.

Having no idea how long she had been sitting there, Melanie jumped when the doctor broke the silence.

"Melanie, you're going to have to talk to me."

Turning in the direction of the doctor who sat in the other chair but avoiding eye contact, Melanie said, "I know. I need a little more time. May I have some more water?"

It was distant déjà vu. She was back in Jackson, Mississippi, sitting in front of Dr. Horton, with her heart in her throat. *Where to start? What to say?*

Fifteen minutes passed before Melanie was surprised to hear her own voice.

"May I ask you a question, a personal question?"

"Certainly."

"Are you…are you…a Christian?"

"Yes." The doctor answered without changing expression or missing a beat.

Surprised by the doctor's response, Melanie immediately chastised herself for making a stereotypical assessment of the other woman based solely on her physical appearance.

"I'm sorry. That was probably rude."

"No. It was not rude. It's a fair question. You forget I'm living in a post-911 world. Most people don't give me the courtesy of asking if I'm a Christian. They choose to make the obvious assumption."

A long silence hung in the air before Melanie could find her voice again.

"Do you talk to God?"

"Yes. All the time."

"You probably think I'm weird for asking."

The doctor cocked her head slightly and gave Melanie a warm smile. "I don't think you're weird, Melanie. Nothing you could say could possibly make me think otherwise. I promise. Let's start talking about what brought you to see me."

"Okay," Melanie said hesitantly. "Do you know who I am?"

"If you're asking me if I know you go by the name Melanie Bridges and not Melanie Baldwin, the answer is yes."

Melanie stared at the other woman and waited for her to say something perfunctory. *It's so nice to meet you… I'm flattered to have you as a patient…* Something!

Saying nothing of the sort, the doctor simply looked at Melanie with a gentle smile.

Melanie's muscles tightened and she fought the urge to flee from the doctor's office.

"You asked me if I talked to God. Why don't we go from there?" the woman asked gently.

"Okay." Melanie fidgeted nervously, wringing her hands in her lap.

"I asked you if you talked to God because I do. A lot. He

blessed me with a tremendous gift when He used me as a vessel to win the Devilland case but my life has gone to Hell in a hand basket since then. I've been professionally and financially blessed beyond most people's imagination. I have no shortage of people who want to hook me up with their brother, cousin, or husband's best friend. From the outside looking in, I live a magical life but the reality is I'm miserable. I haven't been this miserable since my marriage. It's a completely different kind of miserable but it's still awful."

Saying nothing, Dr. Johnson waited patiently for Melanie to continue as she took another long swallow of the now tepid water.

Melanie's efforts to hold her tears completely failed and she broke into sobs. The doctor handed her the box of tissue.

Damn it! She hated being such a crybaby!

Breathing deeply, Melanie struggled against her sobs to find her voice.

"Since the Devilland verdict and even more so since the Supreme Court ruling, other than my family, there are literally four people in this world who don't give a damn that I'm Melanie Bridges, the attorney who defeated the undefeatable."

The fact of the matter was other than Chad, Michelle, Josephine, and her best friend Pauline, everyone treated her differently than before the verdict. Everyone treated her with an odd reverence, bordering on a distorted sense of worship.

"You're wrong, Melanie."

"Wrong?"

"You said that other than your family, there are only

four people who don't give a damn that you are Melanie Bridges. It's five people. I don't give a damn. Our time is up for today. I need to see you next week. You can schedule your appointment at the front desk."

Taken aback by the doctor's frankness, shock and relief simultaneously blanketed Melanie. The doctor was honestly not impressed in the least.

"Praise God!" Melanie thought and stuffed her tear-stained tissue in her purse.

Before opening the door, she turned back toward the doctor. "Thank you. Thank you, really."

"You're welcome, Melanie. Coming here was a difficult leap but we can work through this. That I can promise. I will see you next week."

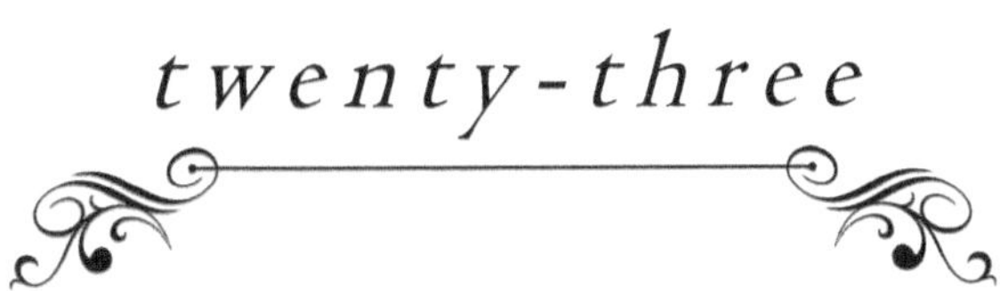

twenty-three

One month passes-August, 2008
Dallas, Texas

MELANIE LEANED BACK INTO THE COMFORT OF the familiar chair and smiled at Dr. Johnson. She had been faithfully seeing the psychiatrist weekly for the last month. As she had with Dr. Horton two decades earlier, Melanie had not confided in anyone that she was seeing a psychiatrist. The stigma could hurt her professionally, especially in light of her position. Even without the stigma, the simple fact of the matter was it was nobody's business.

"What are you thinking about right now?"

"Honestly?"

"Yes, Melanie. Honestly."

"I'm wondering if I'm getting any better. I feel comfortable when I'm here but when I'm working or at home, I'm still bombarded with anxiety and depression. I don't think I cry as much as I did before I came to see you but I'm not sure of that or anything."

"I can tell you that you are definitely making progress.

We still have a great deal of work to do but we've already hit a milestone."

"A milestone?"

"Yes. Today is the first day you have made eye contact with me. While that may not seem like a big deal to you, it is. Trust me." Dr. Johnson leaned forward slightly and cocked her head. "Tell me about your isolation."

How did the doctor know she'd been segregating herself? It didn't matter how. She knew.

"It's hard to explain. I'm not sure why but I prefer to be at home with my dog and cat rather than out with another guy who wants an arm charm. Over the past five years, I've been out with two heart surgeons, three attorneys, an oil man, and my last date was with a Dallas Cowboy. Those are only the ones I can remember. Somehow, I never make it past the third date when it seems every man expects me to jump into bed with him." Melanie's words tumbled out as if the floodgates had been opened. "I feel absolutely nothing when I go out on a date. I'm bored to tears and can't wait to get home. It sounds crazy to everybody. I can basically have my choice of men but I simply don't want one. I'm starting to think something broke inside me after my divorce. After licking my wounds, I jumped right into law school and then immersed myself completely in my career. I have no one to blame but myself. I made a choice to give up everything for my career. I look at my friends at the firm and they seem to have their personal and family life and career in balance. I've got nothing but my career."

"Alright, tell me about your career."

"The Devilland verdict was only the beginning. Once I won the case, my career virtually skyrocketed overnight. I admit, at first I found the partners' attention flattering. Mr. Hunt and Mr. Spencer especially made a point of including me in countless social functions. For a while I did my best to keep up with the charity events, dinners, cocktail parties, and take care of my caseload but it became more than I could handle. Eventually, everything changed. I'm completely hollow. I'm still going through the motions but in reality I'm nothing more than the show pony. I'm no longer practicing law. I'm expected to wine and dine clients. My only job is to be the perfect little rainmaker. Once I do get the clients through the door, I have to delegate the work to other attorneys so I can get back to wining and dining the next prospect. I understand it's all part of the rat race. I'm an asset they use to win business. I get it and don't begrudge them. The partners have been very good to me and I appreciate that. I truly do, but the reality is I've run the race hard for over five years and now I dread going into the office. Something I used to absolutely love, I now hate with every fiber of my body. Basically, I'm not happy anywhere. I'm not happy in my own skin. I sound like a spoiled brat, even to myself. I have it all but don't want it anymore."

Melanie had become agitated talking about both her social life and her career.

Her volume had increased with her bitterness. She rocked back and forth, rubbing her arms.

"When is the last time you went to church?" Dr. Johnson asked, changing the subject.

"I can't remember but even that didn't work for me so I quit going."

"What exactly do you mean? How did church stop working for you?"

"Wow. That sounded awful. Really awful. What I mean is even at church, once people found out I was Melanie Bridges, *the* Melanie Bridges, they treated me differently. I still have my faith and I've already told you that I talk to God a lot, but honestly, I'm a little angry with Him. A lot angry, actually."

Tears welled up, confessing out loud what she had not been able to admit to herself. The peace she had felt only minutes earlier had evaporated and she had returned to her dark place—angry, confused, exhausted by everything—even God."

"Okay. Explain it to me."

"It's hard to explain. I can't even explain it to myself. I prayed so hard all through the trial. I prayed for wisdom, for guidance, for success, for everything, and I got it all. BAM! I realize what I accomplished is great and wonderful. I know I have made a difference, but now all I want is to be normal again. I want someone to want to know me—Melanie. The *real* Melanie whose favorite thing in the world is to feel the mud of the Yazoo River between my toes after spending all morning picking blackberries with my cousins in Mississippi."

"I never tell my patients they are normal or abnormal because there is no such thing, but I can tell you what you are experiencing is *very* normal."

Wiping her tears, Melanie stared into the other woman's dark eyes. Up until that moment, she had always been comforted by her doctor's advice but now she was making no sense. No sense whatsoever.

Suddenly, Melanie laughed, harder than she had in a long time.

"Seriously, how can you say this experience is normal? Look at me. I'm a miserable puddle of tears sitting in a psychiatrist's office and telling you how mad I am at God because He has blessed me beyond imagination. I don't see anything normal about any of this."

"I can tell you that I have seen many, many people experience exactly what you are experiencing. Our society has a dogma if somebody works hard enough and makes enough money then they will be happy but that is the almost never the case. I see this so often where fame and fortune come on suddenly after years of hard work. Suddenly you are living in a fish bowl. Nobody outside that fish bowl can understand because you have exceeded all measure of others' expectations. The harsh reality is none of us were made to live in a fish bowl. Humans crave social interaction. We are wired that way." Dr. Johnson paused to take a drink of water as she swept a stray hair from her forehead. "Trust me, you would be shocked if you knew the names of the people who have sat exactly where you are sitting and told me a different version of your same story. You are like so many people in so many ways but you are also very special."

"Special? Now that's about the furthest thing from the truth."

"No. It's not. I knew it within thirty minutes of meeting you."

Saying nothing, Melanie eyed her doctor skeptically.

"Do you remember the first thing you said to me?"

Searching her memory, Melanie could not recall. Her memories of that first visit were foggy. The only thing she could remember was being nervous. Very nervous. It had been only a month ago.

"No."

"You asked me if I was a Christian and then you asked me if I talked to God. That makes you special, incredibly special. Our culture has become so mesmerized by financial success and material possessions that many, many people have forgotten all about God. You haven't. Even though you say you're angry with Him right now, at least you have Him in your life. I can give you all the advice in the world and help you through this experience to the best of my ability but at the end of the day, you have what you ultimately need. That's your faith."

"My faith?"

"I'm your doctor, not your pastor, but when the first thing you wanted to talk about was God, I knew you were going to be fine. I'm going to be right here for as long as you need me but if you will lean back into what you know, your faith, then this journey is going to be much easier for you."

"Thank you, doctor. I obviously need to be reminded."

"Okay, well that's it for today. We made great progress. I will see you next week at the same time."

Melanie glanced at the clock and couldn't believe how fast the time had flown. Usually, the sessions seemed to drag on forever, but not today. This was the first day she had felt comfortable enough to talk, really talk about what was going on with her.

Dr. Johnson had allowed her to set the pace of the sessions. Melanie was happy with the progress they had made.

"Before I go, I was wondering if you would write me a prescription for something for anxiety." She had avoided the question for weeks and in light of all the talk about

God, she assumed that the doctor would decline her request but decided to ask anyway. "I don't remember what Dr. Horton prescribed for me during my divorce but I remember it helped."

"I can write you a prescription for Clonazepam on one condition."

"One condition?" Melanie asked hesitantly.

"That you stop drinking."

Melanie's cheeks flushed as she considered denying the fact. Maybe the doctor was only guessing. Looking at the doctor, she had no doubt her denial would fall on deaf ears.

"How do you know I'm drinking?" Melanie asked sheepishly.

"You are very good at your profession. I am very good at mine. Do we have an agreement?" she asked with a knowing smile.

"Yes," Melanie replied tentatively, unsure if she would be able to quit the bottle.

"Melanie?" Dr. Johnson arched an eyebrow.

Silence hung in the air for a brief moment as the two women locked eyes.

"Yes. I will quit drinking," Melanie said resolutely. She would not fall victim to the bottle. She would not.

twenty-four

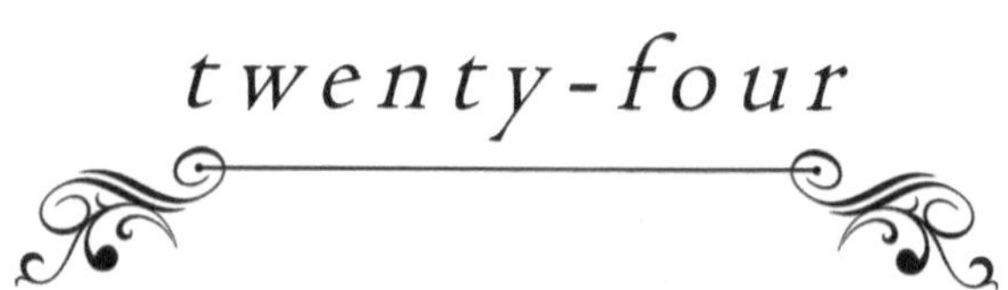

Three weeks pass-August, 2008
Dallas, Texas

ELANIE HAD A FIERCE DETERMINATION TO get better and had been working hard to pull herself through the therapy sessions. She had gained some weight. Not too much, but enough that she no longer appeared as gaunt as she had when she first came to Dr. Johnson. She was sleeping well and the dark circles under her eyes were gone. When looking in the mirror, she saw a spark in her eyes had replaced the vacant stare.

For the first time since their relationship had begun, Melanie felt completely at ease. She, like her doctor, was pleased with her progress. From her past experience with Dr. Horton, she knew full recovery would take a long time but she had finally begun to feel like herself again. She had even started going out with Michelle and other friends and had been surprised she was actually enjoying herself. She had even reached a level of acceptance and appreciation for her new position at Hunt, Spencer & McCoy. Although she missed being able to devote all her time to practicing law, she now looked at her position with new eyes. Socializing with clients and bringing business into the doors was the lifeblood of the firm. What she considered her silver bullet in her recovery was something she hadn't even shared with her doctor.

"You're looking well." Dr. Johnson poured two glasses of ice water and handed one to Melanie. "Is there anything special you want to share with me?" The doctor asked hopefully.

"There is. I have found something that makes me happy, really happy. I honestly can't remember the last time I felt as fulfilled."

The doctor said nothing but let Melanie continue at her own pace.

"It may sound strange but I'm pretty sure not as strange as a lot of things I've said to you." Melanie offered an awkward smile.

"I'm listening."

"Well, I told you my biggest hurdle in everything has been not feeling normal, like a regular person. I started thinking about what you said about leaning back into my faith and then I remembered something Grandmama Tilly used to say. Let go and let God. I've been working down at the homeless shelter every Saturday."

Dr. Johnson leaned back in her chair with a broad grin, proud of Melanie's fierce determination to get better and reaching out to others in the process.

"I throw on a pair of jeans and a T-shirt, put on a baseball cap and I become anonymous. I love the people down there and being in that environment humbles me. I realize I have no right to complain about the way my life is going. I don't have an answer yet but I've been praying for direction on what to ultimately do with my life. Financially, I have enough money to live out twenty lifetimes. I want to use the money to do something great, but I don't know what it is."

"That's wonderful, Melanie. I'm proud of you. You are definitely moving in the right direction. Helping others is fulfilling, but I would like to suggest something to you that I have been considering for a while. I've been thinking about how best to help you take the next step on your journey. We have talked a great deal about you wanting to feel like yourself again, but the reality is your world has changed dramatically over these past few years and you are going to need to accept that change at some point. You need to get to know yourself before you can expect others to get to know you. Your struggle isn't with other people. It's with yourself."

"I don't understand."

"This may seem a little drastic to you but I think it might be exactly what you need. You just said yourself that financially you have more than enough money to live comfortably. What would you think about taking a sabbatical from your career, from everything?"

"What?" Melanie's thoughts raced. How could she possibly take a sabbatical from her career? What did the doctor think she would do? True, she wasn't as happy as she used to be in her profession, but it was all she knew.

"That sounds like you want me to run away from my problems. You're suggesting I go into isolation. I'm sorry but I don't see how that is going to fix anything."

"I'm not suggesting you run away from anything nor do I want you to isolate yourself. I'm simply suggesting you take a time out from the stress."

"I honestly don't see how that can possibly help." Melanie snorted a sardonic laugh and crossed her arms. "What would I do with myself? Sit in my condo and eat bon-bons?"

"No. Let me get you there. Let down your defenses for a few minutes and think about it. This isn't something I would suggest for the majority of my patients but it could be exactly what you need. When you talk about your childhood, there seems to be several constants that made you happy. The biggest one is your family and that makes you very fortunate but the times that captured my fascination the most were when you talked about sailing with your father, especially to South America. Those memories are among your fondest. I can tell by the way your eyes light up whenever you talk about them. You said you still have the sailboat. What would you think about taking off for a year? You could travel and become anonymous for a lot longer than a few stolen hours every week. That's what you need Melanie. To be anonymous. To find yourself again."

An odd, exhilarating tingle crept over her as she listened to her doctor. Was it possible? She hadn't felt it in so long she almost didn't recognize it but it was indeed the feeling she had craved for years now. *Excitement!*

The idea which had sounded ludicrous only moments before suddenly began to take shape. She was captivated by the concept. She would have never thought of it herself. She was indeed intrigued but when she tried to work out the logistics of it all, she was immediately overwhelmed. Would she even have a job if she left for a year? What would she do about her condo, her car? Melanie eyes grew wide and her jaw dropped slightly as she leaned back in the chair and her arms relaxed.

Dr. Johnson didn't say anything for the next several minutes, giving Melanie time to grasp the idea. "I like it. I do, but…"

"But, what?"

"Honestly, it scares the living heck out of me. Walking away from my job, my friends, my home, it seems so drastic. On top of everything else, it's been years since *Quality Time* made that kind of crossing. She would have to be completely refurbished. That's only the beginning…"

"Slow down, Melanie, you're looking at the forest, not the trees. I told you I'm not talking about you doing this tomorrow. I'm merely asking you to consider the possibility and we can take it one step at a time. Will you at least think about it?"

Melanie didn't speak for several minutes as she nibbled her lower lip and considered the doctor's words.

"Okay. I will think about it but I can't honestly say I can do it."

"That's all I'm asking you to do. Our time is up for today. I want to step up the pace of your therapy. We are at a critical crossroads. Let's start meeting twice a week. In the meantime, I want you to go home and start a journal. I want you to start with all the reasons you think you cannot do this. Once you have those identified, we can start looking at how to overcome those obstacles."

The odd tingling filled Melanie's body again as her gaze drifted through the windows and to the tranquility of the atrium. The idea was impossible. No. That was wrong. It was possible. All things are possible.

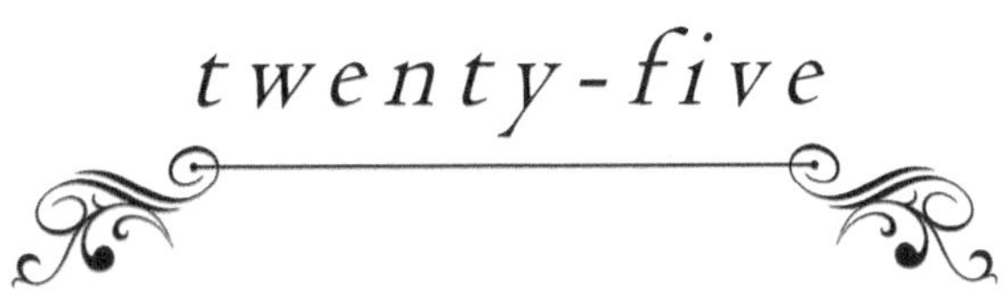

<h1 style="text-align:center">twenty-five</h1>

One month passes-September, 2008
Dallas, Texas

THE SESSION WAS COMING TO AN END AND MELANIE craved a few more minutes with Dr. Johnson. Melanie couldn't believe how much she had grown in only one month. The doctor had helped Melanie immediately knock down so many of her initial objections to the idea of taking a sabbatical. Once the first obstacles were removed, Melanie became increasingly confident with a sense of empowerment for the first time in years. She saw all the possibilities far outweighed what she had considered impossible only a few weeks earlier.

"I'm proud of you, Melanie. Very proud. Honestly, I knew we would get to this day but I certainly didn't expect you to get here so quickly. I can see now exactly how you won the Devilland suit. You've got a willpower I have never seen in any other patient. You truly possess a fierce inner strength." Dr. Johnson wore a triumphant smile on her lips.

"YOU didn't expect it? You should be in my shoes. I have to admit that when you first suggested a sabbatical, I thought maybe we should swap seats—that you were the crazy one." Melanie shared a laugh with the doctor.

"You've come a long way but until you toss off those lines on that sailboat, you aren't there yet. What do you think is your next step?"

"I've thought about that. Actually, it's all I've been thinking about for the last two weeks." A slight tremor cracked Melanie's voice and she shrunk back into the chair.

"I obviously need to give my notice at the firm and need to tell my family."

"Okay and that scares you?"

"Yeah. A lot."

"Why?"

"I'm not sure. I guess because they'll think I'm crazy, that I've somehow gone off the deep end."

"You're wrong, at least to a certain extent. Those in your life who love you will accept your decision and the ones who don't love you truly don't matter in the grand scheme of things. I can't recall who said it but I do remember a great quote I once read. If you fuel your journey on the opinions of others, you will most certainly run out of gas."

"I like that. I need to put a frame around it!" Melanie smiled brightly.

"I won't make light of it. These next steps are going to be difficult but you're ready. Whether you believe it or not, you are ready. Go ahead and give your notice, tell your family. Take the leap of faith. Trust yourself. If you can't trust yourself, trust me. Go be anonymous!"

twenty-six

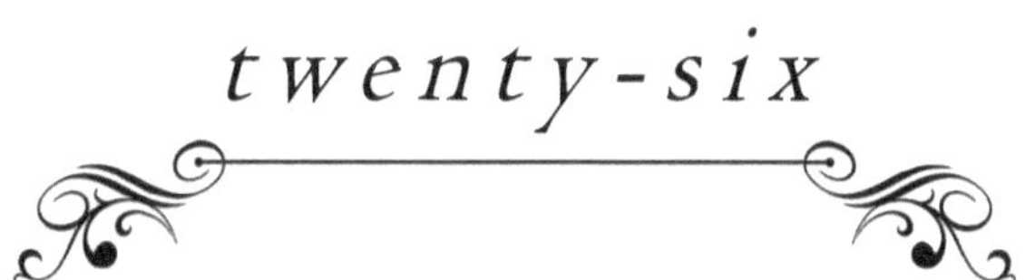

One month passes-October, 2008
Hunt, Spencer & McCoy, Dallas, Texas

"I CAN'T IMAGINE LIFE AROUND HERE WITHOUT you, Mel. More importantly, what are you going to do without me?" Chad's brow furrowed as he shook his head with feigned mystification.

Smiling at her dear friend, Melanie couldn't help but laugh. The truth was she couldn't imagine her life's daily routine without his clever wit and close friendship.

"I have no idea. I'll miss everybody in this place. I know it sounds trite, but like I said at the luncheon today, y'all are my family. It's going to be an adjustment, but re-member you promised to bring Michelle and Taylor to the Caribbean next spring. I'm holding you to it, no excuses, buddy." Melanie gave him the same firm look she had so often given in her closing arguments as she reminded the jury of a particular point to recall in their deliberations.

The two sat in Melanie's office surrounded by card-board boxes. All were neatly labeled and stacked for the movers to pick up first thing Monday morning and deliver to storage where Melanie had already put most of her personal belongings. Josephine had promised to oversee the moving men. Only her basic necessities remained at the condo.

Melanie had insisted her niece Tanner move into the condo when she had told her family she was leaving for the Caribbean. Tanner had been hesitant to make any changes to what still felt like her aunt's home but Melanie had strongly encouraged her niece to make it her own and, slowly but surely, the SMU junior added her personal touches to the posh condo. Everything was coming together beautifully and Melanie was planning a surprise housewarming party for Tanner the upcoming weekend.

"I can't believe it. You're really going. I mean, you are, for all intents and purposes, already gone. What are you going to do, Mel? Day in and day out? You eat, sleep, and breathe the law with the eighty hour weeks, the mind-numbing research, the meticulous preparation. How can you walk away from it all?" Chad asked incredulously.

"That's exactly why I must walk away from it all," Melanie said with a somber smile.

"It's because I do eat, sleep, and breathe the law that I need to take this time, Chad. The last thirteen years have been phenomenal and I wouldn't trade them for anything but honestly, I'm tired. I'm really, really tired. I had no idea how much the Devilland case took from me until it was truly over, when we won in May. That's when I realized I had nothing more than this job. I am nothing more than this job. I am Melanie Bridges, attorney-at-law. Period. I need to be Melanie Bridges, something more. You have Michelle and Taylor. Even with the long hours you put into the job, at the end of the day you go home to your family. You still manage to live a balanced happy, healthy life in addition to having an amazing career. I need that, Chad. I need to find some balance, some meaning for myself." Tears misted her eyes.

Ordinarily Chad would have come back at her with a sarcastic quip but he knew Melanie well enough to know she was baring her innermost feelings to him, her close friend, and he would have never made light of her heartfelt emotion.

"I always thought you led a charmed life, had everything anyone could want. I realize now I was basing my opinion solely on your enviable and successful career."

Melanie dabbed her eyes, freeing them of the wetness gathering there. "You are the lucky one, Chad. Your own career is flourishing, but it isn't the only thing in your life or the most important. You work hard to provide for Michelle and your daughter."

His gaze dropped to the floor. "I treasure them more than I could have ever thought possible. I can't imagine life without them." He looked up, nodding. "I understand your need to find something more than Hunt, Spencer & McCoy. So what's next? How long are you going to be in town?"

"I'm going to be here for a little while."

"What are your plans for Monday of next week? Do you think you could squeeze Michelle and me in for a dinner date? How about we treat you to sushi?"

"That sounds great on one condition." She soberly cocked her head and stared coldly into his hazel eyes.

"What possible condition could you have?"

"The condition you do not tell the waitress it's my birthday so all the staff gathers around our table to sing their birthday chant and beat that humongous drum while everybody in the place stares at me."

"Oh, yeah! Thanks for reminding me. That's always fun. You turn seventeen different shades of red. They do make such a fuss over you every time you have a birthday." He chuckled.

"Thanks to you I have a birthday every friggin' time we eat there—winter, spring, summer, and fall."

"Well, you do get free green tea ice cream and maybe we'll run into Chuck Norris again."

"Wow, I had forgotten all about that! The night was pretty cool. Especially when Michelle and I pulled that hundred bucks off you. You swore it wasn't him but I've watched too many late night reruns of *Walker, Texas Ranger* not to know my man Chuck."

"Good Lord, Mel, maybe you're right. You do need to get out there and find a life if you're still watching that show." Chad hooted as he shook his head.

"Have you had any bites on the house in North Carolina?" He changed the subject as he tossed his empty can in the black wire wastebasket sitting among the boxes.

"As a matter of fact, that reminds me. My realtor called this morning and left a message. A radiologist and his wife saw it this past weekend and are considering making an offer."

"That's great. You haven't had it on the market that long."

"No. We haven't. Jordie and I didn't make the final decision to sell it until after I gave my notice here."

"Deciding to sell had to be tough for both of you. Didn't you tell me that you lived in the same house all your life?"

"Yeah." She dolefully gazed out the window at the gathering dusk. "Mama and Daddy brought me home from the hospital to that house and I never lived anywhere else until I went to Ole Miss. Jordie was only two when my parents built the house so it's the only home she remembers as well."

"I can't imagine. I couldn't begin to count how many houses I had lived in by the time I went to college. My dad got one promotion after another which always came with packing our bags and moving halfway across the States and back again." Chad shook his head.

"Speaking of moving, I wonder who is going to move in here." She gazed nostalgically around her dismantled office.

"I haven't heard any buzz on the grapevine. I guess I should ask Valerie in the morning. She knows everything around here. That girl is like a walking-talking tabloid. You've got one of the best views on the whole floor but it's going to be pretty intimidating for anyone to step into this hallowed chamber where your highness first plotted her strategy to bring the mighty Jack Devilland to his knees."

"Give me a break. I doubt anyone will remember my name a month after I walk out the door. I can hear y'all now, Melanie *who*?" She laughed and threw a wadded up yellow Post-It note at him.

"I wouldn't sell myself short. You, my dear, will go down in the Hunt, Spencer & McCoy Hall of Fame for eternity and I'll be forever proud to say *I knew her when*," Chad said with an exaggerated sentimentality.

"As odd as it may sound, I still can't believe it's really over." Pensively, she added, "It seems like eons ago when I first met the Stanfords."

"It does to me, too. I remember when Eliza Stanford came in for her first meeting with you. I was bored to tears doing title work for one of Spencer's probate cases. I was so pumped when you told Hunt you needed me on Devilland."

"No, no, counselor. I remember why you wanted on the case. You thought Sally Stanford Turner was hot." Melanie laughed as she took a swallow of her now tepid cola.

"Alright, already." He grinned broadly. "Sally Stanford Turner was hot *and* I was numb from doing estate work for three months."

"Men!" Melanie chuckled as she pulled her ringlets into a loose bun, securing it with a lone pencil she found in her top desk drawer.

"What? You can't tell me you don't notice your male clients," Chad said with the innocence of a small child.

"Do I notice? Yes. Do I salivate like one of Pavlov's dogs when they walk into the office? No. That's the difference."

"Aw, come on." He laughed. "I wasn't that bad. Anyway, I was already head over heels in love with Michelle. Sally wasn't anything more than eye candy, a little ray of sunshine to brighten the dismal winter scenery around here."

"Dismal winter scenery, my foot. It was June!"

"Well, probate work makes every day feel dismal and cold." Chad shrugged his shoulders.

"Seriously, Chad. I couldn't have pulled that off without your support, professionally and personally. You were there for me every step of the way and it was a long eight years," she said somberly.

"Ah, thanks for saying so, Mel, but you would have done it, with or without me or anybody else for that matter.

You were driven with a passion I've never seen in you or any lawyer. The victory belonged to you and you alone, regardless of how humble you try to be."

"I admit I did feel something for the case I never felt before or since." She gazed across the room to the cityscape beyond the window, a lifetime of memories flooding back to her.

"It was more about Devilland than the Stanfords. I don't mean you didn't care about them but you cared about something else, too. It was something else that lit you on fire," he said intuitively.

"Yes and no. The Stanfords did touch me deeply but the case became my own personal raison d'être, I have to admit."

Raising his eyebrows in question, Chad said nothing but waited for her to continue.

Biting her lip, Melanie thought of ignoring the implied question. She had hidden Aaron for so many years. She didn't need to say anything. No. That was wrong. She did. Chad had been her biggest supporter during the Devilland trial. She had meant it when she told him she didn't know what she would have done without him. She owed him the truth, at least part of it.

"Aaron. His name is Aaron." Melanie paused and breathed deeply.

"Who is he?"

Melanie shook her head and gazed out the window before looking into Chad's eyes. "The answer to that is complicated. Very complicated. I'd rather not get into it but I will tell you I've never loved another person in this whole world the way I love Aaron. He's an eighteen-karat gold piece of my heart. For the first four years of his life, he was a happy, healthy boy full of energy like any other kid, but then he was condemned to live his life in a wheelchair with nurses around the clock." Her voice cracked as she forced herself to breathe deeply again.

She made no attempt to hold back the hot tears flowing down her cheeks. "He was condemned because someone decided to have one more cocktail before getting behind the wheel of a car. The driver wasn't a hard-core alcoholic, just someone who had one more cocktail before leaving a party on a dark and rainy night. The driver walked away with only the most minor of injuries and went on to live a full and blessed life. Not Aaron."

"Dear God," Chad whispered under his breath as sympathy tugged at his heart. He handed Melanie a Kleenex.

"Aaron never once blamed the driver. He told me that. It was the one and only time in all these years he has ever mentioned the crash that robbed him of so much. So you see, I had to fight for Aaron. I had to fight for Aaron and the life stolen from him."

twenty-seven

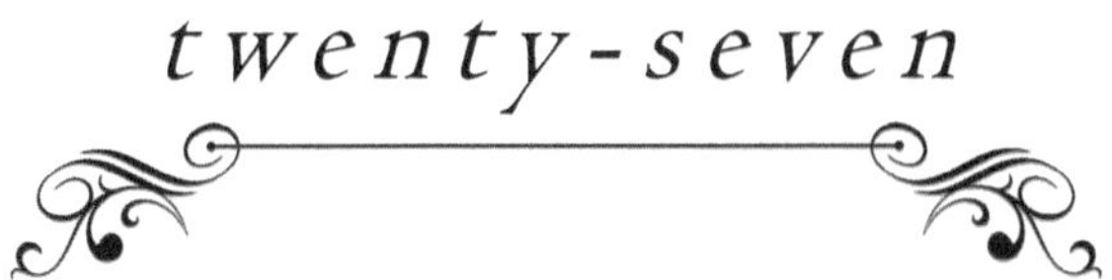

Later that afternoon-October, 2008
Hunt, Spencer & McCoy, Dallas, Texas

AS SHE GAZED AROUND HER OFFICE, SHE STRUGGLED to comprehend that everything was finally happening. In addition to passing her cases on to other associates at the firm, in effect, closing the door on her professional life, she had meticulously sorted through everything she owned, deciding what to keep and what to donate to the women's shelter. Besides her personal belongings, she still had to face the emotional ordeal of packing what remained in the North Carolina house.

Her cell phone chirped. Finding it amid the stacks of boxes, she hurriedly flipped open the cover and breathlessly answered. She instantly recognized the voice on the other end of the line and broke into a broad grin.

"Melanie, I hope I didn't interrupt you."

"Not at all, Captain Ron."

"Great," he said. "I wanted to give you a buzz to let you know I'm already in Beaufort. I moved my bags on board today. My crew arrives later tonight and we plan to check out the systems tomorrow and should be taking *Quality Time* out for a sea trial first thing day after tomorrow. The weather here is perfect and I'm sure everything will check out fine. My plans are to head out soon. We just gotta get us a nice weather window. I'll certainly be in touch before we leave port but wanted to assure you that we'll have this lovely lady in Rockport in plenty of time for them to haul her out and get started on the work you requested. Do you have any questions for me?"

Melanie shook her head and grinned to herself. The man had gotten all of that out without stopping for one breath of air. Although she had never met him personally, the twosome had had many phone conversations and Melanie liked him. A retired career Navy man, Captain Ron had come highly recommended by the marina owner where *Quality Time* had been docked for so many years. Additionally, he had impeccable recommendations from several extremely satisfied clients who had had their own vessels delivered from one port to another by the experienced seaman.

After finishing her conversation with Captain Ron, Melanie allowed herself a few minutes of daydreaming about the new life which awaited her. Since the beginning of the Devilland case, Melanie hadn't had any free time to take *Quality Time* out for a sail and the idea of seeing her thrilled Melanie. Her daddy had bought the thirty-eight foot Camper Nicholson back in 1969 when the vessel was brand-new. He and a friend had flown to England and sailed back across the Atlantic.

There had only been one hundred and thirty-four of *Quality Time's* particular model made. When Melanie recently checked online, she found there was only a handful still in service. Camper Nicholsons, the oldest leisure marine company in the world, was known for the exceptional quality of its yachts, built for some of the world's wealthiest people.

Camper Nicholsons had produced several royal yachts including one purchased by Queen Elizabeth as well as another purchased by Aristotle Onassis which he had given to Rainier III, Prince of Monaco and actress Grace Kelly as a wedding gift.

The unique history of Camper Nicholsons was only one reason *Quality Time* was Charles Bridges' pride and joy among all the material possessions he had owned in his lifetime. His love for *Quality Time* had been passed on to Melanie and she eagerly anticipated the many adventures she would have sailing the beautiful boat. With her wealth from the Devilland case, Melanie could have easily afforded a brand-new yacht, practically any kind her heart desired, but there was and never would be any boat as special as *Quality Time*. What Melanie treasured most about her yacht was the wonderful memories she had of the special times she had spent with her daddy sailing off the coast of the Eastern Seaboard and twice to South America.

A phone ringing down the hall brought Melanie out of her reverie. She sorted through the two drawers of her desk which she had yet to empty. Her hands fell upon smooth glass. Curiously, she pulled the object from the back of the drawer. She grinned as she reread the headline of the framed newspaper article Chad had given her years earlier. *Dallas Star Forced into Bankruptcy.*

Closing the last empty drawer, Melanie gazed at

familiar view of the night sky and the twinkling lights of the city. How many nights had she sat at this desk, toiling away tirelessly? Too many to count. When she had given the partners her notice, they had all assured her she would always have a home at the firm but as she sat here now, she realized her future lay ahead of her—beyond the horizon. She had loved her life here for so long and would always cherish Chad, Josephine, and all the others who had become her second family. She would miss them but life for each of them would move on as life always did. They had all come together for a once-in-a-lifetime divinely appointed purpose. Devilland. She may have led the charge but together they had fulfilled the purpose. Yes, she would miss them all, but the thrill of the journey which lay before her stirred something within her which was much bigger than her sadness at leaving this life behind.

An hour later, the offices of Hunt, Spencer & McCoy were eerily quiet as Melanie, still tingling with a bittersweet feeling of nostalgia, turned off her lights and walked out the door for the last time.

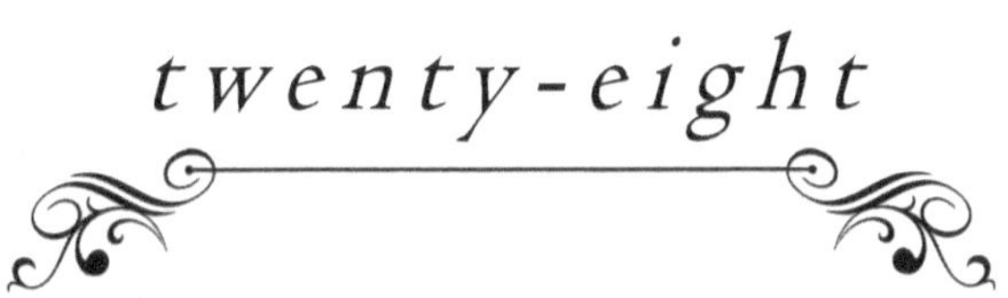

twenty-eight

Two months pass-December 31, 2008
Rockport, Texas

"You have made a wrong turn. Make a correction or redefine your destination," the automated voice announced.

"I didn't make any turn, Simone! Why don't you make the correction?" Melanie pressed the *OFF* button in frustration.

Gazing up from his place on the passenger seat, Fred cocked his head.

"Yes, Fred. Mama has finally gone completely bonkers. I not only carry on conversations with my pets but I'm now arguing with the navigation system and I have somewhere along the way named her Simone. When did I do that? I don't have a clue. We'll get directions the old-fashioned way. I'll stop and ask. It's been a long drive, bud, and I bet you could use a pit stop." She pulled the rented car into the rural gas station.

Although the drive from Baton Rouge had been long and contributed to her tired state, it would have normally been a time Melanie enjoyed. She loved the solitude of long car trips and listening to audio books along the way but Melanie had taken on more physically, psychologically, and emotionally in the last two months than most people could endure in a year. Leaving the firm and her friends in Dallas had been difficult as she had anticipated it would be. What she had not anticipated was the deep emotions of leaving Carlton and her childhood home.

All of these paled in comparison to her last days in Atlanta. Those had been almost more than she could take. Losing Aaron so unexpectedly at Christmas had broken her heart. She had loved him in her own special way. She would always love him. Her heart warmed as she thought of his brilliant smile and imagined him sitting between her mama and daddy on the balcony of eternity, cheering her on to the next leg of her race. No. She would not mourn Aaron. That would be the last thing he would want for her. She would see him again. Melanie would not focus on what had been left behind. She would focus on what lay ahead.

She had made her choice. She was going to embark upon a great journey. The kind most only dream of ever making. Sure it would come with its own drawbacks of leaving family and everything familiar, but she had no doubt what lay ahead of her would soon overshadow all she had given up for this chance. Closing her eyes and forcing herself to take ten deep breaths, she willed herself to be grateful, not regretful. From this moment forward, she would begin each day with an attitude of gratitude. Opening her eyes, she was ready to step out of the car.

"I'll be right back," she said to Fred and Ginger.

Inside the store, a thick aroma of fresh coffee and fried chicken filled the air. Melanie's stomach growled and she couldn't remember the last time she had had anything to eat. It seemed like she had been driving for months instead of hours.

Jordan had begged her to stay in Baton Rouge for New Year's Eve. Nate, Jordan's husband, had been teaching at Louisiana State University for the last several years. Jordan, he, and their children were thriving. Melanie had enjoyed her visit but she had been eager to get to Rockport and to see *Quality Time*.

The effects of the long drive pulled upon her weary bones. She could sleep for a week. Too bad she had so much to do before she could even think of rest and relaxation. At least she could turn in early tonight and start work tomorrow.

Those plans were about to change.

"Hello," the cashier said pleasantly, without looking up from her Harlequin romance novel.

"Hi." Melanie wandered over to the coffee maker and poured herself a large cup before adding two heaping teaspoons of sugar and a dose of vanilla creamer.

Sipping the delicious brew, she mentally ran through the small box of provisions Jordan had packed for Melanie's road trip. After crossing back to the front of the store for one of the small red shopping baskets stacked next to the magazine display, she then wandered the short aisles, picking up a can of chili, a loaf of bread, a small package of sliced cheese, a dozen eggs, a liter of Coke, and a quart of orange juice.

"I've got dog and cat food. This should hold me until

tomorrow and I'll find a grocery," she said to no one but herself.

Back at the front of the store, she got in line behind a man who was chatting with the cashier. He was a tall man dressed in worn camel-colored work boots, jeans, and a red flannel shirt spanning the width of his broad muscular shoulders. Melanie couldn't help but notice how well he filled out his faded blue jeans. She set the small basket of groceries on the counter as he turned and smiled politely.

Melanie swallowed the small gasp before it escaped her lips. Her heart fluttered in her chest. She hadn't been prepared for the glacier blue eyes and dazzling smile; this man was gorgeous. Melanie smiled back, tucking a stray strand of hair behind her ear. She hoped he wouldn't say anything to her. Struck speechless, she couldn't remember feeling this girlish since she was a teenager.

Fortunately he didn't seem to notice. He turned back to the cashier as she rang up his few purchases.

"Hey Inez, how much is the Lotto up to now?"

"It's back down to five million. They had two winners for the eight million last week. That made for a very Merry Christmas, I'm sure. Wanna a buy a ticket?"

"Only five million? I think I'll pass." The handsome stranger handed a ten dollar bill to the clerk as she filled a small paper sack.

"Excuse me." Melanie shocked herself addressing the stranger.

"Yes?"

"I don't mean to pry but that's five million more than you have." She smiled playfully.

He didn't say anything at first, but looked at her

curiously and then chuckled heartily, a delightfully pleasant sound to Melanie's ears.

"You're exactly right. Inez, give me two Quick Picks please."

To Melanie, he winked and said, "Have a nice day and Happy New Year."

"You too."

Inez had already begun totaling Melanie's purchases. "He's a looker. Ain't he?" The cashier raised her eyebrows in question and smiled conspiratorially.

"Uh, well, I didn't…" Melanie stammered.

"Oh sugar, don't tell me you didn't notice. A girl would have to be blind not to notice a man like that."

"You're right." Melanie's face flushed and she quickly changed the subject.

"Could you possibly tell me how to get to the House of Boats?"

"Oh sure, get back on the highway out here take a left and go about three miles. You'll see a sign for the Hooking Bull Boatyard, go a bit further and then turn right at the big black dog sittin' on the corner."

"Turn right at the big black dog sitting on the corner?" Melanie asked skeptically.

"Yep. That's Leroy. You can't miss him unless he's gone inside for lunch. This time of day, he should be sittin' right on the corner," she said cheerfully as she handed Melanie the two sacks of supplies.

"Thank you."

"Happy New Year, hon."

"Happy New Year to you, too," Melanie called over her shoulder as she pushed through the door, both her arms filled with groceries.

"I guess the GPS must not have picked up on ol' Leroy." She laughed to herself as she hit the remote and the car doors unlocked.

After putting the groceries in the back seat, Melanie clipped the leash on an ecstatic Fred and headed back across the parking lot to the small patch of grass she had noticed when she first pulled in the lot.

Fred took care of his business and made himself busy sniffing the grass and picking up the scents of other animals that had passed this way and left their marks.

"Okay buddy, your tank is empty. We don't have time to be reading the P-mail. Let's go."

The two crossed the parking lot to the rental and waiting Ginger.

"*Quality Time*, I presume."

Startled, Melanie turned abruptly and came face to face with the handsome stranger leaning against a black, mud-spattered pickup, the roof lined with hunters' spotlights.

"That's right."

"Tennessee, I presume." She nodded at the peanuts floating in the half-full bottle of Dr. Pepper."

"You got me." He chuckled with a curious look.

"I have a girlfriend whose husband puts peanuts in his Dr. Pepper and he's from Tennessee, but how did you know?" Melanie laughed.

"Well, first of all, the rental car you're driving is packed to the gills. Second, you bought enough provisions to hold you over for a day or two when you can find the grocery store and, finally, the boss man said the captain was getting in town today. We finished putting the barrier coat on this afternoon and are ready to start rolling the ablative paint at sunrise day after tomorrow. We only need to know if you want a cayenne pepper cocktail."

"You must be Rick! I'm Melanie. It's a pleasure to meet you." She laughed and offered her hand. Fred, sitting at her feet, stared up inquisitively at the mountain of a man.

"The pleasure is all mine." His enormous hand completely enveloped her delicate one.

"I'm sorry, but did you say a cayenne pepper cocktail?"

"Yeah. Cayenne pepper mixed with your bottom paint will help keep your hull clean of barnacles but I've got to tell you we have to do it on the Q-T."

"Well, you've got me there. I've never heard of this. It sounds like a Martha Stewart tip." She laughed again as Fred pulled eagerly on the leash, having spied a squirrel run across the road.

"Why would you have to do it on the Q-T?"

"Well, it's not exactly kosher," he explained.

"Mixing cayenne pepper with boat paint isn't kosher. Why not?" Melanie asked curiously.

"Well, some of the people who study such, have determined that over time the cayenne pepper dissolves into the water and the sea creatures that might come into contact with your bottom…" He blushed like a young boy but then quickly cleared his throat and continued. "I mean the bottom paint from your boat. Those sea creatures lose their desire to propagate. I personally don't know if it's true but that's what some believe so it's not something you want to broadcast. There are some who will put cyanide in with the bottom paint and that's illegal because it's poison."

"Well, Heaven forbid, I wouldn't want to interfere with the sex lives of shrimp and wouldn't dream of using cyanide and breaking the law, especially since I'm—"

She stopped herself before she finished the sentence, determined to stop telling people she was an attorney. That was what this whole adventure was about anyway—finding out whom she was beyond the law degree she held.

"What I meant to say is I'm sure regular bottom paint will be fine. Barnacles certainly are a nuisance but I plan to do a haul out every couple of years to redo the bottom, check the propeller, rudder, cutlass bearing, and—" She stopped herself again as she noticed his smile.

"You're quite the experienced seaman. Pardon me, sea woman. Sounds like you know her from bow to stern, better than most men walking around the boatyard."

"Well, my daddy always made sure *Quality Time* was taken care of like a member of the family. I've tried to take care of her, too."

"I could tell that when I first saw her. How long has it been since you've had her out on the ocean?"

"A little less than eight years. I kept her in the water at Beaufort and used to visit three or four times a year but after…" She caught herself again. She had almost mentioned the Devilland case. It was going to be extremely hard to assume anonymity.

"Anyway, after a while, I found I didn't have the time to go up there and give her the attention she needed. I was lucky to have the staff at the Beaufort marina. They took good care of her."

"Well, she's a beauty; that's for sure. Nobody makes them any finer than Camper Nicholsons. You've got yourself a Rolls-Royce, there."

Melanie couldn't help but smile. It was exactly what her daddy had told her about *Quality Time*.

"Thank you. I guess I should be heading for the boat-yard so I can make sure I catch ol' Leroy before he goes in for lunch." She laughed.

"Oh, he doesn't eat for another hour but you can follow me back there." He drained the last of his Dr. Pepper and tossed the plastic bottle into the trash.

"So, Inez wasn't kidding. I do turn right at the big black dog."

"Yep, ol' Leroy has been there for as long as anyone around here can remember." He flashed that movie-star smile again.

"I'll see you at the boatyard."

"See ya there," he called over his shoulder.

As she drove down the road, she only traveled a short distance before Leroy came into sight. Shaking her head, she chuckled as she turned right at Leroy's corner.

twenty-nine

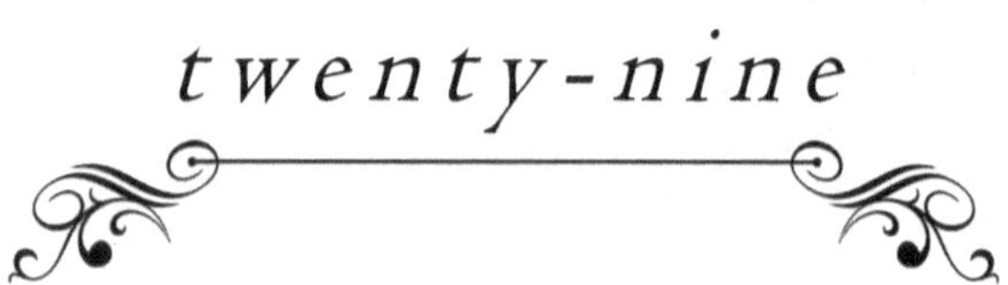

Later that afternoon-December 31, 2008
House of Boats-Rockport, Texas

GLANCING AT HER WATCH, MELANIE WAS surprised to see it was after four. She had been working feverishly for the past two hours unloading boxes and moving her possessions onto *Quality Time*. She had shipped most of the boxes from Dallas and the boatyard owner had stored them for her. She also had her entire car to unpack.

Throughout the afternoon, at least a dozen people had stopped by and introduced themselves. They'd all been delightful and she looked forward to chatting more with neighbors tonight at the New Years Eve party. More specifically, spending time with Rick who had certainly gotten her interest. His passion for *Quality Time*. His smooth, husky voice. That easy, full laughter. Yes. He had definitely sparked something inside her.

Despite being exhausted from the long drive and a hard day of hauling boxes up the twelve foot ladder, she had found her second wind and was energized. She was finally on the coast and was about to embark upon the journey she had been planning for so many months. Rick had stopped by earlier and carried the heaviest of the boxes onto the boat for her but she had insisted she could do the rest herself. She had succeeded in moving all but two small boxes of linens and bath accessories from the trunk of the car onto the boat.

"Okay, Fred, let Mama get the last two boxes and then I'll take you for a walk by the water. We need to scoot, though. I've still got to run to the grocery store." The eager pup watched her climb down the ladder from the boat.

Rick had mentioned everyone in the boatyard would be getting together around seven o'clock for a New Year's Eve celebration and insisted she join in the festivities. Tootsie, the woman on the boat next to *Quality Time*, had told Melanie the store up the road had a nice deli which would be open until six. Melanie had decided to make a tray of cold cuts and cheese which was always fast, easy, and popular.

As she reached into the trunk of the rental, she noticed a third box lodged far in the corner she hadn't seen earlier. Straining to reach the box, she was surprised at how heavy it was. Curious as to what it could be as it wasn't labeled, she pulled back the packing tape and groaned as she gazed at the stacks of family photos she had found at her parents' house.

"Crud! I can't believe I forgot to give these to Jordie." Melanie had been so excited to see the family that the box of photographs had completely slipped her mind.

"Hello, Captain. Can I help you with that?" Rick asked as she struggled to lift the box.

"That would be great. I'm down to the last three boxes, believe it or not," she said proudly and handed him the carton of pictures.

"Well, let's get that taken care of right now and afterwards, you deserve a break. It's New Year's Eve after all."

After delivering the box to the boat's now crowded salon, he climbed down the ladder. "It's almost five. Can I interest you in a cup of hot apple cider? It's my grandmother's secret recipe, guaranteed to be the best you ever tasted."

"That sounds wonderful but I promised Fred I would take him on a short walk and then I need to get something to bring to the potluck tonight."

"Don't worry about the potluck. I've been in the galley all afternoon. I put together a nice platter of hors d'oeuvres, a slow cooker of red beans with rice, and I am fixing to pop a tray of chocolate chip muffins into the oven. I've got you covered."

"Wow, that sounds delicious but I can't let you do that. You've been so kind already."

Melanie smiled at her new friend in admiration. He had been cooking all day. Impressive. Could he possibly be too good to be true?

"I've already done it, no argument."

"At least let me pay you for half of it."

"Not necessary, really," he insisted.

"Okay, but only if you let me fix you supper once I get myself settled. I cook a pretty mean chicken spaghetti, or so I've been told." She surprised herself at how comfortable she felt with a man she had only met hours earlier.

"It's a deal. Take Fred for a walk and I'll meet you down by the water in twenty minutes. It's almost feeding time."

"Feeding time?"

"Yeah, see ya in twenty." He winked and left.

After a short walk, Melanie quickly freshened up and changed into a pink jogging suit. Looking in the mirror at her pale complexion she put on a touch of lipstick and a whisper of blush. It amazed her how much her spirits had been lifted in the few hours since she arrived.

She felt giddy at the prospect of spending more time with Rick. It was funny how she felt about this enigmatic man. As she had told Dr. Johnson, she had dated since her divorce but she never let herself get emotionally involved with any man. She had never felt safe enough to let her guard down, yet she was completely at ease with him. Yes, long ago she had closed the door to any real romance and locked it securely. She had just met Rick and certainly wasn't ready to entertain any possible romantic involvement with him but she welcomed the flutter of butterflies in her stomach. It was a feeling she hadn't experienced for far too long and it felt good. In fact, it felt great! Romance or not, from the little she knew, she imagined she would become good friends with Rick.

Waiting at the water's edge, he waved and grinned as Fred and she approached. There were a half-dozen white plastic lawn chairs arranged around a makeshift plywood table. The rustic sitting area was arranged in front of an enormous catamaran which rested atop the sturdy steel stands on the packed dirt.

"That's one big boat." Her eyes widened as she gazed at the enormous vessel and read the name written on the side. She took a chair, Fred quickly settling at her feet. "*Ma'a salama*, that's interesting. I can't say I've ever heard that."

"It's Arabic," Rick explained. "The literal translation is peace be with you, although it's also used to say good-bye. I met the guy who owns her when he brought her in a few months back. He's a bodyguard for some Saudi Arabian sheikh and is loaded but five of his eight kids are currently in varying stages of college or med school. He said he couldn't afford to keep the boat in the water until at least a couple of them graduated."

"Interesting, I can't imagine having eight kids." The familiar pang tugged at her heart as it did anytime she thought of having children.

"Me neither. Here you go." He handed her a mug. "Careful, it's hot."

"Thank you." Melanie took a sip of the spicy cider. "Yum, you were right; this is delicious," she said appreciatively.

"Thanks." He glanced at his watch and nodded toward the bay. "Hey, looks like they're right on time."

Approximately twenty-five yards away from where Rick and she sat, two dolphins gracefully swam toward them, the sky above streaked with pink and amethyst gossamer clouds. The entire sight was simply magnificent.

"Do they come every day at this time?" she asked curiously.

"Yep. Flipper and Skipper never miss a day. They come twice a day to feed, once right around sunrise and again before sunset."

"They're lovely."

"They are. First time I saw them, they reminded me of a proverb I read awhile back. It goes something like, *Life is not measured by the number of breaths we take,*"

"*But by the number of moments that take our breath*

away." She finished the line with him and they both laughed.

The two new friends sat in a comfortable silence for a long while, enjoying the tranquility of the dolphins as the brilliant orange sun sank into the horizon.

"My daddy said sunsets made you believe in angels," Melanie said wistfully.

"Mmm, I'd have to agree with that."

After a few more minutes, it was time to head back to their respective boats and get ready for the potluck supper.

After dark, Melanie strolled in the direction of where several people lit an enormous circle of tiki torches. Makeshift tables of sawhorses and long boards were filled with a bountiful feast. Coolers filled with ice and beverages were scattered among the folding chairs. Strains of reggae music thumped from a boom box sitting atop one of the makeshift tables.

Following the bright beam from her flashlight, Melanie walked carefully across the terrain strewn with rocks and shells. A black velvet sky with heavy clouds enveloped the night. A chilly wind blew in from the sea and she smiled as she inhaled the familiar scent of brine.

Melanie was surprised by the number of people at the gathering and enjoyed the jovial atmosphere, the easy camaraderie of everyone in attendance, and the delicious food.

The evening flew by and before Melanie knew it, 2009 had arrived as fireworks lit up the sky and the smell of spent gunpowder wafted through the air. A brand-new year. A brand-new life. Excitement tingled over Melanie as the crowd broke into song. It wasn't the typical "Auld Lang Syne" but rather a boisterous rendition of "Celebration" by

Kool and the Gang.

Shortly afterwards, most of the crowd had thinned but a handful remained around the small campfire that burned softly in the cool evening. Melanie reflected on the diversity of people she had met. They had come from all walks of life with one unifying trait, a love of the ocean and the adventure that lay beyond the horizon. Despite their varied socio-economic backgrounds, they were all kindred spirits.

"How did you like our little community?" Rick asked.

"They're wonderful. The people I've met in the few hours since I arrived have been amazing and yet I probably would've never met them in my previous life. So many friendships are based on where you work, which gym you frequent, where you live—all random things. Don't get me wrong. I have some great friends back home but most of them can't imagine doing what I'm doing, leaving it all behind me, casting off the lines, and going to see what's on the other side of the horizon. Tonight, talking to different people about their experiences, their hopes, and dreams of setting sail, I felt so connected and yet I barely know these people. It's weird, but weird in a good way. I feel like in the last few hours I've crossed over to a brand-new world and I haven't even left Texas. You probably think I'm strange." A shy laugh slipped from her mouth.

"Not at all," Rick said. "You hit the nail on the head. You're going to meet some incredible people on your journey. Granted, you're not going to become best buddies with all of them but you'll be glad you met them. Your life will be richer for the experience…guaranteed. Reggie, my business partner, used to have a saying. 'People are kind of like Baskin-Robbins ice cream; I don't like all thirty-one flavors but I'm sure glad they make them.' That's what makes life interesting. Although I think Baskin-Robbins makes a helluva lot more than thirty-one flavors nowadays. You're right about this life we yachties live. We all have an undying love of Mother Ocean and the burning desire to see the other side of the horizon. It makes for some pretty cool friendships, counting this one." He thumbed between the two of them.

She was growing fond of his broad grin. "Ditto," Melanie replied easily.

"Have time for one more cup of cider before you turn in for the night?" Rick asked her after the last of the revelers said their good-byes.

"That would be great."

"I'll be back in a minute. Are you cold? Can I bring you a blanket?"

"No thank you. The fire is perfect."

"I'll keep the little lady company while you're gone." An elfin man with rough, leathery skin sat down and rubbed his hands together over the smoldering fire.

Melanie remembered seeing him earlier in the evening but hadn't met him.

"Thanks. Can I bring you a cup of hot cider?"

"That would be mighty nice of you," the other man replied gratefully.

"I'm sorry but I don't think we've been introduced. I'm Melanie." She offered her hand.

"My friends call me Dodger."

He grinned broadly, showing a mouth void of any teeth and took her hand in his small calloused one.

"It's nice to meet you, Dodger."

"It's an honor, ma'am. I've been eager to meet you ever since I found out you were coming to the yard."

Confused by his choice of words, Melanie replied, "Excuse me, but I don't think I follow."

"Well, first of all, let me say I respect your privacy and nobody's gonna hear anything from me. That's one of the best things about us boat people. None of us knows or cares about last names. Everybody here has got a past, some good, some not so good, but here in the yard, we're all equal."

"Alright, but I still don't understand." Melanie eyed the little man curiously.

"If you don't mind, ma'am, I want to tell you a story about a man I once knew. It won't take long," he said with pleading eyes.

"Okay." Melanie moved closer to the fire, the winter wind nipping at her face and hands.

"The man was a doctor who was well respected and extremely successful by most people's standards. He was the personal physician for a handful of ambassadors and other dignitaries. He traveled all over the world for twenty, twenty-five years. He had a wonderful wife and a beautiful daughter who were the lights of his life. I've never known a man who loved his family more. After his daughter was born, the man and his wife built a home in the Seychelles. I don't know how much you know about that part of the world but the islands are in the heart of the Indian Ocean. A prettier place you've never seen. The islands are granite and coral with amazing forests. Huge cliffs overlook white sandy beaches. It's absolutely gorgeous and the water is like a giant aquarium. You can see forty meters below you, clear as can be." He stretched his arms in the air, his voice animated as he described the beauty.

Tilting her head, Melanie could see the islands in her mind's eye as she had seen amazing places in her sailing adventures with her daddy.

"Well, anyway, this man lived in this paradise with his wife and daughter. He was happier than any man has a right to be. One day, when his daughter was twelve years old, she was walking home from school and was hit by a car. Drunk driver knocked her right off a cliff and never even stopped. If it weren't for a lone witness, her little body might never have been found."

"How awful," Melanie said quietly, her hand resting on her chest.

Vacantly staring at the dying embers of the fire, the petite man stopped for a moment and took a long swallow from a small bottle shrouded in a brown paper bag. Melanie had heard countless heartbreaking stories of children killed by drunk drivers during her preparations for the Devilland trial. Shirley Simms and so many others in MADD had shared their experiences. Others had relayed their horrific tales in the multitude of cards that were mailed to her each year. She had lived through the pain with Aaron. She had always thought Aaron had been dealt the worst hand possible but he had refused to allow her to grieve his fate. No. Aaron's story had been heartbreaking but Dodger's tale was more than she could fathom. Biting her lip to hold back the swell of tears, she stared at the man before her. In his eyes, she saw the hellacious full circle of alcoholism. A life in ruins.

With a shake of his head, he continued. "Man was never the same. When he lost his daughter, he lost his reason for living. He and his wife stayed married for a couple of years but after a while, they couldn't be together anymore. It hurt too much. When they looked at each other, all they saw was the little girl they lost. This man, he crawled inside a fifth of whiskey and never found his way back out of the bottle. The whole thing is ironic when you think a drunk took this man's life from him and now that successful and respectable doctor is nothing more than a shell of the man he used to be. He's nothing more than a pitiful old drunk himself, doing whatever odd jobs he can to buy his next meal, not knowing from one night to the next where he's going to lay his head…" His words trailed off, his desolate gaze lost in the dark night.

Melanie had no doubt the toothless man dressed in rags and sitting before her was the heartbroken father of a young girl killed over ten thousand miles away.

Silence hung in the air as they both stared into the golden orange flames. Melanie could not find her voice.

Dodger spoke first as his pained gaze met hers. "I just wanted to say there's a million people, probably a lot more, from all over the world, who could be sitting in this same chair right now telling you just about the same story—losing it all to the impious demon in the bottle. What you did saved so many people who will never get the chance to thank you, so I'll do it for them. Thank you, Melanie, and may God bless you." Tears glistened in the corners of his eyes.

All the past accolades for her legal victory dimmed as she gazed into the fire, afraid to look into the man's eyes. Afraid she would break into sobs. Afraid she wouldn't be able to stop. She had always thought she understood what she had accomplished with Devilland but she realized in this moment she didn't have an inkling. Devilland had changed society and the change had only just begun.

Choking back tears, she smiled sadly. "God bless you, doctor."

thirty

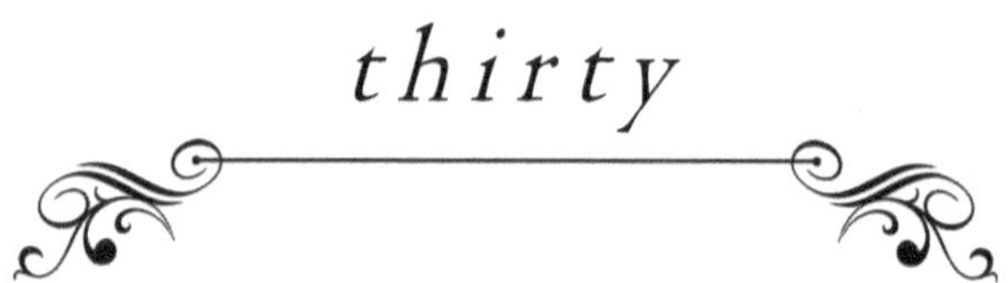

Three days pass-January, 2009
House of Boats-Rockport, Texas

A PELICAN DOVE FOR A FISH AND WOKE FRED WHO had been napping on the deck. Melanie sat down next to the pup and scratched behind his ears. First thing this morning, they had splashed *Quality Time*. She had been put back into the water after almost two months in the boatyard while being completely refurbished. There were still some cosmetics to be done to the inside but all the major work had finally been completed.

Unfortunately, the only available space for *Quality Time* had been on the far bank of the boatyard, across the small bay from an enormous facility with a half a dozen barges blocking most of any scenic view. The day after to-morrow Melanie would be moving the boat to the city marina where there was a wonderful park and long stretch of public beach. She was excited about moving to the marina but would miss the people she had met in the boatyard. She had promised to come back to visit her new friends who were sad to see her leave.

It would be sunset soon and the dolphins Flipper and Skipper would arrive for their feeding. Melanie and Rick had been meeting every morning and evening to admire the majestic creatures. Melanie wasn't sure exactly what she was starting to feel for this man she had met only a few days ago but she did know that she looked forward to seeing Rick every day and enjoyed his company immensely.

She was unsure how long she had been sitting, staring into the horizon and contemplating new life when his voice broke her reverie.

"Just think. The fact it's now four-forty is important to some poor sucker somewhere."

"And Fed Ex arrives at five." Melanie flashed a brilliant smile for her visitor.

Fred jumped up and ran the length of the boat, eager to greet Rick who always had a Milk-Bone in his pocket.

"Come aboard."

Rick followed Melanie below into the salon.

Fred barked wildly from the bow of the boat. In answer, Melanie grabbed a dog treat from the jar and stuck it out the hatch that she referred to as the drive-in window. Fred appeared and stuck his small head in the opening, eagerly taking his treat.

"Good dog, good boy, good boy." Melanie encouraged the pooch as she screwed the lid back on the plastic jar of doggie treats.

Rick chuckled.

"What's so funny? He's getting pretty good at that. I don't want him barking every single time someone walks by the boat but I do want to know when a stranger passes. That little fellow is my first line of defense. He's a lot tougher than he looks." Melanie smirked.

"You're right. Fred's getting good at something, but it's not alerting his captain to strangers. I've been sitting on Jimmy's boat for the last two hours helping him with his GPS and not one single soul has walked by your boat. It's Sunday. The yard is dead but I've been watching Fred sun himself and bark randomly every twenty, twenty-five minutes, run to the drive-in window and get his reward. I'm sorry darlin' but Fred's pulling the wool over your beautiful eyes."

Her heart skipped a beat when he called her eyes beautiful. She had heard it many times before from others but hearing it from Rick made her giddy.

"That little stinker! When I started training him, he was doing really well. I know because I would step in the cockpit and check out who was passing the boat. When I'm down South in marinas, I don't want him to be one of those annoying little yip-yap dogs that bother other boaters but I want him to warn me if someone I don't know is hanging around the dock."

"I agree. I think it's a great idea and one your neighbors will appreciate as well but I think maybe you should explain to Fred the rules of engagement once again."

"Obviously," she said with a chuckle as Fred barked again and suddenly appeared at the open hatch.

Melanie looked questioningly at Rick who raised his head and checked outside.

He shook his head. "Nada."

"You're busted fur-bit! No treat for you. Go lie down on the deck." The pup seemed to understand and disappeared from the open hatch without a treat.

"I hope I didn't interrupt anything. I wanted to stop by and invite you over to my boat for sunset. I'm over on the opposite side of the office and the view is spectacular. We'll be able to see Flipper and Skipper from there."

"Thank you. I'd love that. Can I bring anything?"

"Nothing but yourself." Fred padded into the salon. "Your cunning first mate is welcome to come along, too." Rick reached down and scratched behind the dog's ears.

Half an hour later, Melanie crossed the quiet boatyard and headed in the direction of the office. She hadn't yet seen Rick's boat as she had been so busy for the last few days getting settled on *Quality Time*. Now as she stood on the bank, she was beyond shocked at the sight before her. A stunning sixty foot Hatteras, not more than three years old, sat gloriously in the water. She had never priced such a vessel but had no doubt there had been a seven figure price tag on this *little ol' fishing boat*, as Rick had called it when she had asked him about his craft. Suddenly, everything she thought she knew about her new friend flew out the window. She had assumed he was a supervisor of the day laborers in the huge boatyard. Clearly there was much more to his story.

"Come aboard. Come aboard." Rick held out his hand to her.

"She's absolutely gorgeous." Melanie kicked her sandals onto the dock and stepped up onto the handsome yacht.

Rick beamed as she quietly gazed around her in bewildered appreciation.

"Cubed or crushed?"

Puzzled for a brief moment, she smiled as he motioned to small built-in ice chests.

"Crushed would be wonderful."

After filling two navy blue glasses with gold anchors painted on them to the brim with crushed ice and cola, Rick handed her one and took a seat across from her.

"Well, Flipper and Skipper should be arriving soon," she said expectantly.

Fred had settled at her feet and slept soundly in the cool afternoon breeze.

Melanie and Rick chatted easily for the next half hour. He had offered to ride with her to the city dock and she had graciously accepted. Sailing solo was second nature to her but pulling into a marina was always much easier with an extra pair of hands.

"Where did they put you over there?"

"Right next to the bright pink bait stand. Fleming's is the name of it, I believe."

"That's a great location. You'll be far enough away from the shrimpers that you won't have the wave action every morning and every night. My slip is around the bend, in front of the aquarium and I rock and roll pretty hard sometimes when those guys come back in from the day. You'll have a little fishy smell occasionally but Fleming does a good job of running a clean shop."

"You have a slip over there?" Melanie asked, surprised.

"That's where I usually am. I only moved over here when *Quality Time* came in the yard. It made it a lot easier to oversee the work the boys were doing if I stayed in the yard full time."

"So you don't work in the yard full time?" Melanie knew the answer but she was curious as to why he had taken an interest in her boat.

"No. Fishing is my game but when Jeff said he had a

Camper Nicholson coming in for an overhaul, I jumped at the chance to handle the work. I love boats and yours is a classic. You don't see many of them around and I wanted to make sure the boys treated her right. Jeff agreed; he wanted to make sure *Quality Time* received the greatest of care."

"Well, I truly appreciate your taking so much time to get involved with *Quality Time*. I had no idea, really." She once again admired Rick's luxurious vessel.

"I enjoyed it very much. Things around here are slow this time of year and it was a good change of pace for me."

"How long have you been running charters?"

"A little over two years. I was in the computer game for a long time, if you can believe that."

"What made you make such a big change?" Melanie asked tentatively, not wanting him to ask the same of her.

She was fairly certain no one besides Dodger had recognized her and she was eager to keep it that way. At the same time, she found herself extremely interested in the incredibly handsome man who sat across from her.

"There's not much to tell. After college I joined the Coast Guard for a while. Then my best friend and I started a little software company. He was the brains behind it. I was more into the management and sales. Anyway, Reggie, my partner, was a brilliant guy. Actually, he was more like a machine. Most of our business was for the oil and gas industry with the majority being automation for oil rigs. Reggie was the Bill Gates of computer software for the oil and gas business. I've never known anybody who worked harder than he did. When I got to the office every morning at seven, he had been there for hours slaving away in front of that damn computer. When I left every night at six, he was still going full throttle. Unfortunately, as the years passed, he ended up working to support four ex-wives and a handful of kids he never had the time to see. I didn't fare much better. My wife left me after twenty-eight years of marriage and I barely knew my only son who had gotten married and was starting his own family. One morning, I came into the office and found Reggie—dead. Right in front of his computer. Heart attack. He would have turned forty-nine the next weekend."

"Oh dear God, that's tragic."

"Yeah. I was a mess for a long time. I remember going out to the cemetery one day after I had closed on a big deal. I had sold the last program Reggie had finished before he died and I had been talking to a guy about an IPO. I didn't know what exactly I was going to do so I was considering several different options. I was standing in front of Reggie's headstone, looking around and thinking about how much time we had both spent building our company, and for what? I wandered around the graveyard, looking at all the headstones, reading the names on them, thinking about their families, their dreams. That's when it hit me. All the tombstones were basically the same: somebody's name, the date they were born, the date they died, and occasionally a few sentimental words, *beloved son, adoring husband, loving father*, but that was it. Reggie's entire life had been minimized to nothing more than a dash, a punctuation mark between his birth and death dates. We're all born. We all die. The only difference is what we do with our dash. I sold the company and two weeks later bought this girl." He proudly gestured about him.

Melanie grinned as she noticed for the first time the yacht's name stenciled on a life ring. *The Dash.*

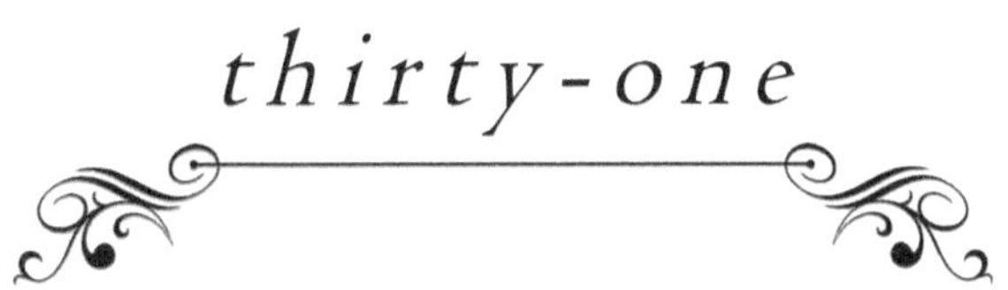

thirty-one

One week passes-January, 2009
City Marina-Rockport, Texas

MELANIE CHECKED THE DOCK LINES AND stepped aboard *Quality Time*. She had eaten a late lunch with Tootsie at the Apple Dumpling Deli. Despite it being almost seven, Melanie wasn't hungry.

Like Rick, Tootsie had quickly become a good friend to Melanie. Tootsie had been a tremendous help to Melanie in choosing new upholstery, linens, and accessories for *Quality Time*. Since the boat would be her new home for at least the next year, if not longer, Melanie wanted to update everything from bow to stern. Over the years, the white walls had yellowed with age so Melanie had decided to paint the salon and cabins with vibrant colors and to reupholster all the cushions to compliment the new color scheme and refinished woodwork.

The two women had a grand time shopping together. Melanie was still becoming accustomed to her new found wealth and was pleasantly surprised at the bargains they found at the different shops around town. Their favorite store—Castaways—was a resale shop benefiting area churches. Melanie had been thrilled with the unique treasures found there. They found several remnants of fabric with anchors and other nautical themes. Tootsie had sewn a variety of throw pillows for the sofa and berths on Melanie's gorgeous boat.

Grabbing an orange from the bowl on the table, Melanie settled down in the salon. As she reached over to open the hatch, her foot bumped the box of photos she had slid under the chart table when she had moved onto the boat.

"Hmm. This would be a good time to start the album. What do you think, Fred?"

The pup gazed up at her with his huge dark eyes as if he understood every word she said. For all her life, Melanie had talked to her animals, but in the past few weeks she had begun to talk to Ginger and Fred more than ever since they were often her only audience on the long days and nights in the boatyard.

As Melanie sorted through the huge box of photos, newspaper clippings, and other memorabilia, she soon became overwhelmed with what she had originally thought would be an entertaining and easy task. She realized she had misjudged the magnitude of the project.

There were easily over three hundred photos that had been salvaged from Grandmama Tilly's multitude of albums. Originally there were probably hundreds upon hundreds, if not thousands of photos taken of the Bridges family over the span of six generations. Unfortunately, most of them had not survived the devastating fire almost twenty-five years earlier.

Melanie decided the most efficient way to arrange the

photos would be to do so simply by date. Grandmama Tilly had been meticulous about recording the date on the back of every single photo. Most of the photos had the names of those in the picture as well, with only a few exceptions.

"Thank you, Grandmama Tilly. I'm so glad you were so extremely methodical." Melanie laughed aloud as she focused on the momentous mission that lay before her. After a few minutes she decided to put the task off for another time.

thirty-two

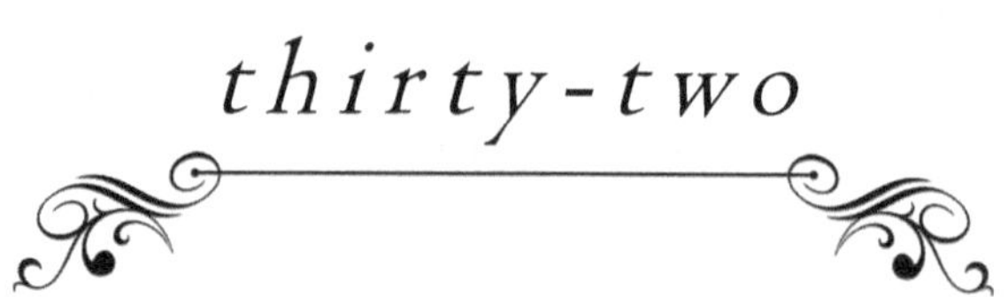

One week passes-January, 2009
City Marina-Rockport, Texas

MELANIE SANG ALONG IN PERFECT HARMONY with the Jimmy Buffett tune as she finished peeling the last of the shrimp. "And an African parakeet and then I'll sit him on my shoulder and open up my trusty old mind; I gonna teach him how to cuss, teach him how to fuss and pull the cork out of a bottle of wine."

She scooped the huge Gulf prawns into the small blue bowl that was already half filled with her special home-made marinade. Opening the refrigerator, she made room for the seafood and took out the red, green, and yellow bell peppers she had picked up at the grocery store on her afternoon bike ride.

"Permission to come aboard," the familiar husky voice called, followed by the customary pattern of staccato knocks.

"Permission granted," Melanie sang through the open hatch.

Cool and crisp, the evening air blew with a hint of sea

salt and the fragrant hibiscus growing throughout the small memorial park across from the city's harbor.

As Rick stepped onto the boat, Fred immediately began his routine barking frenzy and jumped from the sofa to greet the visitor in the cockpit.

"Hey, buddy." Rick scratched Fred's perky black ears.

"Wait. I love this part." Melanie hummed a few notes and then rejoined the lyrics playing.

"Yeah, got a Caribbean soul I can barely control and some Texas hidden here in my heart." Melanie laughed as she danced around the galley.

"Impressive, I hope I didn't interrupt your private concert." Rick chuckled.

"No. This is perfect timing. I need to chop the mushrooms and then we'll be ready to make the kabobs."

Rick gave her a friendly peck on her cheek and held up a bottle of Penfolds Grange wine. Butterflies fluttered in her stomach at Rick's show of affection.

"Thank you! That's my favorite wine ever since my cousin Emily brought me a bottle back from Australia last summer when she spent three months down under," Melanie said, her Aussie accent near perfect.

"It seems I do recall something about that, mate," Rick replied in his own faux drawl.

"What can I do to help?" He slid the bottle of wine into the fridge.

"Open the spice cabinet; the skewers are on the left, behind the salt and pepper shakers." She set the assortment of marinating shrimp, peppers, pearl onions, mushrooms, and pineapple chunks on the tile counter.

As the two placed the delectable bites on the long, thin,

wooden skewers, they fell into easy conversation as though they had been friends forever.

"I didn't know you were a Parrott Head."

"My Parrott Head days go back almost as long as I can remember. My cousins and I even had a band called the *Parakeet* Heads. We would spend hours entertaining my brother, his friends, and the rest of the family—basically anybody who would listen to us. We mimicked quite a few artists but ol' Jimmy was by far our favorite. We probably could've toured with him but were a little young for life on the road."

"You were in a band? What do you play? A guitar? Keyboard?" Rick asked, visibly impressed.

"I played the tambourine. My cousins toyed with the maracas and bongo drums. The instruments were more for show than any great musical talent. Our true talent was that we could lip-sync perfectly to hundreds of songs and had the best moves to go with all of them."

"I'd love to see some of those moves." He winked.

"We'll see about that," she said with a mischievous grin.

The heat of blush crept on her cheeks. She couldn't believe how silly and free she felt with him and quickly returned to the task of cutting the remaining ingredients for the kabobs.

"Wow," Rick said. "That's absolutely gorgeous."

"What?" Melanie turned from her task.

Rick admired the painting she had hung above the chart table earlier today. It was a watercolor of a *Quality Time* on an ocean of aquamarine and emerald green with a brilliant sunset of orange, pink, and a tiny hint of purple, on the horizon.

"Who's the artist? I've never seen anything like it. It's an absolute perfect replica of your boat. The colors are perfect. I'd love to have one done of *The Dash*."

"His name is Aaron. He doesn't paint professionally. It's only a hobby for him. It was my Christmas gift this past year." A lump rose in her throat when she realized she had spoken of Aaron in the present tense.

She hastily continued preparing the meal to stave off the growing tears.

"That's a shame. He could make a fortune. I love art and that painting is one of the best I've ever seen."

Melanie's heart pricked with pride as she thought of all the beautiful paintings Aaron had done in his life. He was always giving his talent freely to everyone he knew, leaving a little piece of himself in each work of art.

Rick quietly refilled their wine glasses, as if giving Melanie a moment to regain her composure, for which she was grateful.

Jimmy Buffett's classic "Margaritaville" filtered through the speakers. The emotional moment passed as the song played. Within minutes Melanie sang along, swaying her hips.

She tossed the last chunk of luscious pineapple into her mouth, and, grinning, returned to her Aussie slang.

"Mate, what do ya say we throw these on the barbie?"

The two chatted easily as they enjoyed a superb meal of shrimp kabobs, cucumber and tomato salad, and mouth-watering chocolate éclairs.

Afterwards, Rick helped her clear the table and wash the dishes, despite her insistence she could do it all in the morning.

"That didn't take long and you shall awaken to a ship-shape galley rather than a pile of dirty pots and pans." Rick finished wiping the terracotta-colored tile countertop and replaced the oak cutting board to its place covering the small stainless steel sink.

"Excuse me, ma'am. I need to see a man about a horse."

"Use the head in the captain's quarters. I started reorganizing my scuba gear in the lazarette and didn't finish before it was time to start supper so my air tanks are in the front head." Melanie laughed as she folded the brightly colored tablecloth and stored it in the locker beneath the refrigerator.

Rick reappeared and stepped back down into the salon as she poured the last of the wine into the two plastic wine glasses.

"Hey, what's with all the pictures spread out on the berth?"

"Oh, it's a long story but basically it's a bunch of family pictures Mama had. I thought putting them back in order in an album would be a good project for a rainy day."

"That's cool. I couldn't help but notice there must be literally hundreds of pictures. It looks like a great project for many a rainy day."

"It will most definitely be that. Luckily, Grandmama Tilly was extremely organized. In today's world, she would probably be classified with borderline OCD so most of the pictures have the dates and people's names written on the back. A lot of them are damaged from the fire but hopefully I'll be able to fill in the gaps of what's missing."

She exhaled a wistful sigh. "One of my favorite memories of growing up is when I spent the night with Grandmama

Tilly. She was my daddy's mama. When it came time to go to bed, she wouldn't read us a typical bedtime story. Instead the cousins each took turns picking out one of the photo albums from the huge coffee table in the living room. Back then, it seemed like she had a thousand albums of every size and color so there were always several I hadn't seen. Grandmama Tilly would let her grandchildren crawl up in the big four poster bed with her and she would open the chosen album and carefully go from picture to picture, telling us in great detail about each person and every birthday party, Christmas, or other occasion that had been captured on film. Because of Grandmama Tilly, I know more about my ancestors and extended family than most people ever learn about their immediate family. She made the people come alive. I felt like I was right back there with them. I could feel the bliss of those special family times. She gave us all so much joy with her stories of our family's history."

Rick said nothing but was captivated by her story.

"Of course, she always told the stories of sunshine and smiles. Much later in our lives, after we were all grown and too old for magical bedtime stories, we each, in our own time, learned the whole truth. Behind those smiling faces that filled Grandmama Tilly's photo albums there were also many trials, tribulations, and heartbreaking tragedies. She used to say life is about looking back and being thankful for not only sharing the happy times but also for surviving the tough times together." A smile crept across her lips as she thought of Grandmama Tilly's wisdom.

"That's incredible. Your grandmama must've been a wonderful woman." He reached across the table and gently squeezed her hand. "I'm sad to say I don't know much of anything about either side of my family. Occasionally, when I can, I still go up to Chattanooga every few years to the family reunion. Aside from my mama, sister, and her kids, I barely even know anyone there except my cousin Randy. We're almost the exact same age and were joined at the hip while we were growing up, but unfortunately we lost track of each other in the years after college."

"What happened?" Melanie didn't know how anyone could lose track of their own family.

"I joined the Coast Guard right after college and he moved to the Midwest for a few years. After that, we both got married, had our own kids and life just seemed to get in the way. My mama used to say, time goes by and distance will work its way into any relationship and that's exactly what happened. I regret not staying in touch with him. He was the brother I never had. When we were growing up in the backwoods of Tennessee, we spent every spare minute we had hunting, fishing, chasing girls, or just hanging out together. We were like this." Rick held up his massive left hand with his index finger crossed tightly under his next one.

"What's he doing now?" Melanie asked, genuinely interested.

Although she didn't say it aloud, she simply couldn't imagine not having a close-knit family. She probably talked to Jordan three or four times a week and never went longer than a week without talking to her cousins. To Melanie, family had been and always would be everything that mattered in the world.

"Oh, the last I heard he was living in Montana, Wyoming, somewhere up there. He runs a big game hunting and guide service. He's married to his fourth or fifth wife. I'm embarrassed to say I can't even remember her name." Rick gazed out the tiny window, across the silent bay, the water like mirrored-glass shimmering in the moonlight as clouds slowly danced across the black velvet sky.

Melanie's heart ached as she imagined Rick's life without family. Surprising herself, she slipped her tiny hand in his and smiled softly.

"How about a late night stroll along the beach?" Her eyes danced with mystery.

thirty-three

The next day-January, 2009
City Marina-Rockport, Texas

MELANIE AWOKE TO THE VIEW OF A SOFT drizzle falling outside the window. In the distance, the sun had begun to color the charcoal sky with pastel pinks and hints of smoky blues and cerulean.

Debating upon getting up for the day or snuggling back down under the canary yellow jersey sheet, Melanie smiled as Fred gave a dreamy yelp and cuddled closer to her.

Reaching down to scratch his belly, Melanie whispered, "Wake up, buddy. You're chasing rabbits again."

Melanie dozed on and off for the next hour. Fred nestled in her lap and Ginger purred softly on the feather pillow next to her.

"Lazy bones, lazy bones, get up. Get up, lazy bones," Rick sang as he rapped his knuckles on the hard top over the helm station.

Awake and laughing, Melanie threw back the bedcovers. "One minute, please. I'm not decent," she said teasingly.

"Make yourself decent and meet me on the porch. Breakfast is served."

Grabbing a pair of Levi's and a lime green T-shirt, appliquéd with the faces of the Seven Dwarfs, Melanie slipped out of her sleep shirt and dressed quickly. After brushing her dark curls back into a pony tail high off her neck, she splashed cold water on her face. She hurriedly brushed her teeth.

In less than five minutes, she stepped from the boat with Fred on his bright red leash and strolled down the long sidewalk toward the Rockport Center for the Arts.

The rain had stopped and the cool morning air was crisp and fresh.

Melanie walked briskly across the street to the renovated Victorian home which had been donated to the Art Association by a prominent family of South Texas. Painted a soft sky blue with a widow's walk atop the roof, the house had become a favorite breakfast spot for Rick and Melanie. From the porch, they had a breathtaking view of the bay and early beach activity. This morning an elderly couple walked two Jack Russell Terriers along the otherwise deserted water's edge.

Rick, sipping his morning coffee, lounged in one of the huge white rockers. A brown fast-food sack and another large cup of coffee sat on the tiny wrought-iron table next to him.

"Hey, Cap," Melanie said, bringing her friend out of his daydream.

"Hey, Disney darlin'. You look like you're eight years old." Rick laughed as he took another sip of his steaming black coffee.

"It's my bon voyage gift from my cousin's twins." Melanie giggled and sat down in the rocker next to Rick. He handed her the breakfast sandwich wrapped in bright yellow paper. "Yum, it smells great."

Peering into the small bag, Melanie couldn't help but smile.

"You remembered my strawberry jelly."

"Of course, I did. How could I forget? We've had McDonalds for breakfast together for how many years?" Rick feigned a quavering, elderly voice.

"Oh, we must be going on thirty years, my dear." She grinned as she spread the sweet red jam on her muffin.

The couple enjoyed their breakfast and then took a walk along the fishing pier. As they crossed the street between the beach and marina, a light rain fell again.

"How about a second cup of coffee? I'll make a pot." They turned at Fleming's Bait Stand and headed back to *Quality Time.*

Once aboard, Melanie grabbed the navy hand towel from the dash and bent down to dry Fred's tiny wet feet.

Melanie stepped into the salon as the sky opened and sheets of water poured down on the tiny harbor. In the distance, thunder rolled.

"Wow, we got on board in the nick of time. Is *The Dash* buttoned down good and tight?"

"Yeah. I closed her up and secured the dock lines. They said on the early news we are in for a soaking over the next few days." Rick gazed outside at the torrential rain. "Looks like I need to find a good novel."

"I still have the bag we got yesterday at the library. You forgot to take your books home. They're in the V-berth."

Melanie blew on her hot coffee.

"Oh, yeah. *Fill a Bag for Fifty Cents*."

"So what have you got planned for the rainy day?"

"Well, believe it or not, I've almost finished organizing and reorganizing every single locker, cabinet, drawer, and cubby hole on this entire vessel. I only have a few cabinets in the captain's quarters and then there will be a place for everything and everything in its place." Melanie beamed with unadulterated pride.

Raising an eyebrow as he leaned back to open the small cabinet next to the chart table, Rick gave an appreciative whistle. Binoculars, sunglasses, flashlights, batteries, all were neatly arranged inside.

"Impressive, very impressive. How much would you charge to come over and do the same for my boat?"

"You mean *Noah's Ark*?"

She had jokingly rechristened Rick's boat, given the size.

"Mmm," she coyly said. "It could cost you a pretty penny."

The truth of the matter was she loved every single minute she spent with Rick. Helping him organize his boat would definitely give her more time alone with him.

"You've got a deal. A pretty penny for a pretty lady." He tossed the shiny copper-colored coin on the table and winked.

How she loved that wink!

thirty-four

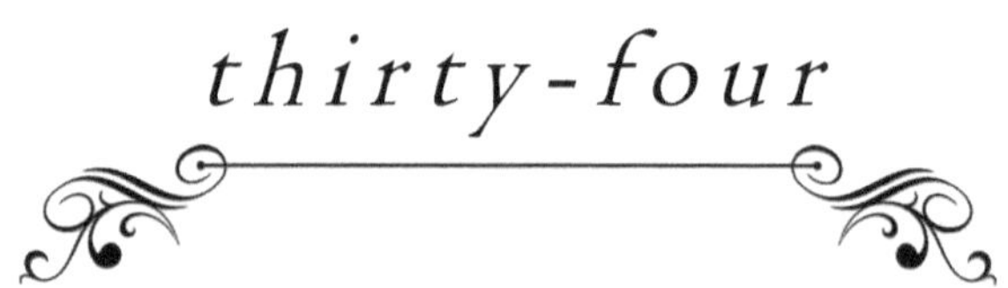

The next night-January, 2009
City Marina-Rockport, Texas

"Wow, is this really..." Rick's voice trailed off as he handed Melanie the black-and-white picture of two stunning raven-haired women and two equally handsome men, all four smiling brightly for the camera.

Glancing at the photo in his hand, Melanie said proudly, "Yeah. That's really them, Senator and Mrs. Charles Bridges."

Smiling mischievously, she added, seemingly nonchalantly, "and the other couple is JFK and Jackie O'—before she was Jackie O'—obviously."

Rick had been helping Melanie sort through her family photographs for the last two hours as the rain continued to tap dance on the deck of *Quality Time.*

Chuckling, Rick handed Melanie another snapshot.

Grinning broadly, in a silver lame' bikini, a towheaded little girl sat on a swing, her tiny feet dangling well above the ground.

"That's my baby cousin Mary Lou. I'll never forget that *beek-a-nee-nee*, as she called it."

Glancing at the date on the back—July 4, 1969—Melanie scrunched her mouth as she often did when she was in deep thought.

"I was seven that summer so Mary Lou would've been almost three. Uncle Jimmy and Aunt Sarah bought that suit in Paris."

Melanie chuckled as she gazed lovingly at her baby cousin's image.

"Wow, this is an old one. Who's she?" Rick handed Melanie the small black-and-white photograph of a young woman standing beside a creek bank.

"Mmm, that's odd. There's no name written on it, just the date. This isn't Grandmama Tilly's handwriting but I recognize the setting. It's on our family's farm, in Mississippi where all my Bridges cousins lived. There are a bunch of creeks on the property but that one was my favorite because down the path a bit was where there were the best blackberries. It's funny I have no idea who she is."

"Well," Rick said. "Obviously she has got a bun in the oven and looks ready to pop."

"Yeah. She's definitely pregnant but that's not the first thing I see. Look at how happy she is. Her smile is absolutely captivating. Even though the picture has faded, her joy still radiates. She's incredibly beautiful, too." Melanie wondered why she had never seen the picture before now. She would ask Jordan about the girl the next time they talked. For now, she set the photograph aside and returned to the stack in front of her.

The next picture showed a ruggedly handsome man, in

his late twenties or early thirties, sitting atop a white post and rail fence. An enormous solid black stallion leaned its massive head over the top rail just to the left of the cowboy.

"Who's this? He looks like the Marlboro man and based upon everything you have told me about your colorful family, he probably is."

Rick chuckled as Melanie playfully glared at him before snatching the print from his hands.

"Hmm." Melanie thoughtfully scrutinized the striking man. She turned the photo over and was disappointed to find both the name and date had faded on the damaged paper.

"This must be my great-uncle Jack as a young man. I've seen other pictures of him and he definitely has the same amazing eyes and strong chin. He was Granddaddy J's kid brother. I don't remember him but always felt like I did because Grandmama Tilly told us such wonderful stories about him. She truly kept his memory alive for as long as she herself was alive. He was a remarkable man personally and brilliant in business based on everything everyone who knew him said. He built one of the largest contracting companies in the South from literally nothing but a team of mules."

Continuing, almost to herself, "From the background, this looks like it could've been taken at Whiskey River, too. It's the same plantation where the picture of the pregnant girl was taken."

"By the way, he wasn't the Marlboro man but since you mentioned it, my cousin Mary Lou, the one in the silver bikini, was named for Marilouise Conerly who was the wife of Charlie Conerly. He was the quarterback for the New

York Giants and one of the first Marlboro men," Melanie said with a false air of superciliousness, her head held high, as if she were the Queen of England.

"Sailor, you're full of it." Rick shook his head disbelievingly as he went to the galley.

"I'm serious!"

Rick returned to the settee with a bottle of water, a canned cola, and two bags of miniature pretzels. "Okay," he chuckled. "I'm impressed, but I've got a little trivia question to test your story."

"Hit me with your best shot," she said confidently.

"What was Charlie Conerly's nickname?"

"Is that all you have, seriously?" Melanie jokingly snorted.

"Stalling for time, are we?"

"No, I'm not! *Roach* is the answer. He ran across the field like a roach running across the kitchen counter. You know how you can never catch those little suckers. Nobody could catch Roach Conerly, either."

"Alright, since Roach played long before you were even born and you don't impress me as the typical football history trivia buff, I'll buy what you're selling. Now I'm really curious. Why would your aunt and uncle name a kid after the Marlboro man's wife?"

"Little Mary Louise wasn't named after big Marilouise because she was the wife of the Marlboro man. Big Marilouise was Aunt Sarah's college roommate and best friend who coincidentally happened to be married to Charlie, the Marlboro man," Melanie said in mock exasperation.

"Okay. I get it but I'm still not sure I completely believe you. I might have to Google that one. You have to admit it does sound a little far-fetched. You've got a great-uncle who looks like he should have been the Marlboro man and a cousin who was named for the wife of the Marlboro man. Interesting. Very interesting."

Settling back against the cushions, he crossed his arms. "You're not the only one with fame in your family. My uncle was Buford Pusser," Rick said proudly.

"As in *Walking Tall*?" Melanie asked curiously, referring to the cult classic about the famous Tennessee sheriff.

"Yep. That would be the one,"

"Wow, that's pretty cool."

"He was a pretty cool dude but I have to say my family pales in comparison to yours and that's based on just by a few short anecdotes about a handful of pictures. You've got stories. A lot of 'em, I bet." Rick grinned and reached back into the box of photos.

"Yeah. I do." Absently she shook her head at the thought of all the crazy turns her life had taken and all the outrageous experiences she had shared with her family, especially Sue Ellen and Mary Louise.

The next picture showed two striking men, in their early to mid-thirties, gazing up into the camera and grinning broadly. They appeared to be in a huge chasm of some sort.

"Who are they?" Rick handed her the print.

As Melanie held the photograph, she had to bite her lower lip to hold back the sudden swell of emotion within herself. Tears misted the corners of her eyes and an unexpected lump rose in her throat.

Noticing her sudden change in mood, Rick raised his brow and reached for the picture.

Trying desperately to regain her composure, Melanie

failed completely as Rick handed her a tissue. "Uncle Eddie and Uncle Jimmy… Before…" She quickly wiped her tears and cleared her throat.

"Before?"

Surprised and obviously embarrassed by her unexpected show of raw emotion, Melanie took a long swallow of cola and cleared her throat once again.

"Before they destroyed each other," she said flatly. "Actually, that's not true. I mean it's not the entire truth. Whiskey destroyed each of them and then they destroyed each other."

Melanie's hands flew to cover her mouth. "I honestly cannot believe I just said that! I…I…never…never ever… talk about it…to anyone…I mean…anyone outside my own family."

Her family's history of alcoholism was something she had kept closely guarded. It was something Southerners did and did exceptionally well. Hide family secrets. Even during the Devilland trial, she never admitted to anyone, not even Josephine or Chad, that she had had a front row seat to what the nefarious mistress in the bottle could do to generations of an entire family. It was a shameful secret she had guarded for decades and now she had just announced it to Rick. Someone she had known for less than a month! The heat of embarrassment quickly crept up her neck and onto her cheeks.

Reaching across the table he took her trembling hand in his own. "Hey, it's okay. Really. I promise. Been there, seen that. You'd be surprised at how many families could tell you the same story."

Biting her lip again, she was determined not to tell him

that she would *not* be surprised. She could quote statistics on alcoholism going back half a century. No! She wasn't going to open that door. Devilland was off limits. She had finally begun to find happiness again and she was determined not to destroy it.

Go be anonymous! Anonymous! Dr. Johnson's advice rang in her ears.

By this time, Rick obviously knew her last name but he had never mentioned any connection to Devilland. She couldn't be sure if he truly hadn't made the connection or more than likely, didn't care. Living as a yachtie for only a brief time, she had learned their world was different. Many yachties made an intentional decision to live *unplugged*—not watching the news or reading newspapers. People who had never experienced life as a yachtie could not begin to fathom the lifestyle. Melanie certainly could not have understood it herself, but already she loved it.

"Why don't we change the subject? Surely we can find a picture of one of your relatives who played Big Bird on Sesame Street," he said casually as he flipped through the photographs. It was a weak attempt at humor but they had waded into some deep waters.

"Now that you mention it..." Melanie wiped the last of her tears and grinned mischievously, grateful for his compassion.

"Next." She sorted a handful of uninteresting yearbook pictures of herself, her siblings, and her cousins into the correct stacks.

Rick continued to sift through the photos in his hand.

The black-and-white print was one of the oldest they had run across all morning. It was actually a photograph of an oil painting that still hung in the parlor of the Bridges family home in Mississippi. It showed a robust and distinguished man standing behind a petite dark-haired young woman seated on what, Melanie knew from the original painting, was a red velvet chair. The regally dressed couple evoked the epitome of proud Southern gentility.

"Wow, this is my great-great-great-grandmother Melanie Anne and my great-great-great-grandfather Otis. I was named after her and my sister was named after him," Melanie said happily.

"You're gonna tell me you have a sister named Otis?" Rick asked with a chuckle.

"No, goofball! His full name was Otis Jordan. My sister's name is Jordan." Melanie laughed heartily, having fully recovered her jovial mood.

"Don't call me a goofball. You said his name was Otis and your sister was named for him. That would make your sister the goofball." He playfully tossed Fred's tennis ball at her which she easily caught and shared his laughter.

"So let me get this straight. You're named for her, your sister's named for him, and your cousin's named for the Marlboro man's wife. Did anybody in your family get their own name?"

"Nah. You know nobody in the South is born with their own name. We Southerners recycle names like the rest of the world recycles paper and plastic," Melanie said flippantly.

Returning his attention back to the stack on the table in front of him, Rick picked up a faded color Polaroid.

"Whoa, ho, ho! Who's this babe-a-licious?"

"Let me see." Melanie eagerly reached for the photo.

Rick pulled the picture back toward his chest, out of Melanie's reach. "No. This one you have to tell me before you have a chance to look and make up some wild story. I will give you a few clues. She's sitting on what looks like a boat dock, has long blonde hair in braids, is wearing a Budweiser halter top, which is amply filled out I might add, and bell-bottoms. She's holding a fifth in one hand and smoking a cigarette with the other.

"Never mind. I don't even have to look to answer. That's the one and only." Melanie hooted at the thought of the image Rick held in his hand.

She could still remember the day she took that picture at Seven Pines. There had been nothing extraordinary about the day except Sue Ellen, Mary Louise, and she had spent an entire carefree day at the lake. Good Lord, that must have been thirty years ago. How it ended up in Grandmama Tilly's collection, she couldn't imagine.

"The one and only?" Rick asked, breaking her reverie.

"My wild and wonderful cousin Sue Ellen Bridges, self-proclaimed to be the one who put the *fun* in dysfunctional."

"Well, so far, out of all your family I have met in these photographs, I must say that Sue Ellen is the winner in my personal curiosity department."

"Oh, the stories I could tell about my sweet, sweet Sue Ellen," Melanie laughed. Rick's smile changed as he focused on her mouth. Melanie cast her gaze downward, suddenly shy.

"I love the sweet melody of your laughter."

Melanie sighed as the heat rose in her cheeks. Oh boy, she could be in trouble with this one.

thirty-five

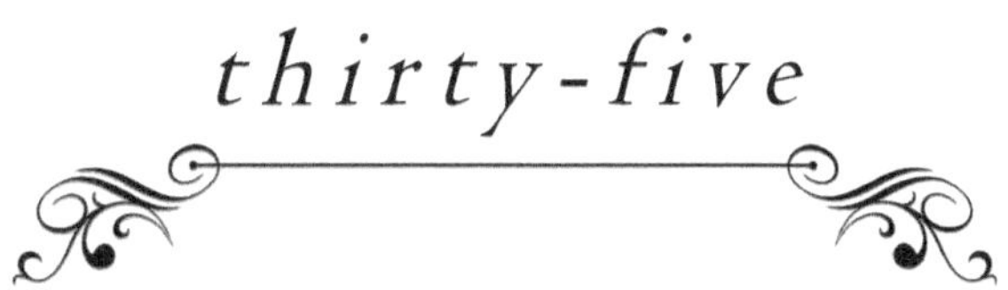

MELANIE HAD SPENT THE AFTERNOON organizing the remaining few storage compartments on the boat. Tomorrow was the big day. She would finally toss off the lines and set sail.

After putting the last cabinet in order, she sat back on the sofa in the salon with an ice cold soda.

"Well, Fred, Mama has gotten everything completely put in order at last. As Sue Ellen would say, I've been 'shuffling shit' for the past month, but it has paid off for us. We'll be much more comfortable now that I know where everything is. How do you like our new home?" Fred laid next to her, his eyes following her every move, his ears tuned to every word she said.

Gazing about the cabin, Melanie smiled at the updates she had done. Everything from the freshly painted walls to the luxurious upholstery, bright bedspreads, throw pillows, and artwork came together to create the perfect home for Melanie, Fred, and Ginger.

Melanie had done her best to minimize everything—from her cooking utensils to her clothes—but was still amazed at how much stuff she personally required on her voyage.

Organization was critical not only because of the limited space on the boat but also for safety reasons. She had to be able to find her flare gun, fire extinguisher, and a multitude of other emergency items at a moment's notice.

Traveling solo would certainly present its own set of unique challenges but Melanie was more comfortable sailing than doing almost anything else in life. As her thoughts drifted to her voyage, excitement surged throughout her body. Memories of sailing with her daddy came back in vivid color. It had been the weekend after her eighth birthday when her daddy had first put her behind the helm of *Quality Time* and allowed her to drive solo for the entire afternoon. By age nine she had mastered the art of navigating by the stars, something very few sailors knew these days due to all the technology available: autopilot, radar, GPS, navigational software such as The Captain, and many other conveniences. While Melanie did have all the modern technological devices aboard her vessel for expediency, she had confidence that, thanks to her daddy's long hours of teaching, she was as well prepared as anyone who had been sailing all their lives. Her daddy had indeed taught her well. At age twelve, Melanie could recite the entire *Chapman's Piloting and Seamanship*, known as the Bible of Boating, in her sleep. Several years ago, Melanie had taken courses and received her Captain's license, passing the final exam with flying colors. Therefore, she had no qualms whatsoever about taking her voyage solo. In fact, she much preferred it that way. She found herself thrilled by the prospect of many long hours of solitude and self-discovery.

Yesterday, as she sorted through her wide assortment of bathing suits, she had to laugh at herself. There was no reason for one person to have such an extensive variety of bikinis, tankinis, one piece suits, cover-ups, and the abundance of beach jewelry and accessories she had brought with her.

Rick had given her a hard time about the mountain of clothes, sandals, and trappings she had packed, saying his entire boating wardrobe fit into a duffel bag.

Melanie adamantly explained to him that while pulling into port, unshaven, in worn cutoffs and a ragged tank top might work fine for men, looking like an old salty dog wasn't something to which she aspired.

In addition to a rather extensive tropical wardrobe, Melanie's other weak spot was her vast collection of brightly colored plastic dishes, glasses, tablecloths, and serving platters.

Entertaining her family and friends had always been something Melanie loved yet had had little time to do in the past several years due to the demands of her career. Plain paper plates and towels were simply too drab for festive occasions. Even in the brief time she had spent in the boatyard, she had learned quickly there would be a multitude of celebratory events and get-togethers among the JBS crowd cruising the islands.

JBS was one of a multitude of terms in a vast dictionary of *Sue Ellenisms*. Throughout their lives, Sue Ellen had quirky words she made up to describe a host of different situations and people. As her thoughts wandered, Melanie recalled the day Sue Ellen had first coined JBS. It had been the day when Melanie told her cousin she was taking a sabbatical from her legal career to sail the Caribbean. Sue Ellen had been sitting on the patio of Melanie's condo with her bright red sundress hiked up just over her knees, her bare feet with perfectly manicured toenails resting on the Meadowcraft iron chair opposite her.

"I think it's a great idea, Mellie. Now that you have more money than God himself, why in the hell should you work another day in your life? I sure as shit wouldn't if I had all that money."

"I have no idea how much money God has but I'm quite certain I do not

have more money than He. More importantly, where are your Southern manners Sue Ellen Bridges? Have you forgotten what we have been taught all our lives? Any discussion of money is rude, crude, and socially unacceptable. It's quite simply vulgar."

"*Vulgar* is my middle name, sugar. You should really know that by now," Sue Ellen said matter-of-factly and winked as she took one long last drag of her cigarette before crushing it in the huge iron leaf-shaped ashtray that had once belonged to their aunt Sarah. She had given it to Melanie as a special housewarming gift when she moved into her condominium.

"Seriously, Mellie, I knew it would be only a matter of time before you were struck with JBS. You and I are too much alike, my love, and I know I would've come down with JBS the day they handed me my piece of the Jack Devilland slaughter." Sue Ellen chuckled as she took a swallow of her cola.

"Okay. I'll bite. Pray tell, what's *JBS*?"

"Jimmy Buffett Syndrome, darlin'. You're gonna be livin' smack dab in the middle of millions of people's screensavers! It's what everyone thirsts for but only the very few and fortunate ever actually taste. It happens when you can sell out and then sail out for the wild blue yonder." Sue Ellen beamed brightly as she picked up her purple lighter to light another cigarette.

"Oh and by the way, JBS isn't something that lasts a few months or even a year. Once you've got it, it's got you. Despite your carefully made plans, you, my dear sweet Mellie, shall never return to this life as you now know it. You'll spend your days island hopping and your nights mattress dancing with some really hot, Latin boy toys. Eventually you will settle down on some private island you've bought with your bazillion dollars," Sue Ellen said in a soothing sing-song voice as though she were a medium gazing into a crystal ball. "I'm thrilled you now have more money than God. At least I know I can have fruit in my Jell-O once I make it to the old age home. I'm pretty sure that costs extra but I know you love me too much to let me go without such a small luxury, right?" Sue Ellen imitated a faux tremulous voice as if she were ninety years old.

Melanie laughed at her beloved cousin. "Yes, my dear sweet Sue Ellen. I will make sure you not only have fruit in your Jell-O but also a dollop of whip cream on top."

The conversation had then taken a sharp turn as Melanie became serious. She had reached across the table and took Sue Ellen's hands in her own. "It's the least I can do for the one who has been with me for my entire life, through thick and thin. You've wiped my tears, made me laugh, sometimes through those same tears, picked me up when I stumbled, and cheered when I succeeded. More important than anything is you gave me strength when I had none of my own left. You're my gift from God and I love you more than you will ever know."

Tears had filled Sue Ellen's eyes.

"Ditto, Mellie."

The pang in Melanie's heart was more intense than usual when she thought of how much she would miss Sue Ellen and the rest of the family during her travels. Every one of them was tremendously supportive of her decision. Dr. Johnson had been exactly right. Those who loved Melanie had completely understood what she needed to do and why. Each had witnessed her struggle after her landmark legal victory. While she had always thought no one would understand what she had faced with the intense media scrutiny and overwhelming attention, she had been wrong. She hadn't given her family the credit they deserved. They loved her and wanted only the best for her.

As she thought about living with JBS, she realized how much her life had already changed in a few short months and smiled to herself. The creature comforts which had once been so important to her had been tossed aside—her luxury condo in North Dallas, her maid, her masseuse, her manicurist, and personal trainer. Sitting right here, right now, she could honestly say she hadn't missed any of it since settling into her new carefree lifestyle.

Once she had taken the leap of faith, it had come exceptionally easy to trade in her tailored designer suit and ostrich skin briefcase for her favorite hot pink bikini and flamingo patterned beach bag. One of the happiest moments had come when she had been freed from having her cell phone attached to her person every waking moment and e-mail wasn't something she had to check every hour on the hour. By far, Melanie's favorite change of all was the most important appointments of the day were watching the sun rise over Mother Ocean to welcome a new day and watching the sun yield its royal reign to the moon and galaxy of stars every night.

Yes, it had been a tremendous leap of faith but one she was confident would be well worth the costs.

Fred nudged her with his cold nose and rolled over for a belly rub. As she stroked the pup's underside, her thoughts drifted back to Sue Ellen and she realized again how much she would miss both Sue Ellen and Mary Louise. What she hadn't expected was how much she was going to miss Rick, his gorgeous smile, his jokes, and his comfortable companionship.

Was *she possibly making a huge mistake? Could the love of her life be right before her eyes? All her carefully made plans…what if they were for nothing? What would happen if she threw caution to the wind and asked Rick to come with her? What would he say?*

Melanie considered the possibilities. She nibbled her lower lip, her heartbeat picked up, and she imagined escaping with him by her side. An unexpected sense of apprehension flooded through her. What if she was indeed making the mistake of a lifetime by not telling Rick how she felt? Within moments, she made her decision.

No. She couldn't do that. Dr. Johnson had told her that she needed to get to know herself first before she could expect more.

Would it be a case of out of sight, out of mind? Or would it be absence truly did make the heart grow fonder? She had no way of knowing.

Yes, she would miss so many people, but she refused to let those thoughts damper her spirit of adventure and self-discovery.

Glancing at her watch, she was surprised to see it was after eight. Weary from the long day, Melanie decided to take a hot shower.

Afterwards, she made herself a cup of peppermint tea and went to sit on the deck. In the silence of the sleeping harbor, she contemplated the thrill of the unknown, that which lay just beyond the horizon. After almost an hour, she realized she needed to get to bed. Tomorrow would arrive soon and with it, her adventure would truly begin.

Crawling under the cool sheets and pulling Fred close to her, Melanie lay perfectly still as the prickle of excitement tingled from the top of her head all the way down to the tip of her toes. Drifting off to sleep, she whispered one word over and over. "*Anonymous, anonymous, anonymous.*"

Author's Note: I hope you have enjoyed meeting Melanie Bridges. Her family's story continues in Book Two—*Bridges Blood*—of the *Rhoades to Bridges* saga.

With gratitude,
Olivia Bridges

A Note from the Author

Tribute to the True Inspiration of Rhoades to Bridges: Eloise Tanner Stanton

She was the greatest woman five children were blessed to call *Mama.* I alone called her Marty. She was my best friend and the wind beneath my wings.

Dear readers:

It is my deepest desire that my work has meant something to each of you as you have been introduced to Melanie Bridges and her family. Th e story of the Bridges family has only just begun. I invite you to join them on their journey over 150 years and seven generations.

Hopefully you laughed. Maybe you cried. Perhaps you simply pondered. Perchance you experienced a flood of all these and many more of your own personal emotions. Most importantly, I hope you that once you have finished the series, you realize that, no matter what battle they faced or their ultimate fate, the Bridges family's Christian faith and family bonds endured above all else. I know this to be true because I am very proud to say this real-life Southern family of survivors is in fact my own amazing family. Each and every one of whom I love with my entire heart and soul.

If you have already begun to wonder which of my characters I am, the answer is many and none. My own personal life experiences have been woven among many characters so there is no "*Olivia Bridges*" in the novels. I have done this simply to provide a veil of anonymity for myself, my husband, and our children.

I give my mama credit as the inspiration for the *Rhoades to Bridges* series, as this is truly her gift. All those who knew our mama pleaded with her to record the rich tales I have recorded in the series as she was an exceptionally gifted and eloquent writer. Unfortunately, Mama never got a chance to write *her books* before she was unexpectedly taken from us. Words cannot express how very deeply I wish she, not I, were the one writing this letter to you.

In conclusion, I feel it important for you, my readers, to know something of my mother because as I wrote *Rhoades to Bridges*, I personally felt her presence with me more than I ever have in the sixteen long years since her death. I feel it is critical for you to understand something about the true soul who, I have no doubt, wrote this series. I merely recorded a legacy my mother somehow left hidden deep within my heart when she left this earth.

Mama was a truly amazing woman. When asked at my mother's seventieth birthday what flower she would have been, had she been a flower, Jarvis Standifer, a dear friend of Mama's who had recently suffered a stroke, simply said, in her garbled and stressed voice, "Weezie Stanton is the original steel magnolia." I will remember those words forever. In her diminished mental and physical state, my mother's beautiful friend summed up Mama's entire being in those seven simple words.

After Mama's death, my family and I kept waiting for someone to step forward from the darkness and breathe life into the stories she never got a chance to record. I never dreamed I would be the one ultimately called for this momentous task.

It was only when a cherished friend gave me a quote from Aristotle that *Rhoades to Bridges* was truly born within me. Aristotle once said, *"Where your talents and the needs of the world cross lies your calling."* In *Rhoades to Bridges*, I have indeed found my calling.

A great man once said, *"Your imagination is nothing more than a preview of life's coming attractions."* My family prays that my mother's magnificent imagination, the basis for the first paragraph of *Rhoades to Bridges*, was indeed a preview of life's coming attractions.

I have no doubt whatsoever that one day all of our prayers will be answered and that this, for now, imagined battle will be waged in a court of law and the triumph will belong to all the people who were taken so tragically from this world by the wicked disease of alcoholism.

I sincerely hope I have done *Rhoades to Bridges* justice but more importantly that I have once again made my mama proud of me.

Yours Truly,
Olivia Bridges

THANK YOU" IS NOT ENOUGH

Rhoades to Bridges is more than a series of novels for me; it represents a long and emotional journey. Over the span of eight years, across six countries, and two continents, I wrote *Rhoades to Bridges* while sailing the Caribbean with my husband aboard our boat *Memory Maker*. Olivia Bridges will be given the credit for this work but the reality is *Rhoades to Bridges* would have never been born without all the wonderful people who contributed their hospitality, knowledge, time, and support of the novels and me. If I were to attempt to individually thank everyone for the role he or she played in *Rhoades to Bridges*, I could easily fill another book. *Thank you* does not begin to convey how much I truly appreciate each of those listed below.

Writing is often a lonely profession, filled with long hours of solitude apart from family and friends. No one sacrificed more for *Rhoades to Bridges* than my amazing husband Bill who supported me every day and in every way. I am eternally grateful that God blessed me with the most wonderful best friend and partner a girl could have.

The others who so graciously donated to this work are listed alphabetically because each person played a part in the *Rhoades to Bridges* experience. Some played a minor role and others a major one but all were equally important. It brings me great joy to finally be able to publicly thank my family and friends who believed in me. My apologies in advance if I overlooked anyone. I assure you it was not intentional.

My deepest gratitude to: Ardath Stanton Francke, Arnold in Cartegena, Ben Giddings, Billie Wilmon Jenkin,

Dr. Bob McClimans, Bonnie Schmiddy, Pastor Brady Owens, Caleb Pirtle III, Carol Ann Smith, Carolyn Higgs Stanton, Catherine L. McClimans, City of Cartegena, Colombia, City of Rockport, Texas, Diane Straub, Doc Caughlin, Dylan Tarver, Elizabeth Tanner, Frances Tanner Swift, Garlon Lain, Hank Hodges, Haydon Lain, Helen Stanton Cullifer, Izzy Rollins, Jenna Rockett and the Rockett.net team, Jenni Stanton Lain, Joe Coomer, John Stanton, Joyce Chastain Roach, Judy Farrish Johnson, Kathy Eppley, Kim Horan Bruner, Kim Liston, Kim Parsons, Kittie Schwebel, Liz Stanton Haskins, Lucy Dougherty, Magdeline Abraham, Mark Andrew Barylski, Marty in Cartegena, Mary Jane De Cutler, Mike Stanton, Natalie Haskins Laukitis, my NCC family, Orlando in Cartegena, Patsy Futch, Paul Roessner, Paul Edward Smith, Pauline Shuler Lewis, Perian Conerly, Russell Smith, Roy Gardenhire, Sarah Stanton Crimmins, Savannah Tarver, Selena in Cartegena, Stella Gold, Tom De Cutler, Tommy Haskins, Tommy Haskins, Jr., Tuitti Nichols, Y&R PR, and last but not least, my four-legged cheerleaders Bruiser, Chanel, Lucky, Mickie, Otis, Rufus, Sugar, and Waffles.

With great love and gratitude,
Olivia Bridges

To Bill-You may now buy that new yacht as I promised when we began this journey.

To Kim Horan Bruner-Did Robert Frost really write *Gulliver's Travels*?

DISCLAIMER

Rhoades to Bridges is a work of historical fiction. Greenwood, Mississippi is a real place; Carlton, North Carolina is not. Other than the historical figures who will be mentioned throughout the series, none of the characters represents a real person but rather a composite of several people enhanced by the imagination of the author Olivia Bridges. Any resemblance between any one character and a real person is purely coincidental. This includes the author and her family members. The events depicted in the novel were inspired by actual events and artistic license has been taken in some instances to add to the novel's entertainment value.

Olivia Bridges

Did you like, or hopefully love *Anonymous*? Did you know that authors need many reviews to help sales and boosting of their pages online?

Reviews can be two sentences to multiple paragraphs.

Please consider leaving a review for this book online.

Thank you for helping an author. We really appreciate reviews from readers and fans.

You're amazing!!

BOOKS BY OLIVIA BRIDGES

Rhoades to Bridges Saga:
Anonymous

www.ingramcontent.com/pod-product-compliance
Lightning Source LLC
Chambersburg PA
CBHW051651180726
48284CB00006B/1960